I0588003

# THE GRAIN MERCHANT

*An Argolicus Mystery*

## ZARA ALTAIR

Fervent
Crux
Press

Cover by Patrick Knowles Design
patrickknowlesdesign.co.uk

ISBN 978-1-7327225-6-9

# TESSERA - GOLD

In the king's new chapel, every morning, the sunlight through the high windows shone on the gold pieces of the mosaic, the tesserae, around the images and the intricate Eastern garments of Balthasar, Melchior, and Caspar, glittering in splendor. At every Arian liturgy, the congregation chanted, "Long life to Theoderic," forty times.

The old king ruled his People and the Romans of Italy with impartial care. It was rumored, and probably true, that under the soft cushions on his throne lay a human skin to remind him that his judgment had the power of life and death. His ten-year captivity in Constantinople under the Emperor Zeno inspired his knowledge of palace architecture and dissenting courtiers but had little bearing on his tenuous connection to the present Emperor Anastasius. He ruled Italy from his palace in Ravenna in the North.

In the South, life went on without much care from the king. Few of the king's People lived there; Italians were Romans, and Greeks, and Syrians. The Church worshipped the Holy Trinity, and bishops raised money with a thriving slave trade. The governor of Bruttium, breadbasket to the North, was young and venal. Occasionally the Prime Minister, a Roman southerner by birth, sent a letter of rebuke from the king, which was largely ignored.

Local patricians lived comfortably and ran the local government through a council that imitated the Senate in Rome. The council selected a magistrate every two years. A treasurer kept track of local monies and duly sent taxes to the governor, who sent them on to the king. Crops and livestock—olives, wine, grain, fresh fruit, cattle, and horses all went north to support the king's country of Italy.

As long as harvest went well, money flowed, and the area prospered.

A rgolicus opened the door of the large stone house to
memories and seventeen years of dust. He peered into
the *atrium* in the early morning light as if childhood
never left, hoping to hear his father's voice. Dust motes floated
above the stagnant *impluvium*, the pool in the middle of the
*atrium*, coated with green moss. No wonder his mother never
came here. The house spoke of his father, despite the dust and
years.

Workmen marched past him into the room in a group. The
foreman started calling instructions. Men went off to other
rooms, leaving Argolicus alone in the room. The early August sun
coming through the roof seemed to light up history: business
conversations in his father's study and office and somewhere his
mother's laughter echoed. He pushed those sounds from his head
as he strode across the *atrium* toward his father's study. A large
table, draped with a cloth, stood in the middle. It looked smaller
than he remembered. Had it diminished with time? Or was he
seeing it as a man rather than a boy?

"Master," Nikolaos, his boyhood tutor and lifelong companion, came up beside him and interrupted his thoughts. "I'll prepare a room for you. Which one?"

"The main bedroom. If I'm taking over my father's house, I might as well move in as the master."

Nikolaos nodded and went off toward the rear of the *domus*, calling to one of the workmen to follow him.

Argolicus wandered through the house. Town. He was in town. No more leisurely country villa life. It was time for him to act as a responsible citizen and throw off the pretense of running a country estate.

The rooms filled with dust as workers swept, shook out cloths, and dusted alcoves and shelves. They covered their faces with cloth to avoid breathing the dust. Argolicus decided to go outside, and reacquaint himself with the town of Squillace just miles from his country villa estate. Now that the family town house was open and people were working, he wasn't needed.

When he stepped out of the vestibule into the street, the summer sun blinded him. He took a few moments to let his eyes adjust. When he blinked, a man in magisterial robes, all silk, stood in front of him. Medium height, but with a carriage that implied importance. He met Argolicus' blinking with unreadable eyes. His perfume seemed to expand in the summer air.

"Sura," he said in a resonant voice. "Caius Larcius Sura, surely you remember me."

Sura. He remembered a gawky, petulant adolescent, full of pretension and ready to latch on to anyone with a good name.

"Sura, I do remember you. It's been years. You look well."

His eyes took in the fleshed-out face with a trace of jowls, squinting eyes that hinted at poor vision, and wrinkles beside his mouth that would soon turn into permanent scowl lines. The man looked ten years older than his early thirties.

"Elected magistrate and chosen civil curator of Squillace just this year. Keeping the town in peace. At least I try." He glanced to the side, where streams of people were filling the street headed toward the harbor. "Lately, we've had this problem." He nodded toward the people in the street. "We're having a council meeting tomorrow. You should come. You've been up in the hills too long. It's time you joined us."

There was no excuse for it. Argolicus had made a decision to enter town life, and here it was, an opportunity on the very first day. One of the marching men in the street shouted, "*quod de nos? What about us?*"

"I'll be there. You can all fill me in on the unrest. I see the people are agitated."

"It's about the grain harvest."

"What about it? It was a good year. No rain." He thought of his fields up at the estate where the grain harvest had ended just two weeks ago. The crop had been excellent.

"You're right about the harvest. But most of it is going north, to Rome and Ravenna. The estate owners and the grain merchants made money. Small farm owners and laborers made none. And since the grain is leaving, there isn't enough for the people who don't own land. Not that it would make a difference. They have no money, so they couldn't afford bread, even if there were plenty of grain here."

"When is the meeting? I'll be there."

"At the normal hour. It's good to see you back in town. I hear you went to Rome."

Argolicus nodded his head.

"And served as *praefectus urbi?*"

Argolicus nodded again. This time a bit irked. If Sura already knew, why was he asking? Then he understood, an appointed magistrate of Rome was a much more powerful title than the elected magistrate in Squillace.

"Yes, it's true. But I retired to come back here. This is my home."

"Ah, it is beautiful here." Sura waved his hand toward the ocean and then up toward the mountains. "People still remember your father. A wise man. We need men like that." Then, as if he were late for an appointment, he said, "Well, I'm off. Good to see you back. I look forward to seeing you at the council meeting." He headed up the street in a swirl of silk and perfume.

It might be smaller here, but politics was the same. Men who jockeyed for position and measured others they met in relation to themselves. Argolicus sighed. Inside the house behind him, a workman was singing as he cleaned. He closed the door to the house and started down the street in the direction away from Sura.

It was still early enough for the shops to be busy. Cooks and slaves bartered with butchers, fruit sellers, and millers. A smith was hammering over an open fire while small boys watched. Restaurants, open since before sunrise, were feeding their last morning patrons.

Argolicus followed the street until he reached the city center. The forum was crowded with more shops, all selling wares to housekeepers and tradesmen. Citizens gathered in small groups, ready to trade gossip. Behind the forum, the town council building loomed over portico columns in front of the entry door. Argolicus briefly wondered why Sura had gone in the other direction and wasn't installed in the city council performing his duties.

He had a sense that Squillace was a normal town, thriving on trade and hearsay. It was his town, and he would find his place here. He turned around to head back to the house, his house. As he walked back on another street, the stalls were busy with locals, but there were fewer discontents marching. His childhood haunts returned. There was the milk stall where they'd given him cream when he was a boy. But the man in the stall was not the same.

"Argolicus? Young Argolicus? Is that you?" a voice called from across the street. "It's me, Rufus. Rufus the One-Eyed."

Argolicus would recognize that gravel voice anywhere. The best fruit in all of Squillace. "Rufus, yes, it's me. A bit larger now," he said, laughing. "What do you have today?"

"Look at these figs. Oh, no, they're not good enough. Hold on." He bent down under the stall table and pulled out a golden peach. "The last of the harvest, but ripe and very, very tasty." He handed the fruit to Argolicus.

"Rufus, you're still the same, always a cheerful word for everyone and a surprise for the boys. You do still give treats to the boys, yes?"

Rufus chuckled. "Of course. They grow up to be men who are willing to pay, just like you." He chuckled and then asked, "Have you moved into town? Come down from the hills?"

"Yes, I'm opening up the house. The men are there now blowing dust around, but soon it will be livable."

"And Nikolaos? That feisty tutor, is he still with you?"

"Nikolaos is still with me. Feisty as ever and just as wise."

Rufus nodded.

Argolicus asked, "Are you content here in this stall?" And before he could think, he added, "Would you consider moving?"

Rufus paused. "Moving?" Then his face broke into a smile. "You are inviting me to take up my old stall at your *domus*?

"Yes, the stalls are empty. The house is open."

"I pay for my space here. Let me think about it," Rufus said. "My old spot." He grinned. "I'll see what I can do. Who is your housemaster?"

Argolicus was not ready and laughed. "I don't have one yet. It's time I found staff for the house. In the meantime, you can talk to me."

Argolicus cradled the peach in his palm and started back to the house.

⊗⊗⊗

The afternoon August sun beat down on the slave market as Argolicus and Nikolaos entered the crowd. Some people were eyeing the slaves; others were bidding on the men and women on display. Several slave masters lined up their goods on platforms proclaiming strength, or youth, or beauty depending on the slave.

Nikolaos stopped as if frozen. Argolicus turned to him. "What is it?"

"Joram!" Nikolaos said under his breath, nodding his head toward the farthest platform. "He is not a good man."

The slave master, a large man whose powerful muscles were hidden by the flesh of overindulgence, was describing a pubescent girl standing naked in the blazing sunlight. "...she will grow into a delightful companion or a sturdy worker." He brought his arms down, defining imaginary curves. "Turn around. Let them see all of you," he said to the girl. Tears ran down the girl's cheeks. An involuntary shiver ran down her back as she turned on the platform.

Argolicus noticed nothing different about this slave master from the others, but he caught Nikolaos' distress. "There are plenty to choose here. We don't have to deal with him."

"He was...," Nikolaos started. He tried again, "When your father bought me. It was from him."

Argolicus thought of the young Nikolaos, imported from Greece. A fifteen year old in the large man's stable of slaves.

"I was treated well," Nikolaos said as if reading his master's thoughts. "I was educated and valuable. But girls like her had rough treatment with only enough food to keep them alive. They slept crowded in tiny rooms. Look at that girl there, probably fresh from the farm. The way things are these days, her parents probably sold her to make ends meet."

"We'll find a housemaster, a doorman, and a cook from someone else," Argolicus said.

## 2

A rgolicus slid onto a bench in the council hall amid nods
from fellow town members. The long stone bench was
one of two that edged the walls of the meeting hall. The
town principals sat in chairs arranged against the far wall on a
slightly raised stone dais. Sura was in deep conversation with a
graying man with squinting eyes. Argolicus tried to remember the
man's name but couldn't.

During the years he had been away in Rome, it seemed as
though the membership had dwindled. There should be close to a
hundred men here. As he did a quick headcount, he noticed fewer
than fifty men in the hall, including the principals up on the dais.
Wide spaces on the benches testified to members who were not
there. He understood now why Sura had invited him.

Sura was waving at Argolicus, gesturing for him to come up to
the principals' dais, mouthing, "Come, come."

Argolicus hesitated, thinking he would just watch and observe
in this meeting. But, Sura was right; he was a principal of the
township and belonged on the dais. He rose. As he mounted the
dais step, all eyes followed him as he made his way to Sura. Not

the beginning at the council he had imagined. He was in the thick of politics. All his misgivings from his time in Rome as Praefect swirled inside his stomach. Father would not have been hesitant. But, Father had not experienced the Senate in Rome.

And now he was his father's heir, and it was time to take his place.

Sura smiled. "You remember Donicus. He was our taxman before you left." Argolicus now remembered the man who was grayer and squinted more than before.

"Donicus," he said, "keeping track of everyone and everything?"

Donicus looked up, squinted, and said, "Argolicus, has your wisdom grown in Rome? Did you bring back knowledge you can share? I'm the last to hear any stories. Tell me you are here now in Squillace."

"I am. I am. As you can see, this is my first time at the council since I left. Today I'm here to observe and learn. I have years to catch up. But I'm wondering, why are so many seats empty in the benches?"

Donicus shook his head. "Too comfortable in their country villas to come into town for business. Almost everything is left to us to decide." He waved at the group of principals on the dais.

"Everyone's role seems different now," Argolicus said. "Look at Sura. He's a magistrate."

Sura expanded under his silks. Then he motioned for Argolicus to sit in an empty chair next to Donicus.

Donicus nodded his head. "Indeed. We need strong leaders. This year we have, Vespasianus." He nodded his head toward the central chair on the dais. A tall man in a richly embroidered, fine linen tunic sat with pomp surveying the room. He turned his head covered with dark, almost black hair, cut in a fashionable Roman-style cap, to survey the room, frowning at the empty seats on the benches.

Donicus continued, "You see, we have leaders, but now we have..."

He was cut off as Vespasianus rose with pomp from the chair to begin the session.

"Citizens, we have several issues to discuss today. I'm hoping we can get through them all with a minimum of discord. Vopiscus Aurius Macro, our treasurer, will explain the new tax levies and how they will be paid to our governor, Venantius, as well as the funds to improve the warehouses and ongoing maintenance of our city streets."

Donicus pulled out several vellum sheets and began reviewing columns of figures.

Vespasianus continued, "Caeso Rabirius Donicus, our *curator civitatis*, will report on the success of the markets in general and the success of the grain harvest this year. We can all be grateful for our harvests."

Donicus gathered the sheets of vellum and prepared to rise, but Vespasianus continued, "Missing from us for several years on his appointment by the king in Rome, we welcome back Gaius Vitellius Argolicus." Head turned toward the dais, searching for the new face. "The town of Squillace is grateful for the leadership of his father, Gaius Vitellius Maximinus, and looks forward to continued guidance from Argolicus."

Men nodded in agreement and then burst into brief but hearty applause. Argolicus rose and then sat.

A man swathed in silks rose from the benches and walked toward the dais to address the principals. Argolicus cringed at his neighbor Bartholomaeus, a man of strict principle and growing wealth. Bartholomaeus nodded toward Donicus and Macro and then addressed the room, standing with defiant widespread legs.

"We have an urgent situation that must be addressed today. More immediate than warehouse improvements or even taxes. I am speaking of the unruly rabble disturbing our streets, defacing property, and causing civil unrest. In spite of our foreign king, we have our eternal Roman laws."

Argolicus noticed heads nodding agreement along the benches. But the principals on the dais seemed inured to tirades like this. Bartholomaeus continued his impassioned rhetoric.

"We need the town warden to keep peace in the streets, so we can go about our business undisturbed."

There were a few murmured calls of agreement on the benches.

"Most importantly, we need to hear from the arbiters of grain supply like Pompeius Severus Quintinus. We need to know why the town is short of grain when the harvest was good. Not only good, one of the best in years. Why are we short of grain? Who will quell the hungry mob? Where can we get grain now? I call on Quintinus to speak."

The heads on the benches turned toward the dais. There was a hum of voices and then silence. Argolicus recognized the empty chair was not for him but for the missing town principal Quintinus.

Around him, the principals muttered and exclaimed in sotto voce. "Where is Quintinus?" "Not like him to miss a town meeting." "Just when we need him."

While the principals flustered, Argolicus knew that he might see Quintinus this very afternoon. He had an appointment at his house. He would ask him then about the grain and why he wasn't at the town meeting.

A scrawny man stood on the dais. His angular face held the trace of Greek ancestry not uncommon here in the south. "Perhaps I can give a brief explanation."

Vespasianus waved his hand for the man to continue.

"Citizens, Vibius Horatius Bartholomaeus, I am not Quintinus, but I speak with him often about these matters. The grain harvest was plentiful this year. The weather was kind to the fields.

There was suspicion about normal shipments to Ravenna and Rome from Egypt. Quintinus stepped in. He brokered almost all the grain from here in the south to meet that demand in the north."

Men grumbled on the benches. Several stood up to speak.

Vespasianus turned his regal head from one side of the hall to the other. He held up his hand. "Let Sextus Gabinius Pennus continue." Bartholomaeus frowned. The men at the benches sat down.

Pennus continued. "Quintinus knows best where the grain comes from. He is in communication with the growers — the large estates and the small farms. We'll need to wait for him to let us know if more grain is available."

Bartholomaeus interrupted. "We can wait. Meanwhile, something must be done. If we can't appease the people... the hungrier they are, the more they will turn to disruption. I call on the principals to settle this matter as quickly as possible."

All the men on the benches stood. Cries of "Now" and "Stop them!" rang through the large hall. Some raised their fists in anger others ran toward Bartholomaeus and stood next to him in front of the dais. On the dais, the principals began whispering questions and shaking their heads.

Thoughts and questions ran through Argolicus' head. Was Bartholomaeus doing this as a play to become a principal? He was richer than some men on the dais, like Pennus, the wine merchant. But he was not from an established family. Although he had property, much of his wealth stemmed from the slave trade.

Argolicus was surprised by the crisis in the council. He had never seen the citizens of Squillace so out of order. They were as disruptive as the people in the streets, just in a different way. It seemed as if the entire town was erupting in chaos.

Vespasianus rose from his chair and raised his hands. As he turned his head to look out over the town membership, the men on the floor grew quiet. Those at the benches lowered their fists and hung their heads. One by one, the men around Bartholomaeus returned to their places. Finally, Bartholomaeus walked to take a place on a bench.

Vespasianus lowered his arms and said, "Citizens, nothing will be solved without order. We can discuss our situation rationally and reach our conclusions. Grain distribution cannot be solved until we hear from Quintinus. Let us, for the moment, continue with the other issues of today's meeting." He turned around and motioned toward Donicus.

Argolicus stood. "I have an interim proposal." Donicus tugged at his tunic, waving his sheets of numbers in his other hand. Argolicus turned, "In a minute," he said.

Vespasianus frowned, sure that Argolicus wanted to prolong the discourse. Men on the dais looked on with shock. On the benches, men murmured and furrowed brows.

"Citizens," Argolicus continued, speaking to everyone in the hall. "In the matter of the grain shortage, I will speak with Quintinus. I have an appointment at his home later today. I recently returned from Rome, where I settled disputes regularly. Correct information is the basis of sound decisions. Let me gather facts from Quintinus, our grain merchant. I will report back to the magistrate Vespasianus. If we need to confer with other principals of Squillace, we can do that once I have the facts. Then we can set up grain dispersal for the people. Once they know they have food, I am sure their fractious behavior will subside."

The men on the benches settled back. Heads nodded. Everyone on the dais turned to Vespasianus. Bartholomaeus frowned but finally nodded in agreement.

"A reasonable solution," Vespasianus said. "Once we calm the populace, we can return to regular town affairs and the prosperity of Squillace. We look forward to your answers." He nodded to Argolicus. "Now let us turn to the matter of the tax levies..."

Argolicus listened with half a mind through the tax levies, dickering over the warehouse improvements, and Donicus' explanation of the markets. He was focused now on how to approach Quintinus about the lack of grain for the region when the main purpose of his visit was to meet Quintinus' daughter. His mother had arranged with the woman's mother for the two to meet. It wasn't quite an arranged marriage since both were adults, but a maneuvering to unite two families—the wealthy grain merchant without old Roman family ties and the established principal family whose representative was Argolicus.

His most difficult concern was how to approach Quintinus. If the merchant had oversold the local harvest leaving no grain for the town, then the council would be pressed to find the grain. Would they pressure their most important merchant to make arrangements? Would Quintinus make good to the citizenry for his zealous bargaining? Was the local shortfall truly due to the merchants overselling the entire harvest? So much of southern Italy's grain went through the warehouses of Squillace. Even if Quintinus were to blame, how would the town provide for the people? The grain came here from all over the South. It wasn't as though the town could call on the next valley over to provide grain.

Vespasianus was bringing the council meeting to a close. Donicus turned to Argolicus. "Congratulations on your resolution. That Bartholomaeus causes a stir at every council meeting."

"Well," Argolicus said, "it's not resolved yet. I don't know how the town will make up for the shortfall. It seems that Quintinus is the one who brought us all to this dilemma."

"Remember that Quintinus is a bargainer. You will have a hard time getting a straight answer from him, especially if what you ask costs him." Donicus squinted into the emptying hall. "You can trust only his prices, nothing else."

"I'll keep your words in mind," Argolicus said, putting his hand on the man's shoulder. "Thank you for your warning."

He left the hall, nodding to those who were still in the council room. Men grouped in clusters of two or three talked in low voices. Some nodded back while others ignored him. Ah, politics. Always the same. And he had voluntarily stepped into the middle. As he headed back toward his house, he hoped he would maintain his father's good name.

## 3

Argolicus shifted on the bench in the entertainment room of the vast town residence. His mother's choice for a new wife sat across from him. Her name was Proba. She was small and delicate with brown eyes framed above by graceful eyebrows. And, she was the daughter of Quintinus.

Her father, Pompeius Severus Quintinus, was obviously well off. Multicolored rich mosaics covered the floor in intricate weaving strands of leaves and geometric patterns. The bright frescoes on the walls were themed with musicians playing harps, flutes, and drums. The slaves moved easily around the room, bringing various tasty snacks. A plate with thin bread rounds and a bowl of honeyed herb apricot sauce sat on the table by the side of his bench.

Proba broke off a tiny piece of bread, dipped it in the honeyed apricot sauce by her side, and chewed silently. The silence was the cause of Argolicus' shifting. His mother had spoken to Proba's mother about a possible marriage match. The two of them now sat opposite each other without a word to say. Each time Argolicus asked her a question, she answered with a polite yes or no and let the question drop into the pervading silence.

It wasn't that she wasn't good-looking. The light green tunic with embroidered strips down the front and on the sleeves revealed a shapely form. The idea of spending days—the rest of his life—with someone with nothing to say dismayed him. What was the point?

Proba broke the silence. "I'm going to be honest. Here we are sitting together in a moment arranged by other people. The purpose is marriage and I'm not interested in marriage. Our family has money. I'm comfortable. My mother, discontent as she is, thinks I would be happier married. I'm not unhappy."

Argolicus felt his body relax. Not only was she not trying to trap him into a marriage he didn't want, she was not interested in marriage.

"I'm not unhappy either," he said. "My mother was happy in her marriage and wants the same for me. My father died seventeen years ago. She doesn't want to marry again. We're both old enough to know what we like in life. Can we agree that this marriage idea for the two of us is not a good one?"

Her composed face lit up with a smile, and her eyes glowed with warmth. She broke her silence with a stream of chatter. Her opinion on all those people in the street flowed into the importance of guarding wealth, and that changed into the responsibilities of principals toward the general populace.

Argolicus burst out laughing. She stopped and frowned. "No, no. I'm not laughing at you. I'm laughing at myself. I agree with your ideas. It was just that minutes ago, I was wondering how we could have a conversation about anything."

"So was I," Proba said, smiling. "Look how just the idea of marriage kept us from talking. Now that you've heard my grandiose ideas on the principal's role in civic life, tell me about you. How do you spend your time?"

"I don't know how to answer that. My life is changing. Just yesterday, I left our villa in the hills to move into town. I went to the town council meeting this morning. I don't know what my routine is yet but I do have one thing I do every day."

"Oh, what is that?" Proba tilted her head and raised her delicate eyebrows into arcs.

"I read. I have a book collection and spend time reading each morning before I begin the rest of the day. Then, in the evening, I read out loud, often in Greek, to practice." Argolicus shifted again, leaning forward. "My slave has been with me since I was a child. He was my tutor and now supports my daily activities."

"Oh, I had a tutor when I was young. He is long gone to another family. I read little. I prefer numbers. I like numbers. They give you answers."

"Answers? I never thought about mathematics that way. What do you mean, answers?"

Proba's eyebrows lifted again, this time in surprise. "It's simple. They add up. Sums give you information. Then you act on the information. That's why I love working with my father. We check the numbers and then make decisions."

Well, here was a way of approaching numbers different from the squinty-eyed Donicus. Proba found them useful while Donicus just kept track.

"What kind of decisions?" Argolicus asked. "I'm used to people like Donicus who keep track and make reports of totals." His evaluation of this slight girl was changing.

"Donicus," Proba said. "He keeps columns."

Argolicus smiled. "Indeed, I saw his lists this morning."

"Well, Father makes arrangements all over Italy. With the grain trade, he has to make predictions. Then he bases his offers on the predictions he makes. It's quite simple, really. How much grain was harvested this year? Compare that to how much grain last year? Who were the biggest buyers last year? Then match them up."

"It would make my head swim. I thought it was a matter of knowing the right people."

Proba smiled. "That, too. It takes years. That's my father's special skill. I do the numbers, and he manages people."

"You do the numbers?"

"Yes, what did you think I was talking about?"

Argolicus dropped his eyelids and nodded. He had underestimated Proba. It was as if he had opened a spigot to a woman he didn't understand, and out flowed someone completely different from his first perception. Her mind worked in a way opposite to his. He had thought he had a grasp of logic and reading people, but she lived in a different world.

"I've never met a woman who worked with numbers."

"Not until today," Proba said with a grin. "I can tell you are a philosopher at heart. But you are also curious. If you like, I can show you. First, you examine numbers. Then, you talk about them."

She smiled and held out her hand.

"Come, I'll show you. It won't be like mathematics with your tutor."

Argolicus tried to remember the last time he had taken a woman's hand. Some dinner in Rome, he decided. He reached out and took her hand. She led him from the entertainment room, across the warm garden sunshine of the *peristylum*, through a hallway, across the *atrium*, to her father's study.

The room was much like his father's study in the town home with shelves and shelves of journals. The large table was stacked with neat piles of vellum and several open journals. Proba let go of his hand and stood behind the table.

"Father is gone most of the time, creating his connections and setting prices. This is officially his office, but it has been my domain for almost ten years. I have a system. I keep track of the numbers for his business dealings here," she tapped a vellum sheet with columns of numbers. "I list the name, the place, the amount of goods, usually grain, the source, the transportation method, usually by ship, its cost, the name of the ship and the captain, the port warehouse, the delivery, and the delivery date. Then I make a note here," she pointed to the bottom of the sheet, "of where the agreement is stored."

"I think I understand," Argolicus said. "Each sheet represents the transaction for his business. The actual agreements are stored separately. Where?"

"Oh, those are kept in these journals." She pointed to a row of leather journals on the shelf. Then she swept her arm up and down. "All these shelves are copies of agreements organized by date and name."

"No wonder your father is out sealing agreements. You are the backbone of his operation. He can negotiate costs at every step of the transaction from buying grain to delivery."

Proba did not blush or simper, she just nodded her head.

"It more than keeps me occupied. I enjoy keeping track and organizing. I know most women don't have a 'vocation,' but this is mine. I couldn't give it up. That's why marriage seems impossible for me."

Argolicus nodded. "I understand. You are a unique woman." Then he decided it was time to change the topic. The promise he had made this morning at the town council meeting tugged him to action.

"I was hoping I could meet with your father while I'm here. Something came up at the town council this morning."

"Well, if it's about business, I'm sure he will want to meet with you. My strength is numbers, not making the agreement."

"Yes, well, is that possible? Could I meet with him now?"

"Oh, no. As usual, he is traveling." A small frown furrowed her brow. "But, he was due back last night. He planned to attend the same town meeting. Some terms of agreement must have delayed his return. He doesn't stop until he's reached the terms he sets. He is quite the bargainer. That's why we make such a good part-nership. He is firm with people, and I'm solid with numbers."

"If you could…"

"Oh, I'll tell him." Then she actually winked. "I'll tell him to give you a special rate."

"No, no. It's not about a transaction. The overseer at the villa makes all those arrangements. I need to talk to him about..."

"Oh, Proba! What are you doing?" A woman's voice cut him off.

Fabia, Proba's mother, scurried into the office. "This is no place to entertain a patrician. You must learn to..."

Argolicus could see where this was going. He cut her off.

"Fabia Pompeia, I asked to see what Proba does. She was showing me the system she developed. I'm quite impressed."

Fabia gave him a huge smile. "Oh, I'm so glad the two of you are getting on. It was my idea to talk to your mother about a marriage. It's good to see the two of you together like this." She gave an approving smile to Proba.

"Mother, we're not getting married. We both agreed that it wouldn't work."

"Oh? I'm sure you can iron out little difficulties. That's what all couples do. The differences fade with time..."

"Mother. We are not getting married. We both agreed."

"But, but," Fabia spluttered. She turned to Proba and spoke with approbation. "Take him back to the entertainment room. Honor our guest. Let go of business for one afternoon."

She turned to Argolicus. "My daughter is headstrong even if she is tiny. I apologize for..."

"No need to apologize," Argolicus said. He looked over to Proba, and she winked again.

"A good idea, Mother," Proba said. "Tell the kitchen to send us more food and some honeyed wine."

She strode out of the office back toward the entertainment room. Argolicus followed, leaving the perplexed Fabia wringing her hands in the office, hoping for a marriage that would not happen.

Once they were back and seated, Proba laughed. "She doesn't

understand. You handled her so well. I usually end up in an argument."

Argolicus smiled. "Years in Rome. I'm sure she thinks she has your best interest at heart. Mothers want what they think is best for their children. Sometimes that means overlooking who their children really are."

"You are a remarkable man." Proba spoke without thinking the words, then shook her head. "No. I mean you are, but I didn't mean to blurt it out like that. I don't spend much time in the company of men. I'm sure you can tell."

Servants entered with a new platter of *gustum*, clear glasses, and a pitcher of wine. They set down the platter with a bowl of melon pieces cooked in spices and two small omelets filled with tiny fish, raisins, and oregano.

When Proba took a bite of her omelet, she smiled. Argolicus wondered at how quickly she had gone from the earlier glazed look to her smile now. It was only a matter of minutes.

"Without giving your mother false hopes, I think we could be friends," he said.

"I like that idea. Mother's life is full of female friends. They gossip. I have no interest in gossip. I don't have friends. You know, friends to just talk and spend time with."

Argolicus nodded. He remembered how he'd had similar thoughts about himself. Friendship was hard to find. Except for his neighbor Ebrimuth, of the king's people, he relied on Nikolaos for companionship.

"Good," Argolicus said, thinking he had just made his first friend in town. "These melons are delicious."

He nibbled while Proba talked. He decided that moving to town was a positive action. Not only that, he wasn't a dealer like Proba's father but he knew he wasn't cut out to manage a country estate.

They spent the rest of the afternoon in friendship.

$$ \text{❧} \quad 4 \quad \text{❧} $$

Outside, the evening air encouraged people in the street, but they were not happy. They jostled and shouted. Clusters of men yelled in angry voices. Over and over, Argolicus heard *What about us?* Low murmurs to loud chants. Even though it was not dark, some carried torches. The feeling was fierce and eruptive.

Events like this didn't reach the peaceful villa in the hills. Argolicus understood that in whatever form—town meeting, an afternoon of talk, or out in the street—contact with people was a new element in his life. As he was lost in thought, a group of young men pushed him. They made it seem as though it were unintentional, but their looks told him the action was deliberate.

He found himself in a small alley between two large homes, a passageway for slaves to carry goods in and out. A stack of boxes was piled up against a wall, waiting to be taken inside.

He heard a sobbing noise behind the boxes and took a step into the alleyway. At first, he saw nothing. Then a pair of red-rimmed eyes peered at him above tear-stained cheeks. The young girl cringed and pulled back against the wall. Her brown hair was matted. Her tunic showed worn seams.

"I won't hurt you," Argolicus said, thinking she was a slave from one of the buildings. "Just go back in. Everything will work out." He knew that wasn't always the case, but it seemed the right thing to say to get her to stop crying. Children baffled him. They seemed to turn emotions on and off in minutes.

She stopped sobbing. "There is no go back in. I have no place to go. I don't belong anywhere." Then the sobs erupted again.

Argolicus started with the simplest, most straightforward thing. "What's your name?"

"Severa," she said, wiping tears off her cheek and smudging her face in the process.

"Severa, you don't have a home?"

She shook her head. "They... I heard them... they... slave master." She looked up from her incoherence. Her eyes were deep brown filled with pleading. "My parents. They found a slave master. I heard them. I heard them talking. They weren't going to tell me. They were going to take me into town and then hand me over. I know what happens to girls. It's worse than being poor on a small farm. That's just work." This time the tears rolled down silently. Her shoulders trembled.

"Your parents were going to sell you, so you ran away? Is that right?"

She nodded her head. "Don't take me back home. I won't go. A place where they sell their own children is not a home."

"Would you like a home? A place where you wouldn't be sold and nothing bad would happen to you?"

She nodded again, then stopped in thought. "But where would that be?"

"Up in the hills. I know a very nice woman who can always use help."

"Oh, I can do so many things. I sew. I clean. I work in the kitchen. I harvest crops..."

"I can take you there tomorrow. First, have you eaten? Would you like something to eat?"

She nodded and wiped her cheeks again. "I'm very hungry."

"Good. I know just the place where we can go and get you food. It's not far from here. My new home. I just moved in yesterday." He reached out his hand. "Come on, I'll take you there."

She hesitated, then stood up, and reached out her small hand. When she stood, Argolicus realized she was older than he had first thought. Her tiny breasts pushed against her tunic. No wonder she was afraid. He took her hand and led her back into the street.

"Stay close to me. There are many people in the streets tonight."

Severa tightened her grip on his hand. "What is your name?" she asked in a small voice.

"Argolicus, Gaius Vitellius Argolicus. We're going to my father's house. I'm trying to get used to thinking of it as mine. It's safe in there and there's food."

He heard the sound of horse hooves on the street and made sure they stayed to the side. The horsemen were calling, "Disperse. Disperse." The street crowds pushed Argolicus and Severa forward as the horsemen approached. The girl tightened her grip even more if that were possible and pressed against Argolicus. He could feel her trembling.

"Don't be afraid. The horsemen are trying to clear the streets of all these people. Just stay close and follow me."

As the horses drove the people forward, the street filled with the people urged on by their shouts of "Disperse."

Argolicus said, "We'll stay to the side of the street, out of the way of the horsemen. We'll be there very soon." Severa nodded her head, but her eyes were wide with fear.

Argolicus could hear the horses panting now. The crowd pressed on every side. Suddenly, a voice called, "Argolicus."

He turned his head. The horsemen were right behind them. In front was a large, muscular man with a wild mane of blond hair, guiding his horse with his thighs. He pulled on the reins and signaled the men behind him to keep going.

He hopped down from the horse, sword and long fighting knife hanging from his belt, and gave Argolicus a hug. Then he pushed back and said in a burst of energy, "What are you doing here? Look at these crowds. Where are you going? Who is this?"

He turned to survey the crowd while Argolicus answered.

"I'm moving to Father's house. I'm going there now. This is Severa, she's coming with me."

Ebrimuth towered over her and smiled. "Severa, a nice name. You've found one of the best men in all of Bruttium."

Severa nodded her head but kept her eyes down.

"Now," Ebrimuth said, "you need to get home and stay off the streets. Things are getting rough. There was a fire down by the warehouses."

"First, I have a question," Argolicus said. "Why are you patrolling the streets? Isn't that the work of the peace warden?"

"Our friend, Cassiodorus. That's why." Ebrimuth moved his massive shoulders to loosen them. "I've been appointed by the king."

"Appointed? What do you mean?"

Ebrimuth stood his full height, inches taller than Argolicus, and said, "You are looking at the *comes civitatus*. You may call me Count, if you like." A grin spread over his chiseled face. His energized body seemed ready to bound up or away, filled with drive and vitality.

Argolicus smiled at his friend. "Ah, Cassiodorus. Leave it to him to remember his childhood friends. Be wary. I was appointed to Rome and wasn't happy. I'm glad to be back here."

A new group of ruffians marched toward them, chanting. They glared at Ebrimuth and his horse as they walked past. Silently they broke up and walked off to side streets and alleys.

Severa continued to grip Argolicus' hand. She looked up at the tall, blond Ebrimuth.

"Don't worry, little one. No one will harm you. You have Argolicus to stand firm and me to defend you."

Severa nodded but said nothing.

"She's hungry," Argolicus said. "We were on our way to the house to get her some food."

Ebrimuth raised an eyebrow, wanting to know but not asking.

"I just met her," Argolicus said, partially answering the unasked question. "She'll be up near you soon. I'm taking her to the estate tomorrow."

"Aha, we'll be neighbors," Ebrimuth said.

Severa nodded. Then gave him a timid smile.

Ebrimuth focused his attention back on Argolicus. "You shouldn't be walking the streets alone. These are unsettled times. I know you are used to your freedoms but right now you need a bodyguard or two. I'll send you two."

"I don't need a bodyguard."

"You do. You live with your books. You have no idea what is happening not just in the streets of town, but on the roads. People are unhappy and groups are turning violent, especially against landowners and the clerics. You may not carry weapons under the king's law. It's foolish to go without bodyguards. These are troubling times."

Argolicus shrugged his shoulders in exasperation.

Ebrimuth continued, "I'll send them to your house tonight. I have a couple of fellows in mind. They are loyal, trustworthy, and fierce." He gave Argolicus a salute, leaped on his horse, and rode down the street to catch up with his men.

"There you are, Severa. Two protectors. You don't need to be afraid. Now, let's get you some food."

He led her down the street to the town house. They were greeted at the door by the imposing doorman, with dark, impenetrable eyes.

"See, Severa," Argolicus said as they stood in the vestibule, "you have a protector here, as well." He turned to the doorman. "Tell me your name, again."

The massive man bowed his head and answered, "Boden, Your Sublimity."

"Boden. This is Severa, she is staying with us."

Nikolaos appeared with news. "Master, all the rooms are cleaned. Your bedroom is set. Your books are in the library. Your notes are in the study. You see the doorman is here. The cook is making dinner."

"Good," Argolicus said. "Let's eat in the *peristylum*. We have a hungry guest. This is Severa."

Nikolaos eyed the girl and gave Argolicus a questioning look. Argolicus mouthed the word 'later'.

In a few minutes Argolicus, Severa, and Nikolaos clustered around a table with a salad of olives, bread bits soaked in vinegar, and greens, flatbread, and cheese. Severa's eyes opened wide.

Nikolaos had found a woman in the kitchen to help the girl wash and lend her a clean tunic. Her face was symmetrical, classic, and fresh from cleaning. Her skin was even-toned except for her pink cheeks.

"Go ahead, eat," Argolicus said, encouraging her.

She broke off a piece of bread and tested the salad with a tiny bite.

"We made good choices at the market," Nikolaos said. "The cook has organized his staff, and they've been working since early morning. The housemaster, Crispus, is the one who readied the entire house. You'll find it turning into a home."

"Well, the food is good," Argolicus said.

A servant came out holding a tray with steaming bowls of stew.

"There's more?" Severa asked. Her eyes opened wide again.

Argolicus chuckled. "You won't have to go hungry again. You will see that my mother keeps the best kitchen. She loves food."

They heard voices at the front door and Boden's voice saying, "Around the back."

Severa peered into the stew and sniffed. "What is this?"

Nikolaos who had just taken his first bite said, "Seafood. Oysters and mussels. Herbs. Dates."

She dipped her spoon and sipped.

Argolicus felt the gap between this girl's life and his. Food was something that happened daily. For Severa, food was a scarcity. Bread and vegetables were her regular fare.

"I like it," Severa said, dipping her spoon again.

"Master, your bodyguards," a voice said from across the courtyard of the *peristylum*. The housemaster stood in front of two large men. A redhead and a man who was dark for The People. They towered over the small but thick housekeeper. Argolicus knew if he stood, the men would both be taller than he was.

"I'm Kunimund," the dark one said in Their Language. "We've pledged to Ebrimuth to defend you against any and all. This is Eboric." He nodded toward the redhead.

Argolicus rose. "I'm grateful to Ebrimuth. But as I told him, I'm not certain I need bodyguards," he said in Their Language. Then he switched to Latin. "Do you speak Latin? That's what we use here in my household."

They nodded.

"Not well," Eboric said.

"Well, you'll have practice here. Have you eaten?"

They both shook their heads from side to side.

"Go in the kitchen," Argolicus said. "You'll always eat well here. Tell the cook who you are. Remember, Latin."

They headed to the kitchen in a clatter of long knives and swords, leather creaking

Crispus, the housemaster, said, "I'll give them a room across from yours." He headed in the direction of the main bedroom at the back of the house.

Nikolaos smiled. "Master, your household is growing. Will we be trailed by those two from now on?"

"So it seems," Argolicus said. "Ebrimuth thinks they are necessary. You've been inside today. The streets are filled with restive groups—marching, chanting. I've seen the *What about us?* graffiti all over the walls. Unless I solve this problem of the grain shortage, it will get worse. Let's get this little one to bed."

Severa was drowsing over the food. Nikolaos stood and lifted her over his shoulder like a little child. "Where to, Master?"

# TESSERA - CHALK

Boden could understand Latin, even though he didn't speak it well. But for a marketable slave, language skills were not a high priority.

He stood on the platform, naked to the blazing sun, far away from his home country north of Italy.

The market for large men had dwindled after the close of harvest. The two other men on the platform stood abject, but Boden decided that his Burgundian pride would never let him be like that. No matter how little food he had or the rough treatment from the slave master, they could never break his spirit.

As the slave master presented four girls on another platform, the crowd turned away uninterested, except for one man. He was a curious fellow, small, lithe, compact, and dark except for the touches of gray at his temple. A pampered slave, from his looks. He studied Boden.

"Has this man served in a household?" the little man asked the slave master, nodding his head toward Boden.

The slave master eyed the small man and answered, "These are strong men destined for heavy work, you'll find the household slaves over there." He gestured toward another platform crammed with men and women.

"These men barely speak Latin, they're good for fieldwork, not much else." He looked at the little slave again. "I'm sure you'll find something for your master over there."

The little man raised an eyebrow, then turned to study Boden again. "This one will serve my purpose."

The slave master shrugged his shoulders. "Very well, then. Of course, since you want him for your household, the price is higher."

The small man raised his eyebrow again. They started bargaining.

❄  5  ❄

The next morning, Argolicus and Nikolaos headed out to take Severa to the villa. Her face glowed after rest and food. Kunimund rode ahead while Eboric followed.
Argolicus noticed even in the early morning the road was filled with people heading toward the town. How could it all have changed in just two days? He had done nothing to discover what Quintinus had done to get the area in such a fix.

The pedestrians made way for the party, eyeing the weapons on the bodyguards. Many gave Severa a curious look. She was perched behind Nikolaos. The four horses made their way through the foot traffic up the hill. When they reached the villa, Argolicus turned around to look toward the sea.

"I love this view," he said. "I will miss this living in town."

"It's not as though you can't visit," Nikolaos said. "You made the right decision."

A large white dog bounded around the corner of the villa. He ran up to Argolicus as he dismounted.

"Pup, I miss you already," he said, scratching the dog under the chin and then behind the ears. "You are keeping everything safe?"

The massive dog leaned against his thigh.

The door opened. A swirl of blue tunic and a long, blonde braid rushed out the door. Amalina, Argolicus' mother, smiled and gave him a hug.

"Changed your mind already? Couldn't stay away?" she said.

"Mother, this is Severa." He pointed to the girl as Nikolaos helped her from the horse.

"Severa, welcome." Amalina gave Argolicus a questioning look.

Severa reached out to Pup, who sniffed her hand and then gave her a friendly lick. She started talking to the dog in a low voice.

"We met yesterday," Argolicus said. "This is the best place for her to be."

"And bodyguards? You've taken your new role seriously."

"On loan from Ebrimuth. I'll tell you everything in a minute."

"Come in, we'll have a snack. Are you hungry, Severa?"

The girl looked up from the dog and nodded. Minutes later they were all in the courtyard of the *peristylum* nibbling bread and cheese and dates while the bodyguards stood watching from two corners of the yard. The fountain burbled against the growing heat of the morning.

"I have to get back to town. I pledged the council I would look into the matter of the grain shortage. But first, I want to know that Severa will have a safe place."

"Of course, there's always something to do here," Amalina said. "But you. You've been in town two days and already have an assignment from the council."

"Yes, it's tied to this year's grain harvest. Even though the harvest was plentiful, there's not enough for the people."

"We only sell the excess," Amalina said. "We keep enough to feed everyone here first."

"That's just it. The principals are stocked, but all the people—the small farmers, the laborers—who don't grow wheat, have nothing. People are poor. Look at Severa. Her parents were ready to sell her for money. And even with money, they can't buy bread. There's no grain for the municipality to make bread for the people. I don't remember this ever happening."

Two women came in to lead Severa off to her new life. She got up then turned around to give Argolicus a hug. He leaned down as her thin arms wrapped around his chest. "You'll be fine here. Amalina keeps a good house."

She nodded her head, clung tighter for a moment and then left with the women.

Amalina said, "You did the right thing for that girl."

"I have one more task," Argolicus said. "I'll find her parents, tell them where she is, and give them some money."

"So now you can tell me all about Proba."

Argolicus knew he would disappoint her.

"We are not getting married. We both agreed for different reasons. She's an interesting woman. Beautiful, too. We've formed a friendship."

Amalina nodded, but her face had the mother's look—I'm disappointed, but you make your own decisions.

☙❦❧

Argolicus settled into the chair in front of the table in his study and opened an old journal. Seeing Proba with her father's books had inspired him to look at his father's journals. Nikolaos quietly arranged books on the bookshelves.

"Leave my father's journals," Argolicus said. "I want to look through them."

"What about your Greek collection?"

"We'll keep that in the library upstairs and use that room as the reading room."

"It will be good to settle into routines. We can read tonight. And, tomorrow morning we can practice in the courtyard by the stables. We used it when you were young. I had it cleaned out today."

Argolicus chuckled inwardly. For years the little tutor had bested him when it came to martial arts. Even though under the king's rule as a Roman he could not carry weapons in public, he welcomed the practice. As the classic education intended, physical activity kept him supple and sharpened his reflexes.

They heard Boden's northern accent at the door. A moment later he arrived in the study accompanied by a slight woman. Argolicus was surprised to see Proba.

"Proba," he said. "Welcome."

"Argolicus, it's not welcome news. My father has been killed. I need your help. You are the first person who came to mind." Her face was a mask. Argolicus didn't know if she was holding in sorrow. She said it like it was a fact, in the tone you would say how much grain was harvested in the Bruttium area last month.

"Your father, Quintinus?" As soon as he said it, he knew it was not a bright question. He was knocked off guard. He'd been waiting to talk to Quintinus, and now this. He recovered and said, "I'm sorry. Tell me what happened."

"First, his horse returned without him. Soon after his servant came back and said they were ambushed by the river. It's all so unclear."

"The servant, what did he say?"

"He said it happened so quickly he's distraught. His injury is severe. They were in the river canyon, someone came out, struck the servant, and then knocked my father off his horse onto the rocks. My father's body is there. I was hoping... Would you come with me? Maybe you will see something. I hear you are good at this sort of thing."

"Proba, I am truly sorry. I think my reputation is larger than my skills. But, if you want me to help you with the body, I can do that. I have two strong bodyguards. What about your mother?"

"Mother," Proba said, her voice even. "Mother is being the

grieving widow, shrieking, crying, summoning her friends. She is useless. It's not as though she loved him. He was her convenience."

Nikolaos slipped out of the study.

"I see," Argolicus said. "What do we need to bring your father back?"

"Horses, a way to carry him, possibly a cart once we bring him up from the river. I haven't been there, yet."

Nikolaos came back with two sturdy slaves. "I have two men. We'll get a cart from the stable. Kunimund and Eboric will be waiting there."

"Proba, this is Nikolaos. He's been with me since I was a small child."

She nodded at Nikolaos. He nodded back and headed for the servant corridor, followed by the two men.

"Do you have a horse?" Argolicus asked.

"At home. I walked here."

"We'll find you a horse in the stable. Do you know how to get there?"

"Yes, it's the canyon in the river. The place where it flows over the rocks."

Argolicus nodded. He remembered going there as a boy. It was a popular place for boys to dare. The rushing water and the boulders made it dangerous.

Soon, everyone was assembled in the stable. Nikolaos and the two men had hitched a horse to an old cart. Kunimund stood silently by his horse. Eboric looked as though he couldn't wait to get started. He tossed his mane of red hair and then helped Proba up into the saddle.

"We'll meet you there," Nikolaos said, flicking the reins. The cart rolled out into the alleyway.

"Are you ready?" Argolicus asked Proba.

Her face set, Proba said, "Ready."

Kunimund led the way into the alley.

Everything that had been fresh and green in spring was dry and gold. Spikes of grass shot up between rocks. The horses picked their way down the steep slopes to the river. The farther down the slope they went, the sound of the water rushing over rocks seemed to fill the canyon. Boulders rose from the water as it threaded its way on its course.

"He's here, somewhere," Proba said, her voice wavering.

Argolicus could tell that now that they were here in the August sun with the rushing water and the rocks, finding her father's body was becoming a certainty. The servant had described the waterfall over the boulders.

Eboric scanned the river, raising his shoulders high. "Over there," he raised his voice above the rush of the water, pointing to a large boulder jutting up among the other rocks.

Argolicus said, "You wait here, Proba. I'll call you. Kunimund can lead you down."

The dark man nodded his head and moved his horse closer to Proba.

"But I want to see him," she said, not whining, just making a statement.

"You will. A dead body can be unsettling. Let us find him first."

He prodded his horse with his knees and it picked its way through rocks on the steep bank. Argolicus joined Eboric who led them further down to the edge of the river. Here, boulders crowded together so that no horse could pass. They dismounted and left the horses as Eboric led the way to what he had seen. They edged through several large boulders and came to the bank of the river. Quintinus' body lay on a small muddy patch between two boulders.

"Here's the man," Eboric said as he strode over the mud to the body.

"Don't touch him, yet," Argolicus said, coming up beside Eboric. In the shade of the boulders, the air was cool. He looked down at the body twisted on the ground. "If it weren't for the servant, you'd think he'd been thrown from his horse."

Argolicus turned around and gestured to Kunimund and Proba waiting above on the steep slope. "He's here. Be careful on the rocks."

In a moment, Proba forced her small body through the two rocks. Her eyes focused on her father's crumpled shape face down in the mud. She turned to Argolicus, "You're so practiced, tell me what you see."

"Tell me what you see," Argolicus responded, not rising to her challenge.

Proba raised an eyebrow. Then, she looked down at her father. "I'll start with the obvious."

Argolicus nodded.

She continued, "His body is twisted. He looks like he was thrown from his horse."

"Good. And?" Argolicus asked.

"The side of his head is bloody. It's... It's like a hole." Her voice started to break.

"Can you go on?"

Proba took a deep breath and nodded. She walked around to the other side of the body. "His hand is scratched. And his arm. You are right, it's unsettling."

"It is. No matter how many times I see a body, I have a sense of all humanity affronted. And a deep sorrow."

Proba nodded. "His leg is twisted..." She gulped and then turned away to vomit on the mud.

Argolicus went to her. He put his arm around her trembling shoulders. "It's normal. You'll be all right. Death is ugly, especially violent death. I shouldn't have pushed you to look so closely."

"No. No, I need to know. I want to find the person who did

this. I'm just..." She burst into tears. "My father." Then she leaned on Argolicus and cried.

Eboric called from behind a rock, "I found something."

Proba untangled herself from Argolicus. She wiped her eyes and then headed toward the fiery redhead. Argolicus and Kunimund followed.

"There," Eboric said, pointing to a small glistening piece of gold on the ground. "You said not to touch anything."

"Right," Argolicus said. He noticed footprints in the mud near the gold object. "Stand back," he said. "I want to look closely."

He leaned down. "One set of footprints. One man. A large man. Good shoes." Then he walked over to the glint in the mud, reached down, and picked it up. "A bead. A gold bead... But, it's just one. Not a broken necklace. It must have fallen off something else." He rolled the bead between his fingers, wiping away mud. No engravings, just a plain, round bead.

Above them, they heard the cart trundle to a stop. Nikolaos called down, "We'll be there shortly."

Argolicus waved. The summer sun heated the air even in the dark crevices between the boulders.

"We know some things," he said. "A large man, probably alone. The gold bead and the shoe imprints suggest he is wealthy. So, we don't need to consider brigands."

"I would not have thought of these things," Proba said. "I know I chose the right person to help me." She smiled at Argolicus.

"Here you are," Nikolaos said, emerging from the boulders. "I brought water."

## 6

The sun's heat grew as they rode back to town. Eboric's red hair flickered in the light like a beacon leading them to Squillace. Kunimund followed behind the creaking cart with Quintinus' body covered in cloths. Sunlight glistened on the stubble in the empty grain fields on both sides of the road.

Argolicus looked at the fields. His first promise to the *curia* at the council seemed unreachable. He would never have a conversation with Quintinus about the over-pledged grain. Proba rode by his side in silence.

"I wanted to talk to your father," he said.

"I remember," Proba said. "Something about contracts."

"Yes, not specific contracts, but the shipment of grain away from Bruttium."

"Ah, number totals. Maybe I can help. What do you need to know?"

"You've seen the people in the streets?"

As he spoke, they approached a group of ragged men in the road. They turned belligerently at the sound of the horses, then resumed their plodding toward town when they noticed Eboric and his sword.

"Like those men," Proba said. "Yes, they march in the streets, stand in groups at street corners, and write graffiti on walls. What about them?" She peered ahead at the group on the road.

"They are unsettled because of the lack of grain. There's no bread for the people. So you've seen the graffiti? What about us?"

Proba nodded.

"Well," Argolicus continued, "with a good harvest, we should have plenty of grain for the community. Your father controlled most of the exports. I'm uncomfortable saying this now, but he seems to have sold all the local grain without apportioning grain for the community."

Proba sucked in her breath. She shifted in the saddle as she glanced back at the group on the road.

"My father. He was about the contract. How much money was involved in the agreement was his priority. He promised grain shipments to the north. I need to go back and look at the contracts. I can't answer your question. If he calculated incorrectly, it may have been up to me to discover the difference. He would never have deliberately shorted supplies to the community."

"Why was it up to you? You weren't physically present when he was negotiating. If he was at Portus or Rome arranging shipments, you weren't there."

"Before he went on each trip, I gave him the numbers. What was available, how much we had sold so far, and what was remaining."

"So, with that information, he could make arrangements without exceeding what was available?"

Proba tipped her head and pursed her lips, puzzled. "Yes. I don't understand how the community grain supply is short. Do you think this has something to do with...?" She turned her head back to the cart carrying her father's body.

Argolicus shook his head. "Anything is possible. At this point, we don't know. But, murder? It's unlikely. Murder is usually personal, very personal. A grudge or jealousy or greed. Can you think of anyone?"

She shook her head.

Eboric motioned for them to come closer as the road led into town. People marched in groups crowding the street but stepped aside as Eboric forged their way toward Proba's home.

"Where was he going on this trip? Who was he going to see?" Argolicus asked.

Proba shook her head again. "He told me this was a personal trip. Something about a local grower, but he didn't need new numbers. He said he knew everything he needed to know."

They rode through town, Eboric clearing the way through the people in the street. They were greeted with raised fists and followed by grumbles. At last, they entered the alley beside the town house. Nikolaos supervised the two men as they lifted the body and the draped covers from the cart. The side door burst open as Fabia's tiny body hurtled toward the body. "Husband! Husband! What has happened to you?" she cried, grabbing the cloth as she tried to uncover Quintinus' face.

Argolicus pulled her back from the covered body. "Fabia, let us take him inside."

She nodded and then followed the two men and Nikolaos who trailed Proba as she led the way to a room set with a large table. The men laid the body on the table. Two slaves began removing the layers of cloth.

Fabia stood by silently, her frenzy quelled by the sight of his body covered in mud and the gobs of blood clinging to his head.

Proba clutched Argolicus' hand. "Now that he's home, it seems so final."

Argolicus nodded and squeezed her hand. The slaves began to cut away the clothing, respectfully removing pieces.

"I can't look," Fabia said. She turned away and headed toward the *atrium*.

"I'd like to talk to your mother," Argolicus said to Proba.

She nodded. "She's quite emotional. But I can't tell if it's for show or not. I saw three of her friends in the *atrium*. None of them is crying."

She led him into the *atrium*. Fabia and her friends were gathered on chairs by the pool, murmuring.

"Mother," Proba said. "Argolicus would like to speak with you. Could you spare him some time?"

Argolicus watched as a procession of emotions blazed across Fabia's face—anger, bewilderment, a fleck of sadness—until she composed a matronly mask. "Very well. We'll go in my writing room."

She turned to whisper to her friends and then led Argolicus to a *cubiculum* several doors away from the place where the slaves cleaned Quintinus' body.

Frescoes of young women in flowered fields adorned the walls. Vines covered with leaves wound in scroll patterns on the mosaic floor. Two chairs faced each other in one corner, while a small table with writing tools stood in another.

"We'll sit here," Fabia said, gesturing toward the chairs.

They sat facing each other. Fabia was dressed in a plain *tunica* of brown linen and wore no jewelry. Trinitarians used the days of mourning before burial to receive friends after the body preparation. Fabia was looking at three days of being a hostess to occupy her first days of grief.

"First, thank you for going with Proba to claim the body. I couldn't do it. I feel as though my life is turned upside-down. Who will continue the business? I don't know how much he put aside for our welfare. I'll have to rely on Proba to sort through everything."

"An unexpected death causes confusion. Grief comes later after the rituals and the arrangements. This is not only an unexpected death but a violent killing. Proba asked me to help find the person or people who did this to your husband."

"She would. I don't understand you two. You seem to get along well, but you have refused marriage. Your mother and I..." She trailed off. Then she gathered her thoughts. "Well, you aren't the best marriage prospect. Your mother. It's complicated."

Argolicus caught a glint of greed in her eye, greed that over-looked his mixed heritage in favor of wealth. The glint dimmed as she looked at him.

"My mother married for love. My father married for love. They were fortunate that at the time a union like theirs was not illegal as it is now. My reasons and Proba's reasons are different. You need to talk to her about her reasons. But that's not why I need to speak to you now. I need your help."

Fabia fidgeted with a fold in her garment. She frowned, then looked at Argolicus. "I'm disappointed in Proba, but I will help. Our life was so settled. Murder. I don't know how to think about it. What will I do next?" She waved her hand in a broad gesture, as if the plan for the next steps in her life was somewhere outside the room. "How can I help?"

"Tell me about Quintinus, not his business, but as a man. Who were his friends? Did he have enemies?"

"His friends? I'm not sure he had friends. He knew everyone. The principals. Everyone knew him. They came and went here at the house. But he traveled so frequently. He didn't entertain. We didn't have rounds of dinners and then reciprocate. He filled his life with business. He was always trying to make the best contract possible. For him, that meant money."

"Can you think of anyone who disliked him? Anyone who held a grudge?"

"Proba would know more about that than I do. I didn't follow his business dealings." She paused. "Our marriage was... it was... We lived separate lives. I have my friends here in town. We social-ize, but as women. What Quintinus did, who he met, who would hold a grudge—he didn't share that information. I learned more about him from my friends than from what he told me."

"Did you hear anything from your friends? Some story about how he had wronged someone or caused them harm?"

She shook her head. "No. Only..." she paused again. "Well... women's things. He had a mistress, Martina. She is a woman of property here in town. She lives by herself. I hear she's young from my friends. She entertained him regularly. He never told me about her. As I said, we lived separate lives. I've seen her in the forum. He thought I didn't know... or pretended I didn't know. Either way, it makes no difference. Our marriage was contractual and solid, but not loving."

She stopped, her mind off on the other woman.

Argolicus pulled her back. "Did he ever mention anyone or an episode that made him angry?"

"He wasn't an angry man. He was driven. He would get frustrated. The most he talked about was a deal that wasn't going his way. But that was usually in letters. He made most of his agreements far from Squillace. When he was home, here in town, he still traveled to meet with growers. They talked about this year and last year and the next year. I didn't pay much attention."

"Those growers, were any of them disgruntled?"

"No, no. The growers loved how he got the best price, especially in harvest years like this. Even I know that it's easy to get good prices when the harvest is low. No, nothing, no one." She shook her head again.

"Fabia, I know you are distressed and confused. Let's stop this conversation."

A look of relief passed on her face. Her forehead relaxed from the frown and her mouth softened.

"I haven't been much help. I'm realizing that even though he was my husband, I don't know much about him. I've been selfish. I thought we had a good arrangement, but I relied on him to provide yet didn't know him."

Her face crumpled.

"Death brings regrets even to the best marriages. I'm not sure what defines the best marriage. You did what made your marriage acceptable to both of you."

Fabia gave him a small smile.

"If I think of something, remember anything he said about a particular man, I'll tell Proba. You two seem to be friends. If you think it is important, you can come and ask me more."

"Agreed," Argolicus said. "Thank you for speaking with me in such a troubled time. I've promised Proba I will help."

Fabia rose. She headed toward the door, then turned around, "I think I see why Proba likes you."

## TESSARA - LIME

"Cadmus, I'm going to find you."

He hid in the alley between two large houses, listening to his sister, calling in a teasing voice.

"Here I come," she said. But he heard her walking away.

In the alley, shaded from the summer sun by the tall buildings, refuse stood ready to be carted away.

Cadmus crouched between two piles of rubble. He stepped back to press himself against a wall.

"Ouch," a voice cried out from the foot of a rubble pile.

"Shh," he said, whispering. "I'm hiding from my sister."

"I'm hiding too." The voice belonged to a boy a little older than his sister. He was dressed in a plain tunic, dirty from cringing against the rubble.

"Are you a slave?" he said, in the forthright way of children.

He jutted out her smudged chin, "Never."

Before he could ask why he was so dirty, his sister's voice rolled down the alleyway. "I know I'm getting closer now. Here I come."

And then she was there.

"Found you! Come on, it's time to go home." She grabbed his arm and tugged him toward the end of the alley.

Two enormous men blocked the way out. Cadmus had to tilt up his head to see their faces. One was a patrician like his father, dressed in an elegant tunic covered with embroidery. The other was a slave and larger.

"Out of my way," the patrician said, annoyance and disdain aimed at Cadmus and his sister. "Go home."

The immense slave shoved Cadmus' sister. She stumbled and fell, letting go of his hand.

Cadmus stood frozen in fear. Then his sister was up and holding his hand again. They ran out of the alley.

## ❧ 7 ❧

"I don't know enough," Argolicus said.

"Master, you've just begun," Nikolaos said, shelving a book.

Argolicus and Nikolaos were in the study. The tutor arranged more books on the shelves. Argolicus had set a pile of his father's journals on the large table, but they lay unopened as he thought about his pledge to Proba.

"Quintinus is like a cipher. Proba tells me his business dealings. His wife knows next to nothing. I know next to nothing. And, now I have nothing to tell the council. What was I thinking? My second day in town and I plunged into a commitment to something I know nothing about."

Nikolaos shelved another book in silence.

Argolicus stared at the desk. He didn't know how he would fulfill his pledge to the council. A simple conversation with Quintinus about the grain was not possible. He needed to find another solution. But now he was confounded with no simple solution. He slapped his palm on the table in frustration.

"Whatever we do about Quintinus, I need to see Vespasianus first. Come."

Vespasianus' house was just as large as his own. But, when they entered the *atrium*, Argolicus encountered an ornate surrounding. Marble statues flanked each corner of the pool—a nymph, a satyr, Minerva, and some god from the ancients he couldn't identify. Patterns in gold leaf adorned the bench facing the pool.

Vespasianus entered from his study, preceded by a large slave who lumbered off toward the back of the house. He wore a tunic adorned with rich embroidery of gold and silver threads. He ran his hands through his dark hair, frowned in annoyance, and then settled on a look of contentment.

"You have news already?"

"Yes," Argolicus said, "but not what I was expecting. The grain market needs to wait. I am here with unpleasant news. Quintinus is dead."

"Dead? When?" Vespasianus ran his hand through his hair again and shook his head. This time his frown was sincere.

"Yesterday. The news is even more unpleasant, he was murdered."

Vespasianus' brows pulled together. He put a finger to his lips, then gestured toward his study.

"In here," he said, leading Argolicus toward the study. Nikolaos trailed behind and chose a corner.

Vespasianus gestured toward a chair as he settled into a gilt chair behind the table. He folded his hands on the table and looked at Argolicus. "Tell me."

"His daughter, Cocceia Proba, asked me for help. We went to the creek to recover his body. It looks as though he was hit on the head. His servant escaped and made it back to town, but he is wounded. He doesn't remember much. He must have been struck first."

"This is Squillace, these things don't happen here. We live in a town of peace and prosperity."

"Wasn't a bishop murdered just a couple of years ago? I wasn't here, but I heard about it."

Vespasianus nodded. "Yes, and I heard about your friend, Lucas, Bartholomaeus' son who was killed." He shook his head. "Bartholomaeus tries so hard and offends everyone."

"Murder happens everywhere. Squillace, Rome, it makes no difference. But for the council, this raises a problem. I have no answers about the grain or how to retrieve the stores. Until we find a solution, the people will continue to protest. Just this morning, I saw more groups of people coming into town, ready to complain."

"I see how that would frustrate you. You, like your father before you, don't dabble in trade. Perhaps you took on a role that isn't suited. I know you want to quell the rioters, just like we all do. Have you thought of getting a helping hand?"

Argolicus shook his head. "No, who would you suggest?"

"Well, Donicus could help. He is in charge of the markets as well as the finances and administration. You sat next to him. You seem to know each other. Why don't you go to him? He will know other people."

Vespasianus glanced down and flattened a fold in his tunic, so the embroidery lay straight down his chest. The metallic threads sparkled in the afternoon light.

"Donicus," Argolicus said. "A good suggestion. I'll see him. Anyone else? I'd like to get to the bottom of what happened with the grain."

"Donicus is the right place to start since Quintinus is gone. Quintinus owned the grain market. The smaller dealers ultimately went to him. He traveled. He could get the best prices by meeting buyers face to face. Other merchants here, all did a much smaller volume. Donicus can tell you more. And then there's Macro, the treasurer. He may not know about grain but has a keen eye for money."

"I see."

"Are you sure you want to take this on? You are new to the interconnections here. I understand why you did it, but there is no shame in setting this query aside."

Vespasianus fidgeted with the hem of his sleeve.

"Yes, I do," Argolicus said. "I plunged into investigations in Rome without knowing anyone. And, I gave my word before the entire council."

Vespasianus nodded. "Yes, your family. Your father was the same way, committed once his word was given. Always trustworthy. If you are used to Rome, you will find politics the same here. Few honest men."

"I'll make my way. Before I go, I have another question."

"Yes?"

"When I said Quintinus' daughter asked me to help, she asked me to find who killed him. You knew him. Did he have enemies? Was he liked? Disliked? What can you tell me?"

"Quintinus was more than a grain merchant. He was a man who contributed to the town. Even though he was away much of the time, he knew everyone and everyone knew him. He had dealings with almost everyone. Money was a commodity. Everything was a commodity. He had a price, and he named it. If a man needed a favor, a short loan or capital for investing, Quintinus did not hesitate to make an arrangement."

"An arrangement?"

"Yes, he made small loans, particularly loans on future events —a ship that was due, a harvest in several months. You are probably one of the few men in the *curia* who did not have dealings with him."

"He practiced usury?"

"No, no. It was more subtle than that. He would loan money based on some guarantee, usually a piece of property. Sometimes it was livestock or a portion of goods. He didn't charge interest. He arranged... fees."

Argolicus was unclear about the difference, but he nodded and asked, "Fees? What does that mean? He took a portion of what came in?"

"Well. Yes. So, he made a little from his generosity. I'm curious. Since you didn't know Quintinus, how do you think you can discover who killed him?"

"I'm not certain if I can."

Vespasianus ran his hand up and down the intricate embroidery on his tunic. "And, so?"

❧

"Something doesn't ring true," Argolicus said as he and Nikolaos headed home led by the fiery Eboric and followed by the stony Kunimund.

"His pride in Squillace? Even though people are close to rioting? That?"

Argolicus clapped his tutor on the shoulder. "Yes. Exactly. It feels as though he's told himself these stories about Squillace so often he believes what he says. Perhaps he lies to himself to embellish his position as a magistrate. Well, that task is done. We've told him about Quintinus. Now we have to find the killer."

Groups of men stood in the street mumbling. They glared at Argolicus and the bodyguards as they walked by.

"When we return, I'll send a note to Proba letting her know Vespasianus knows about her father."

They skirted a group of twenty that almost blocked the street.

Argolicus continued, "But that doesn't get us any closer to the killer."

As they approached the house, Argolicus made out activity in the front. Two of the stalls were open with goods stacked. A few household slaves still out shopping in the late morning, gathered around to sort through the goods.

"Argolicus," Rufus called from one of the stalls, "it's all

arranged. I paid your housemaster. This is Ezio. He can get you any plate or platter you need, and he has glassware."

"Rufus," Argolicus said smiling, "it's good to have you back. Ezio, welcome." The slight young potter blushed and bowed his head.

"It's the same here," Rufus said, gesturing toward the street. "With all these ruffians in the street, the patricians are not out buying. The slaves hold the purse, but the owners make the selection."

He passed some plums to a slave and took his coins. The slave scurried away with his purchase.

"Now, only the slaves come. And they don't linger. There's no extra buying. This unrest is slowing business." The potter Ezio nodded his head.

"I can't tell you much," said Argolicus, "but I'm looking into the grain shortage. The sooner this gets resolved, all of us will have a better life."

"Good. I'm glad you are back. Always conscientious. If you are dealing with this, I have hope that this will all go away." He gestured toward the street again. "And, soon, as I spread the word to the right people, I'll have these other four stalls filled. It's good to have you back in town."

The doorman Boden closed the door behind them. Town life faded as Argolicus' heart skipped a beat. The house was freshened and scrubbed, gleaming with care. The pool in the *atrium* was full of fresh water and sparkled in the summer light shining from above. It was like stepping into his childhood. He listened for his father's voice from the study, "What have you been up to?" And just like when he was a child, he didn't know how to answer.

## ❧ 8 ❧

**D**onicus, the squinting *curator civitatis*, welcomed Argolicus into his study. The table was strewn with sheets covered in columns of numbers. An stylus rested under his left hand.

"Jumped into the fray, didn't you?" he said as Argolicus settled in a chair across the table. His creaky voice was just above a whisper. "Stood right up at your first council meeting and bit off a huge bite."

Argolicus smiled at the jumbled metaphors, and nodded. "That's why I'm here. Vespasianus said you should be the first man I see."

"You know my appointment is honorary." He blinked as if trying to clear his thoughts. "I keep track of the numbers others give me. Look at this desk. It's like a repository of numbers. But really, I don't know what to do with them, other than report at the council."

"How do you keep track?"

"Twice a year I ask the members of the council. It's quite a job connecting with over one hundred members. But, they are polite, for the most part. They come here to report. Some bring sheets with numbers, others keep the numbers in their head. I write them down—so much oil, so much honey, so much garum, so much grain, so many horses. Like that. Most of them can supply a value. If they can't, I have a rough idea."

"What about people like my mother? My father died. I was in Rome."

"Oh, your mother is fortunate. She has the overseer Lucius. He's one of those who keep all the numbers in their head. But, he is exact and knows the value of everything. Of course, everything is recorded in your name."

Argolicus nodded. His father had found Lucius before he died and Lucius ran the estate well. And he had recently discovered that as much as he enjoyed life at the villa, he had no interest in how the estate was run. "I see. That means of all the people in Squillace, you have the best idea of how much each person is worth."

"That's the idea when it comes to taxes. We must report to Governor Venantius, who reports to..." he paused, "the King Theoderic."

He lowered his already wheezy voice. "Sometimes I think the numbers change with Venantius." He closed his squinting eyes and nodded his head.

"Mmm," Argolicus agreed.

"But," Donicus continued, opening his eyes, "you are right. I do have a good idea of how much each person is worth."

"And the markets? What do you know about the markets? You perform basic administration for the town. Surely you must know them as well as the individual wealth of each member of the *curia*."

Donicus closed his eyes again and nodded. "It's true. I know what goes into the warehouses, where it comes from, and eventually, where it is going. It's more difficult to compile because it involves tracking several stages."

"This is where I am confounded," Argolicus said. "I talked to

Quintinus' daughter Proba about the grain, and she can't remember anything out of place. While you were 'tracking' the grain, didn't you notice a discrepancy between what was here and what was shipped?"

Donicus closed his eyes. His eyebrows contracted, forming deep furrows on his brow. Then he opened his eyes, shuffled the sheets on the table, and collected them all into a stack. He rested his hand on the stack. "I have what people give me in the same way I gather information about members of the *curia*. I rely on what people tell me about shipments and goods in storage at the warehouses."

Argolicus asked, "So, since Quintinus was the major grain dealer here, your figures came from him?"

Donicus opened his eyes. "Was?"

"Yes, you've been sheltered away with your numbers. He was killed."

Donicus, pulled back, his face unreadable. "Killed," he murmured. Then as if returning to the room, he nodded. "Yes. I rely on the information provided. Merchants like Quintinus and others give me the amounts being shipped. I record those amounts and report to the *curia*."

"But, you know the grain on hand for the community. You got those numbers from Quintinus as well?"

Donicus relaxed his face. "Yes, yes. Exactly."

He raised his hand from the stack of numbered sheets and waved it palm out. "I was appointed by the magistrates, and I keep the numbers. I know the principals expect more of me, but I can do what I can do. Someone else must make sense of all these numbers." He put down his hand and shrugged his shoulders.

Argolicus sighed. Would he have to interpret the numbers to find the answer? "Donicus, where do you keep the tallies for the city stores?"

"Over here," Donicus said, rising from his seat and reaching for a ledger on a shelf. He brought the book back to the table and opened it. "Here," he said, pushing the open ledger across the table toward Argolicus.

"Where are the numbers for the grain?"

Donicus took back the ledger and leafed through sheets. "Each section denotes the city stores. Oil..." He turned the leaves with his index finger. "Horses... Ah, here it is, grain." He turned the book around again and pushed it toward Argolicus.

Argolicus looked at the page. The listings showed amounts of grain placed in the warehouse, the dates delivered, and the source. He noticed most of the source notations were Pompeius Severus Quintinus. "Where is the total?"

"Total?" Donicus whimpered.

No, the man was not a match for the position.

"Donicus, you heard me tell the entire *curia* I would investigate the shortage."

The old man nodded, his face once again creased with a frown.

"I want to take this ledger. I'll keep it safe. But I plan to add the numbers, and, with the help of Quintinus' daughter, I will check these totals against the merchant's records."

"The books are in my trust," Donicus whined. But he did nothing to retrieve the ledger.

"Yes, well, if you entrust this one to me, I will keep it safe." Argolicus closed the ledger and rose. "Thank you for your time. I will let Vespasianus know that I have the ledger in trust."

Concern crossed the old man's face. He grimaced briefly and then smiled. "Thank you. If you can make sense of it all... I have all the documentation here." He pointed to the loose sheets stacked in front of him. He rose. "Your Sublimity, I think Squillace will benefit from your return."

Fabia rose from a small group of women seated by the *atrium* pool. The women peered at Argolicus and began whispering.

Fabia rushed toward Argolicus. "Argolicus, Argolicus. You're here so soon. Have you found something?"

"Fabia, I'm sorry about Quintinus. But, no, I have nothing to report. I'm here about another matter. Is Proba here?"

"Oh, yes, yes. In the study as always."

Proba emerged from the study. She smiled and then her face became quizzical. "Argolicus? News?"

"No. No news about your father. But..." he gestured to Nikolaos who pulled out the ledger they'd brought from Donicus.

Fabia interrupted. "You will come to the funeral? I know you didn't know him but..." She gestured toward Proba.

"The funeral?" Argolicus hadn't thought about that. He turned to Proba. "Would you want me there?"

Proba looked down at her hands. "Yes, a friend is just what I need. I still haven't taken it in. I keep expecting him to come home. I have so many questions for him, and they will go unanswered."

She glanced at the women by the pool engaged in their lively whispers and glances. "Let's go in the study."

Argolicus took the ledger from Nikolaos and placed it on the large table in the study, which was covered with journals, some open, others stacked.

"Have you found out anything about the grain shortage?"

"No," Proba answered. "I've been poring over the ledgers and all the numbers seem credible. From my tallies, it seems the city should have plenty of grain." She frowned and tapped the stack of ledgers. "It doesn't make sense."

"Maybe this will help." Argolicus pointed to Donicus' ledger. "Donicus kept records for the city, but he didn't add any totals. Poor man. He seems out of his depth."

"Yes, that's what Father said. An honorary title but with no ability. Why did you bring it here?" Her thin, dark eyebrows contracted as she opened the book and glanced at the columns.

"For help."

"Ah, the son of Gaius Vitellius Maximinus, lately praefect of Rome, needs my help." She smiled.

They both laughed. Nikolaos watched his master as one eyebrow twitched.

Then Argolicus went straight to the point. "Here, I've marked the section about the grain. Since Quintinus was the major grain merchant, I'm hoping you could check the numbers here against your records."

"I can do that, but it will be several days." She took the ledger and placed it on the table in front of her. "Father's funeral is tomorrow. Mother is in a flurry. Those women...," she gestured toward the *atrium*, "get her worked up. Then when they leave, I have to calm her down so we can make arrangements. I don't know how she will make it through the liturgy. She will be surrounded by them."

"Each person grieves in their own way. Whatever they say to her, she feels surrounded by friends."

Proba's face became solemn. "While Father was here, she was off in her own world. I'm not used to tending to her."

"Maybe you don't need to tend to her. She lived without your attention before. Give her time."

Proba nodded. Then she looked at Argolicus and her face spread into a grin. "Here you are, my new friend, and at such a strange time." She paused. "Friendship. That's why I'd like you to be at the funeral. Just knowing you are there."

It was the best reason to attend a funeral Argolicus had heard. Since his own father's death, he avoided funerals. He would over-come this. "I'll be there."

A wave of relief flowed over Proba. "Thank you. None of this makes sense. I'm having a hard time looking at my life without

Father." She came around the table and hugged Argolicus. Then she rested her head on his shoulder.

"I have a request," Argolicus said.

"Yes." She nuzzled his shoulder.

Nikolaos stood silent, but his eyebrow twitched again.

"Your father's body is here. I'd like to look at him without the mud of the river."

Proba drew back and looked up into his eyes. Argolicus glimpsed vulnerability and sorrow. "If you think it will help. Follow me."

They crossed the *atrium* under the watchful group of women by the pool. Proba entered a small room. "There."

Quintinus' body lay on a table. The body was clean and, from the scent in the room, rubbed with herbed oil. Although the body was covered in a plain tunic, Argolicus could see the bruises on the arm. The right side of the body was colored with blotches of deep red, almost purple.

"Now he looks like a body, not my father," Proba said. "I don't like this to be my last memory of him." She clasped her hands at her chest and stared, and then she said, as if a realization struck, "I don't know what this means for me. I keep numbers. I am not a negotiator."

She slumped against Argolicus. He put his hands on her shoulders and murmured, "Proba. Everything will work out. Let's get through the funeral first."

She nodded and pulled back. "My life was so settled. Now this. I'll wait for you in the study. This is not the vision of my father I want to remember." She turned with a swish and left Argolicus and Nikolaos alone with Quintinus' body.

"Did I miss something?" Argolicus asked, gently turning the head of the corpse and inspecting the wound.

¾ 9 ¾

A rgolicus slumped onto a bench in the *peristylum* in the town home. The garden grounds were dug to receive fresh plants, but the garden was bare. He gave in to exhaustion and extended his body the length of the bench. "I feel like an outsider. In Rome, where I was an outsider, gossip bubbles up by the next day. Here, I've learned nothing."

"Master, you had an official capacity in Rome," Nikolaos said. "Here, you are a recent arrival. Only the members of the *curia* who were at the town meeting know you pledged to investigate the grain shortage. It's not general knowledge. You have no official capacity."

Argolicus sighed. "You are right. So far, in the little time I've had, no one knows why the numbers are wrong. Everything seems straightforward, but grain is missing. There's no denying the reality of that. Even Proba, who worked directly with her father, can't find anything. I hope when she looks at Donicus' ledger she'll find the error."

The afternoon sun slanted in on the bare ground casting shadows from the statuary and the benches. Argolicus lost himself in thought wondering how he could recreate the old *peri-*

*stylum*. He could remember every shrub and plant as he played as a child. He remembered his father having conversations like this one in the *peristylum* with his house manager and confidant.

"Proba," Nikolaos said. "Not a wife, then?"

"No, don't get any ideas. We settled on friendship. I like her. That is all."

"Did you see anything new when you re-examined the body?"

"Nothing new. The same marks on his arm that meant he put up a fight. And the severe blow to his head. Cleaned up, it was easier to see it was deep and the object, whatever it was, wielded with force."

"With so many unsettled people about, maybe it was ruffians with no particular motive other than robbery." Nikolaos pulled a small book out from a pocket in his tunic.

"Those shoe prints said differently," Argolicus mumbled. Then he sat up. "It's late enough in the day for the woman Martina to be receiving visitors. Men often tell their mistress things they would say to nobody else."

Nikolaos put away the book.

❦

Martina's house was large, situated in the area between the town hall and the warehouses. The neighborhood was not patrician, but Argolicus could tell that many merchants lived here with enough money to live comfortably. The well-stocked shops were opening up for the evening and a comfortable hum pervaded the streets.

Argolicus noticed that the ruffians that crowded the streets where he lived and the forum were not haunting these streets. He didn't see "What about us?" painted on the walls. Only a few streets away from his home, yet here the feeling was relaxed.

Eboric knocked on the door. When it opened, he and Kunimund stood to the side. A large doorman peered out at Argolicus. "It's early."

ZARA ALTAIR

"I've come for something else. Gaius Vitellius Argolicus for the mistress Martina."

The doorman arched his eyebrows. "Wait here." The door closed.

The door opened. "Your Sublimity, I am Martina. Enter." A scent of wildflowers in the sunlight came through the open door. The woman was breathtaking. Slender and soft, draped to the ankles in a thin linen tunic topped with a stola cinched below her full breasts, so through both layers of the thin fabric her nipples were barely visible. Her voice was soft and intimate as if they had known each other for a long time. Dark hair tumbled over her shoulders and down over her breasts. Her dark brown eyes were shaded by the longest eyelashes Argolicus had seen.

She led him across the *atrium* and past the *peristylum,* lush with flowers, to the entertainment room at the back of the house. Argolicus watched her body sway as she walked. He realized the scent of flowers came from her. Frescoes of young men and women covered the walls. Two small tables set with bowls of fruit sat next to benches covered in cushions.

"It's cool back here. I'll have some wine brought in. How can I help you?"

"Your friend, Quintinus, was killed two days ago and I..."

"I heard," she said. Her lips turned up at the corners, so she seemed to be smiling even when they were at rest.

"Ah, then I am not bringing you news. The main reason I am here is I have questions."

Her naturally arched eyebrows raised. Argolicus felt his body respond. He concentrated on the information he wanted. The smiling tips of her lips curled up more.

"Ask." Her lips parted into a genuine smile. "But, then, I don't know how much I can help. Everything here is confidential. Even this conversation."

"Ah, then, if it is confidential..."

Two slaves entered with wine goblets and laid them on the

table. They poured from a large pitcher and left. Martina handed him a goblet, then picked up the other.

Argolicus sipped the wine, honeyed sweet. "Quintinus' daughter..."

"Proba. He mentioned her often. That is not really confidential. Everyone knows he relied on her."

"Yes. She has asked me to help find the person who murdered him."

Her dark lashes swept down over her eyes as she blinked.

"So it was murder. I heard only rumors."

"Yes. He was killed. Violently hit on the head. He was traveling. Do you know where he was going?"

Her perfectly arched eyebrows rose again. She shook her head. "No. It was a private matter. That's all I know." She sipped her wine and gazed at him over the rim of the goblet.

Argolicus turned his eyes toward his goblet to avoid her gaze and took another sip. She was the opposite of Fabia; relaxed, sure of herself, and inviting.

"Did he ever mention any enemies? Someone who might want to do him harm?"

"Enemies? No." She shook her head again and her dark hair flowed over her shoulders in waves. "He never mentioned anyone like that." She looked down into the goblet.

"But?"

"He was a negotiator. That's why he liked coming here. Everything has a price. He understood transactions." She smiled again. "I will miss him. But I am not sad. His wife didn't love him. She led her own life. But, what you want to know is he made arrangements with many people."

"I've heard," Argolicus said, wondering how many arrangements Quintinus had made, and how many were outstanding. He needed to ask Proba if she kept track of those arrangements as well as the grain.

Martina shifted in her seat. Her breasts pressed at the thin layers of fabric as they moved.

"I can tell you why some men disliked him, but it was their own doing. I don't have any names if that's what you were looking for. He mostly referred to them as 'that old fool' or 'the young fool.' He told me about situations."

"What kind of situations?"

"When Quintinus made an arrangement and the other party was unable to pay, sometimes things became unpleasant. But, Quintinus, the negotiator, always came up with a solution. The solution was usually not to the other party's liking. Quintinus would end up owning a part of their business or even their home or property. It depended on the amount owed and the man's ability to repay."

Argolicus nodded. "Many men?"

Martina put her goblet down on the table. "Yes, many. Quintinus told me these stories to brag about his acumen. That's why I don't know the names. It was always about Quintinus. From the number of stories, I would think half the patricians in Squillace owed him something, or he secretly owned parts of their livelihood."

"That gave him power."

"Yes, he liked that too, almost as much as money. Is that what you wanted to know? I don't think there's much else I can tell you." She smiled again and Argolicus' body responded involuntarily.

"Do you have a woman? I heard you were going to marry Proba. But then I heard you weren't."

"No, we're not going to marry. But we've developed a friendship."

"In that case," Martina moved again in her seat, jostling her breasts. "I always welcome handsome men... with money. Come again when things are less pressing." She glanced at Nikolaos. "And, come alone."

"Nikolaos goes with me wherever I go."

Her smile turned into a pout. "Oh, into the bedroom as well?"

Argolicus laughed. "No, not the bedroom." Then he rose. "I must go."

"With your slave," Martina mocked.

"I must go. It's been a long day, and I'm certain you have a guest arriving soon."

She smiled. "Yes, that is true. Life here is hard for single women."

Argolicus thought of Proba and wondered what she would do now that her father was gone.

"I have one more question, but not about Quintinus."

Martina adjusted the folds over her breasts. "Yes?"

"This is the first part of town I've been in that isn't plagued by ruffians in the street jostling people, painting graffiti, and chanting slogans. Why is that?"

"Oh, that's easy enough. People in this neighborhood do not control anything, and certainly not the grain markets. Our bakers store grain for us. But what could we do to help them? Nothing. It's people like you, the Principals, that must give them what they need."

"A wise answer. Thank you for seeing me unannounced."

"My pleasure and you are welcome any time."

She rose and Argolicus followed her swaying body back to the front door and the waiting bodyguards.

# TESSARA - COBALT

Grania's hand trembled as she swept the mosaic floor. Two more slaves were gone this morning. She did not want to be next. She stopped sweeping to pick up scattered pieces of torn vellum strewn on the study floor.

The master had been moody and sullen for weeks, yelling over small matters or brooding in his study. Fortune had turned against him. She did not know why or how, but she learned to stay out of his way.

When she had first come to the large town house, there had been over thirty slaves, and now there were only ten. At first, she hadn't noticed but then one morning she spotted the housemaster take a boy from the kitchen and lead him out the side door. The boy never returned. And over weeks, others left to never return.

She placed the pieces of torn vellum in a basket. Then picked up the broom and continued sweeping. Now she knew that the slaves were being sold one by one. She looked down at the girl in the mosaic, soft and bucolic, feeding a peacock. The idyllic image contrasted with the dark feeling in the household. But, however dark it felt here, the idea of being sold at the slave market was what made her hand tremble. It could be worse. Here she had food and clothes and a safe place to sleep. She'd heard about terrible things that happened to young girls. No, she'd rather be here.

She swept up the last corner of the study and placed all the dust and debris in the basket. Then she found the jug of water and sluiced some over the floor. She grabbed a rag, knelt on the edge of the peacock's tail, and began washing the tiles.

## ❦ 10 ❧

**A**rgolicus thrust up to parry Nikolaos' sword. Nikolaos had become adamant that a murder and a market shortage inquiry were not excuses to avoid practice. They were out after daybreak in the space in front of the stables.

"Good, you are getting better," Nikolaos said, signaling a stop. "What's even better is you are not panting."

Argolicus rested his sword against the stable wall and dipped a cloth into the large water barrel. "What concerns me," he said, wiping his face with the cloth, "is how we can use this if the unrest turns into something more violent. Roman citizens are defenseless against armed ruffians, even if they have pitchforks and staves."

"A sound reason for you to discover the discrepancy and how it can be remedied," Nikolaos said.

Argolicus picked up his sword and started down the alley toward the house. "Today, we focus on Quintinus. At the funeral, even though Proba asked me to come support her, I will be a public figure. You do what you do best, watch and listen. The church is as good as the forum for gossip."

Nikolaos nodded.

The church was cavernous with a cupola that seemed to reach to the sky overhead. People stood in small clusters waiting for the liturgy to begin. Nikolaos held back on the left side of the nave where he could watch. Argolicus turned toward the opposite side where Fabia and Proba stood receiving quiet condolences.

Candles glittered in two large chandeliers suspended by ropes that fastened on hitches on each wall. An icon of Iacomus, for whom the church was named, stood on a stand on the coffin in front of the sanctuary. Two large candlesticks stood on the floor next to the coffin. Along the side walls were other icons. The gold leaf in the halos glittered in the candlelight. As people entered the church they bent a knee or prostrated and then kissed the icon, before going to greet the widow and her daughter.

Argolicus looked around and noticed many of the principals who had been at the town meeting. Vespasianus and Donicus were clustered in a group of magistrates and principals.

Vespasianus ambled away from a group toward Argolicus. Although his robes were more somber than usual, they were embroidered in rich tone-on-tone designs. Argolicus met the tall magistrate eye to eye. Vespasianus briefly glanced at the marble floor and then up again to meet the gaze.

"I didn't expect to see you here," Vespasianus said. "Your mother, your heritage…"

Argolicus avoided the issue of the natures of Christ and two churches. "Proba asked me to come."

"Ah. Since you are here, a brief word."

"Yes." Argolicus sensed a warning.

Vespasianus glanced at the floor again.

"When you offered to explore the cause of the grain shortage, a noble proffer, I was grateful, we all were grateful, for your help."

Argolicus waited for the but.

"I didn't expect you to disturb our civil servants. Donicus told me about your visit. He says you implied a shortcoming in his service and even took away a ledger."

"Yes, I took the ledger. Proba will compare the numbers after all this," he gestured around the church filled with funeral mourners, "is over. Donicus may have overreacted. Do you want me to return the ledger?"

"No." Vespasianus paused, glancing around the church. Then he lowered his voice to almost a whisper. "But you must be sensitive to other principals if you meet with them. Keep your opinions to yourself. Concentrate on information."

Argolicus was certain that was how he had been with Donicus. What he knew now was that Donicus was aware of his shortcomings and was sensitive about having them discovered.

"Do you want me to stop?"

"No, no. Just take more care when you ask questions. We must quell this unrest before it turns nasty."

Vespasianus laid a hand on Argolicus' shoulder. "I appreciate what you are doing. Just keep me from hearing complaints." He turned to rejoin the group, leaving Argolicus inwardly fuming.

Argolicus joined the line of town dignitaries queuing in front of the icon on the coffin.

The perfume hit his nostrils before the voice, "Argolicus, I hear you've taken on the murder as well as the grain problem."

"Sura," Argolicus said, turning to face the magistrate. "Yes, all true. One is a private matter, one public."

Sura sniffed as they moved closer to the coffin. "Just a few days in town, and you've taken on a great deal. Are you looking to take your father's place?"

"My father's place?" Argolicus was bemused. For all the perfume and silks, Sura was still the sulky boy underneath.

"Yes, a grand reputation for fair and honest dealings," Sura said as if it were something to be avoided. "And, here you are, a worshipper of the two natures of Christ, at the funeral here." He raised a questioning eyebrow, hoping for advance information.

It was as if he had not grown out of childhood cruelty. But before Argolicus could reply, Sura kept on as they moved closer to the coffin.

"What are you doing here? Did you even know Quintinus?"

And now he was asking probing and unnecessary personal questions. Before Argolicus could answer, Proba slipped her arm through his.

"At last, you are here," she said with a smile. "Come. Keep me company. You don't need to pay your respects to Father."

Her smile was like a shield against the magistrate's probing. She tugged at his arm and led him back to where Fabia stood looking befuddled, leaving Sura to ponder more questions.

"Argolicus," Fabia said. "Proba told me you would be here. There are even more people here than were at the viewing last night. I had no idea how respected he was."

That and an innate love of gossip and rumor. But he didn't say it aloud. He glanced to the back of the nave and caught sight of Nikolaos watching Vespasianus and the others.

The priest came down from the sanctuary. "Blessed is the Kingdom of the Father and of the Son and of the Holy Spirit, now and forever and to the ages of ages."

Fabia and her group of women turned toward the priest. Proba squeezed Argolicus' arm. She whispered, "I think every man here owed my father money at some point."

"We can talk about that when all this is over. I need to talk to you about several things."

She smiled and turned her attention to the priest.

By the time they had followed the casket and the priest to the cemetery, only half of the congregation remained. As Argolicus suspected, many came to church to be seen and collect gossip, even at a funeral.

Proba was tiring. Her steps faltered. Surrounded by her friends, Fabia alternated between great sobs and wails.

Vespasianus, Donicus, and their circle of principals were not in the procession.

The ceremony was brief. After the priest had sprinkled dry, summer earth in the sign of the cross over the lowered casket and chanted one last time, the mourners began to disperse.

Proba sagged onto his arm. "All I need to do is get Mother home. Then I can collapse. I think all these funeral arrangements and public appearances keep people from facing the fact of death. There's so much to do. It's exhausting."

"Give yourself time. Grief lasts a long time." A quick flash of his father lying on the ground. "It doesn't go away, it just lessens in intensity."

"Thank you for coming today. I know you didn't do anything specific, but your presence was calming. This friendship, I didn't realize how much I was missing. My life has been numbers. People do make a difference. Especially, someone like you."

"I understand. My adult life has been solitary, too. Except for Ebrimuth, there's no one I could call a friend."

"Who is Ebrimuth?"

"Ah, he is sort of like family, one of The People. Somehow, he is related to my mother. It's all vague. But we've been friends since childhood. You may have seen him. He's been named *Comes civitatus* for the region, appointed directly by King Theoderic. He's taken on keeping the streets clear."

"I've been too preoccupied to be out on the streets. Now, I'm going to take Mother home. Then I'll sleep. I'm grateful you were here today. It made a difference." She stood on tiptoe and kissed him on the cheek. "Let's meet in a few days. By then I'll have had time to look at all those numbers you brought."

Argolicus watched her delicate frame walk away. Friendship with a woman. Baffling but somehow warming. He smiled.

Nikolaos appeared at his shoulder. "Married or not, she seems good for you."

"There, I think you are right. I'll be glad when we've found the murderer. Then we can focus on the friendship."

A man emerged from the departing funeral crowd. He was in his mid-fifties, medium height, brown hair, brown eyes, unremarkable except for a white scar that blazed down his right cheek.

"Argolicus, I would know you anywhere. Just like your father except for the blond hair. It's your bearing. I am Vopiscus Aurius Macro. Your father was with me when I got this." He pointed to his cheek.

Something buzzed in Argolicus' head, but he couldn't get a fix. He made a mental note to search through his father's journals.

"Macro," he said. "Apologies, I don't remember you."

"Oh, you wouldn't. That was before he married. Not just his bearing, his manner. Formal, yet polite. You knew Quintinus?" He nodded at the mourners wandering away from the cemetery.

"No, I didn't. I've recently met his daughter. She asked me to help find her father's killer. All new."

"My, my. That and investigating the grain shortage. I heard you speak at the town meeting."

"Yes, that too."

"You must come to visit. My estate is up on the ridge. About a mile from your father's estate."

"I shall do that. I plan to go up to the estate soon. You knew Quintinus? I have some questions."

"Yes. But I trade in wine, not grain, so our dealings were few. Come and visit. I'll tell you about your father... and this." He rubbed his scarred cheek.

In another minute, after Argolicus assured him he would visit, Macro left. With the mourners gone, the afternoon was quiet. The sun beat down on the cemetery as two slaves filled in the grave.

The mourners were distant figures on the road back to town.

Heat shimmers glistened on the pavement like miniature mirages. Argolicus longed for the cool *atrium* and the pool.

"Am I right, he was the only person who approached you?" Nikolaos asked.

Argolicus thought back over the last several hours. "No. You saw them. Vespasianus and Sura. Macro's was the only friendly approach if that's what you mean."

"You need allies in the search for the grain problem. Macro may be able to point you in the right direction."

"Perhaps, but that still leaves the issue of finding a murderer. For that, I have no idea."

"Yet."

"Yet. I need to grow my whiskers."

"Your whiskers?"

"The cat without whiskers won't cross the threshold, or something like that. Didn't you tell me that proverb when I was young?"

"A cat without whiskers cannot go through the door."

"That's it. And I know why—the cat can't feel the space. I don't know the space around Quintinus. I must grow my whiskers until I feel something."

## ※ I I ※

When Argolicus entered the *peristylum* the next morning, Crispus, the stubby housemaster, stood, fists on hips, elbows out, directing slaves planting.

"Master, we'll have this looking fresh in no time. I'm planting herbs for the kitchen. Nikolaos gave me a list. I found some flowers for color. In a few days, it will look settled. In a few weeks, the shrubs will be growing. Next year you'll never know it was neglected for years."

"There you are," Nikolaos said, coming from the *atrium*. "I've just finished with the books. Have you eaten?"

"Not yet. I'm recovering from our practice session this morning, and now I am hungry. All these years at swordsmanship and you still have something new to teach me."

Nikolaos smiled. "I'll have food sent out here. You can eat before the day gets too hot."

Argolicus sat on a bench and watched the workers with the plants. He had been preoccupied since his move. It was as though he hadn't moved in yet. Everything was here, but he had spent little time in the house except for eating, sleeping, and his practice sessions with Nikolaos.

Nikolaos arrived followed by two slaves from the kitchen carrying a tray with fruit, bread, and cheese. They set up a table and laid out the food along with a glass of honeyed milk.

Argolicus broke off a piece of bread and reached for the cheese. "Crispus," Argolicus said, "where does the bread come from? Does the cook make it here?"

The housemaster turned from supervising the planting. "No, master. You have grain storage at the bakery. They bake the bread each day and one of the kitchen staff picks it up. Look, you can see the mark on top of the loaf."

Argolicus nodded. "And the grain they store, it came from the villa?"

Crispus furrowed his brow above his round face. "Yes, master. Is something wrong with the bread?"

Argolicus looked at the bread still sitting on the tray. "No, it is fine. You are taking care of everything."

Crispus looked relieved and returned to supervise the planting.

Nikolaos arched an eyebrow. "You are thinking of something."

"The best place to start with this grain problem is home, the villa. How did we manage the grain? Did we sell any? And if so, who bought it?"

"Lucius will know. He oversees the agriculture, just about everything that is outside the villa."

"So, we will go tomorrow. Today I'm going to read Father's journals. I need to know more about this town."

☙❧

The massive white dog, Pup, ran up to Argolicus as soon as he dismounted. The dog's tail went in frantic circles as Argolicus leaned down to pat his head.

"Big boy, all is well?"

Pup bounded away and ran back.

Eboric and Kunimund nodded approval. Eboric's red hair glinted in the early sun. "A large dog. A good alert." He struggled with the Latin, but kept to Argolicus' request to use the language. "We will scout." He nodded his head at Kunimund, and they trotted off.

"Bodyguards," Amalina said, coming out from the villa. She shook her head. Her long, golden braid swung against her back as her eyes tracked the two riding off. "I can't believe it has come to that here."

A few minutes later they had settled in the *peristylum*. The fountain burbled and splashed in the morning sunlight.

"Tell me about Proba," Amalina said. "You are friends, but not marrying her. And you are looking for her father's murderer. Yes?"

"Yes, to both. You and Father married not because of an arrangement. After my marriage with Julia, if I marry it will be for something else. I don't know what to call it. A connection? You and Father had that connection."

Amalina smiled. "We did."

"You haven't remarried even though it's been seventeen years. You've had suitors. I've seen them. But you want that connection. I've never had that connection, but I know it's what I want."

"Now that you've explained, I understand. You know that if you and Proba spend time together, people will talk."

"Let them. There's nothing but friendship. And now I'm trying to solve a murder and have no hint of who did it."

"How is the house? Are you feeling settled?"

"The house. I've been so busy I haven't spent much time there. But it is clean, and thanks to a housemaster things are running smoothly. Nikolaos is skilled at choosing the right people. I started reading Father's journals. He was a keen observer of people. Many of his entries are about the fathers of men I'm meeting now."

Amalina smiled. "He was meticulous and dedicated. He seemed to know everyone."

"People keep mentioning him when they meet me. I feel as though they measure me against him, waiting to see if I'll meet the mark."

The day was warming but the sight of the fountain and its burbling water trickle made the space refreshing. Argolicus understood why Amalina loved it.

"You will," Amalina said, giving him a mother's pride smile.

"We'll see. I want to see Severa. How is she doing?"

"Oh, that girl. She is sweet, cheerful, and kind. She's developed a friendship with Pup. She sings to him."

"Sings to him?"

"She sings to herself when she is working, and it cheers everyone around her. But in the morning and evening, she sits with Pup, and sings just to him."

"So, she is happy here. I'm relieved. Where is she?"

"I'll send someone to fetch her." She signaled to a slave, gave a brief summons, and the slave disappeared.

"Also, I need to talk with Lucius," Argolicus said. "I think he can help me understand, at least from our aspect, how grain is stored here and how it is sold. I don't understand how the community has a grain shortage."

"The best time is siesta. He keeps accounts in a room near the barn. You'll find him there."

Severa came in, saw Argolicus, and ran to him. For a moment he thought she would hug him, then she pulled back and smiled. The girl was transformed. Her cheeks glowed with health, her bearing was demure but solid as if she knew who she was. The haunted look was gone from her eyes.

"Severa," Argolicus said. "You look happy."

"I like it here." She glanced at Amalina. "Mistress Amalina is like you, kind."

Argolicus laughed. "Oh, if I am kind, it's because of her."

"Well, she is. And there's always something to do. This is a large villa and so many people."

"You understand that you can stay here as long as you like. But, you are free to go at any time. No one is keeping you here."

"Yes, thank you."

"I want to talk to your parents."

Severa's face clouded.

Argolicus continued. "I'll tell them you are safe. That is all. Can you tell me where I can find them?"

Severa looked at the ground and shook her head.

"I don't want to see them. Ever."

"I understand. You don't have to see them. But I will feel better if I can tell them you are safe. Do you understand?"

She nodded. "The farm is past the second hill." She pointed northeast. "There's an estate on the hill, a patrician Macro, then just on the other side, in a valley, that's where they are."

That made it easy. Argolicus planned to see Macro tomorrow. He could go both places.

"Thank you, Severa. I promise you don't have to see them. We already made that agreement, remember?"

Her body relaxed. Amalina smiled.

"It's just when you said you wanted to see them. I thought... I thought you had changed your mind."

"Now, let's go visit Pup." He turned to Amalina, "She has time for that, yes?"

"Of course. With a visit from you, everything is flexible," Amalina said.

Argolicus took Severa's hand to go outside.

"How is your shoulder?" Argolicus asked Lucius, the overseer. A few months ago, Lucius had accompanied him to the governor's estate and had been thrown from a new stallion startled by a thunderclap.

The overseer was tall and sturdy, his face weathered by the sun. He sat at a table writing in a ledger.

"It still aches, and I can't move my arm up and down." He stretched out his arm and raised it slightly up and then down. "But each day it gets better. I have someone help me with the animals. That Mercury's Flame, he's a handful."

"But, you are happy with the purchase?"

"Oh, yes. I have breeding dates set up for the fall. We'll make money with that one."

"It was a strange event, dealing with Venantius and that odd family. I'm glad you went with me, and we made a good purchase."

Lucius said, "There's something else you want to talk about?"

"Yes. Yes, there is. Tell me how our grain is handled after harvest. I know nothing about how it all works. We rely on you."

Lucius took the compliment in stride. "What do you want to know? We store the grain here. Any extra, like this year, we sell. It's straightforward." He shrugged his good shoulder.

"Tell me more about the extra. How do you find a buyer? What happens to the grain?"

"That's pretty easy here in Squillace. There are minor buyers, but the first person to contact is Quintinus, the grain merchant. He drives a hard bargain, but everything works well."

"I need to tell you that won't be an option in the future. Quintinus died. He was murdered."

Lucius frowned. "That's not good news. The other merchants might give a better price, but they are often harder to work with or leave the grain here until it's too late. There's that fellow Pennus and Vespasianus deals in grain. Quintinus knew the ropes."

"A hard bargain? Was he difficult to deal with?"

"Not if you stand your ground," Lucius answered with pride. "He always started at a low price. A very low price. Then we negotiated. It was like a game with him. He enjoyed the bargaining."

"What happened once you agreed on a price?"

"That was another good thing about Quintinus. He paid. On the spot. No 'I'll bring it next week' or 'I'll pay you at the warehouse.' He paid cash with no hesitation. So, once we worked through the negotiation, everything else just worked."

"What was the everything else? What happened to the grain?"

"Oh, usually the next day a team would come, load up the grain, and take it down to the warehouse—he had a large complex for storage—down by the harbor. Most of it got shipped up north."

"So, once the grain left here, you were done?"

"That's it," Lucius said. "We made a bit of money by selling our excess."

"How do you calculate what is extra?"

"That's pretty simple, too. We have a household and the estate slaves. I figured out how much grain we need for a year when I first came here. I looked at the last overseer's records." He pointed to the ledger in front of him. "That's why we keep records."

All the time he'd been growing up and even as an adult, Argolicus had not thought about how it all worked. Lucius was more than just an animal handler, he made the estate run.

"I'm doing two things right now—trying to find Quintinus' killer because his daughter asked me. And, hoping to discover why the community is short of grain in a good harvest year."

"I can't help you with the murder." Lucius shook his head. "Too bad. I respected Quintinus. Once the grain leaves the estate, I don't know what happens to it. I can't help you with that, either."

"You've already helped me. You explained why you preferred working with Quintinus. Your reasons are probably why he was the biggest grain merchant in the area. A hard bargainer, but fair."

"That's about it."

"Tell me one last thing. Since I didn't know Quintinus, I want to learn as much about him as possible. What was he like?"

Lucius pondered for a moment. "I only met him once a year, so I can't tell you much. He didn't lose his temper. No matter how hard the bargaining was he didn't get angry. Like I said, it was a game to him. As long as I played the game, he was easy to work with. He paid. He picked up the grain in a timely manner." He shrugged his good shoulder again. "Now the others, they could wheedle and whine, balk at paying, or leave me wondering when they would actually pick up the grain. That's it. All I can tell you."

## ❧ 12 ❧

The next morning, Argolicus found Severa and Pup in front of the villa as he was riding away for the day. Her head was down and the white dog nuzzled her face.

"You two have made friends."

"Yes, he's learning tricks. Watch."

She brought her arm up. Pup followed the movement with his eyes. She lowered her hand. Pup immediately lay down.

"Now watch. This is his new trick."

She turned her hand sideways. Pup rolled over on the ground.

"We're off. Have a good day."

Severa looked up from the dog, her face beamed. "I like it here."

He looked at her eager face, the fresh cheeks, and the innocent delight and shuddered at what happened to girls sold as slaves.

"I'm glad you are here."

Argolicus looked at Nikolaos riding behind him. "Do you have your note equipment?"

Nikolaos started to reach into his tunic.

Argolicus laughed. "Not now. Just keep it handy today." He put on a straw hat for sun protection and nudged his horse forward.

Eboric led and Kunimund followed as they approached the trail.

☾☊

The treasurer Macro's villa was nestled against the side of the hill. The grounds were green with trees and shrubs and stood green against the surrounding dry grass of summer. The estate was old and well established. There had to be a spring to keep everything so lush. As Nikolaos led them up the hill, Argolicus noticed the trees were unpruned and patches in the stucco walls were not repaired.

They gathered in the entertainment room to stay cool and out of the sunlight. The walls were covered in bright colors with several frescoes of sheep, grapes, and wheat. A mosaic of intertwining leaves covered the floor. Macro's slaves brought honeyed wine, fruits, and herbed cheese balls, set them on tables near their seats and left.

"Your father was an exemplary member of the curia. I remember how all of us who were younger looked to him and hoped to be like him. He was honest, fair, and spoke with deliberation and wisdom. I heard you at the town meeting. You are quite similar. And he would have done the same, taken on a problem unbidden for the good of the community."

"Can you help me with that problem? The grain? Surely as treasurer, you would know about goods for distribution."

Macro closed his eyes briefly and smoothed his tunic over his thighs. "Sadly, that would be Donicus. But his vision is not broad. He is best at keeping track, but not interpreting the accounts."

Argolicus nodded. "Yes, I've been to see him and noticed that right away. In fact, I borrowed his grain ledger. I asked Quintinus' daughter to check the amounts against her records. She is not only meticulous, but able to grasp the significance of the totals."

Macro sucked in his cheeks and shook his head. He looked down at the leaf pattern on the floor.

"There, you see. Your father would have done something like that. Take matters into his hands to solve a problem. I am a wine merchant, you understand, and I talked with Quintinus from time to time. But it was general things about being a merchant, dealing with reluctant sellers, managing shipments, things like that. We weren't friends."

Argolicus tapped his fingers on his thigh impatient to get to the town's grain storage.

"And the grain? Surely grain is part of the treasury."

"Oh, there you are. No, it's not. The treasury is about money. Goods are definitely in the realm of Donicus." He shook his head again. "For all I know, Donicus could be at the root of the problem. Far be it from me to cast aspersions on another principal, but you met him. His honorary title does require some capabilities. Just like your father, you seem to be on the right track. Once you get those reconciled amounts from Quintinus' daughter, what a wonder she is with numbers, you will probably have your answer."

"Now I really must tell you about my cheek," he rubbed the scar, "and how your father saved my life."

"That I want to hear."

"We were young, but even then, your father abhorred altercations. He thought everything could be settled with rational discussion. We were walking around the streets, as young men do, looking for action, something to do, and hoping some girls might look our way. A group of lads from the country started pushing and shoving and name-calling. Not unusual for young men. I pushed back. I was angry and full of energy. "

He waved his hand in front of his body as though Argolicus could see the impatient young man.

"But you must remember that our current King Theoderic was still far away in another country and young men were armed. There was no law against carrying weapons. That ruffian from the country had no qualms about using his dagger. He whipped it out ready to cut me. But your father, he was just as large as you are, pushed his arm up and away and the blade cut my cheek, not my chest. Of course the wound festered and left this mark. But, if not for your father, I think that would have been my last moment."

Macro shook his head again and then stared at the floor as though the entire scene were alive before his eyes. Then he blinked and returned to the room.

"Your father and I drifted apart in the following years. I was out here. He established that house in town. But whenever we saw each other it was as if there were no years. Until his untimely death we were comrades in spirit. But there was one time I was in town..."

Argolicus grew impatient with the storytelling, but could tell Macro had not finished. Watchful Nikolaos shuffled his feet on the marble floor in the corner of the room.

"You see, your father never lost his sense of justice and fair play. Just before he died, he stopped an altercation between young boys. They were much younger than we were when he saved my life, but boys. One boy in particular, I think you've met him, Sura. He was maybe twelve years old but his tendency to irritate was well in place. Well, Sura was picking on three younger boys, calling them names and throwing street rubbish at them. Your father walked up, sent the young boys away, and then dressed down Sura in no uncertain terms. A crowd gathered, nodding and urging on your father. By the time it was over, Sura was publicly disgraced."

It all made sense now. Sura's digs about Maximus and taking his place. Macro's story put it all in perspective.

"Yes, I've met Sura. He was the one who invited me to the

town meeting, but I don't think he was prepared for the consequences."

Macro rolled his eyes. "Indeed. That man carries grudges. Be careful in your dealings with him." He shifted in his seat and put his palm to his chest. "The grain shortage remains a mystery."

"Yes, I thought it would be a simple matter of talking to Quintinus and straightening out the shortage. But he'd already been killed when I made that promise to the *curia*. And every place I look has no answer."

Macro looked at a shepherd in a fresco as if seeking an answer. Then he turned to Argolicus. "You've jumped in the middle like a careless youth diving in a pool. Before you left for Rome you were not in politics."

"That's true. I learned a lot about politics in Rome."

Macro nodded his head. "But before you left you had a reputation as a reclusive scholar. Now you are leaping into local politics without knowing the depth. Listen and be careful."

Then he raised his shoulders and tilted his head to the side. "So, tell me about Quintinus. What happened?"

"He was on his way to visit someone, but even Proba doesn't know who that was. He and his servant were attacked by the creek where the water runs over the boulders."

"I know the spot," Macro said. "The sound of the rushing water deafens everything else."

"Yes, that's the place. He was lying between the boulders in the mud with a large wound on his head."

Macro leaned back and shook his head. "Such a powerful man. Struck down for no reason."

"Oh," Argolicus said, "there was a reason, but we don't know what it was."

"Do you think it was personal?"

"Yes. I think it was personal. Not robbers. Not disgruntled peasants. Someone with a grudge."

Macro rubbed his hands on his thighs then rested them

curling and uncurling his fingers. "So many people disliked him. Well, I'd say they didn't dislike him as much as begrudged him."

"What do you mean?"

"He wasn't particularly likable. But, he never failed to help. If someone was experiencing financial difficulty, he was more than willing to help out. And then... they owed him."

"And then they begrudged the owing."

"Yes, exactly. That is why I invited you here. I know you are trying to find his murderer, but it will not be easy. When you ask, everyone will say a good word about him. He helped. He helped just about everyone. A few are grateful, but most don't like to think about their failure and so begrudge him. They will hide their financial relationship."

Argolicus formed a tent with his fingers and pressed them to his lips. "I see. I'm grateful for this information. You are right. People have so many ways of hiding true feelings. I must be careful."

He needed help from Proba. She would have a record of all the loans. They would have to go through them one by one.

"I need more immediate help. Do you know the farm of the three trees? I must pay a visit."

Macro raised his eyebrows. "Yes, it's not hard to find. Go over the north hill behind the estate, and you will see it down in the valley. Not the extensive pig farm. The small one to the east."

Argolicus answered the unasked question. "I found a child in town who ran away from her parents. I'm going to give them money because the child is settled with my mother. I want to give them news of her safety."

"You are so like your father. You'll have no trouble finding it. Come, now, let's have lunch. It's laid out in the *peristylum*."

The farm of three trees was just where Macro had sent them. The three oak trees stood out from the barren ground. The house was stucco, cracking from neglect. In front of the small barn, a lean sow grunted at piglets. The bodyguards left to ride the perimeter of the farm.

Argolicus and Nikolaos led their horses to the barn fence. A man in his mid-thirties came out from the barn. His patched and dirty tunic covered his thin body. He pressed together his lips and nodded.

Nikolaos said, "Gaius Vitellius Argolicus to see the parents of Severa."

The man pressed his lips more firmly and then nodded. "I don't see her. Did you bring her back?"

"She's not coming back," Argolicus said. "Are you her father?"

"Yes, ungrateful, disobedient girl. Where is she?"

Two boys, both under ten, ran from behind the barn and stared wide-eyed at the horses and then Argolicus and Nikolaos. They made it obvious that not many people visited this farm.

"Go inside," the father growled at the boys. Then he turned to Argolicus. "You'd best come inside out of the heat. You can tell me where I can find her."

In the house, they gathered around the table on simple chairs, the only furniture Argolicus could see.

Severa's mother was as thin as her husband. Her bones showed beneath her skin. "I'm Anna Maria. My husband, Marcellus... We don't have many visitors." She waved her hands in the air.

"So, where is she?" Marcellus grumbled.

"All in good time," Argolicus answered. Poverty was no excuse for bad manners, and Argolicus could tell Marcellus knew it. He was honor bound to Severa, but this man was aggravating. "My understanding is you wanted to sell her to the slave master for money."

"Yes," Marcellus said, gesturing around the empty room. Then he cast down his eyes and mumbled. "We are starving."

Anna Maria burst into tears. The boys clung to her arms. "Where is she? Where is Severa? I miss her."

"I have news I think you will like," Argolicus said, feeling for the mother despite the father's gruff ways. "I've come to pay you for your loss."

"What do you mean?" Marcellus asked. "Is she dead?"

"No, no. She's not dead. She's doing well. She's living as a free person. I want to give you what you expected from the slave market."

Anna Maria redoubled her tears and sobs. Marcellus widened his eyes.

Nikolaos reached into his tunic and pulled out a small leather sack. He handed it to Marcellus.

Marcellus opened the sack. His eyes widened even more. "But, this is more than..."

"Severa is a wonderful child, full of compassion, gentle, and eager to pitch in. She wants to know that you are safe. She didn't want to cause you harm. She wanted to be safe, too."

Anna Maria nodded her head. "She is. She is a good girl." She wiped her cheeks with her palms. "She is with you?"

"No, she is with my mother. She will be fine. You don't need to worry."

Tears flowed down her cheeks again, but this time in relief.

# TESSERA - RED

Geberic luxuriated in the quiet of the hunting lodge in Faventia when the nobles were away. Miles away from Ravenna, tucked in the woods, he stoked the fire in the forge. No drunken revels, no friends of the king getting lost in the woods. A pair of doves pecked outside his shed.

He plunged the bar of iron into the fire and waited until it turned red and then yellow.

Every once in a while, like today, he wondered what happened to the knives he made. Who would buy them? Where would they go? Each knife was like a bit of his life made up of the days of heating and hammering, heating again, shaping, the tang, the point, smoothing, hammering, plunging into water, polishing. If he saw the knife again he would remember the days, what had happened, who was nearby, and what season it was. His life was captured in the blade.

A group of sparrows flitted in the bushes, twittering at each other. He heard a hawk cry far overhead.

The iron glowed bright yellow. He grabbed it with his tongs and laid it on the anvil. He raised his hammer and gently pounded the glowing metal, flattening the bar and marking the place where the tang would begin as the iron cooled. Then he placed it back in the fire.

The sparrows flitted away and the doves were somewhere out of sight. He heard a cuckoo calling in the trees.

The iron was bright red. He pulled it out of the fire and swung it over the anvil. Time to shape the tip into a point. His hammer strike broke the summer silence.

## ❧ 13 ❧

The evening heat wilted horses and riders on the way back. The road to town swelled with people jostling and shouting. Kunimund and Eboric cleared their way surrounded by shouts and insults. "Barbarians!" "You don't know!" and "What about us?"

Argolicus was ready to relax at home. As they passed the front of the house, Rufus was closing up his shop. Two slaves scrubbed unsuccessfully at graffiti on the wall, "What about us?"

"Argolicus," Rufus said. "It's been an eventful day. You missed the ruckus."

"What ruckus?" Argolicus asked as they all pulled their horses to a halt.

Rufus pointed to the two slaves. "The streets have been unruly. A group of thugs tried to overturn my goods. I've just finished packing away everything. You'd best be inside. I hear rumors of more trouble tonight. We've all," he waved to the closed shops in front of the house, "decided to stay home at least tomorrow. This is bad for business."

"Good luck to you," Argolicus said. "Hungry people will miss your goods. Stay safe, Rufus."

The older man closed his shop as Argolicus, Nikolaos, and the bodyguards headed for the stables.

Argolicus stretched on a bench in the *peristylum*. "Everyone says the same thing about Quintinus. But, no one has any details."

Nikolaos nodded his head as he fussed over the tiny plants that would soon be his herb garden. "Do you have any suspicions?"

"None." Argolicus sighed. "None on either front. I've no idea who killed him and no idea what happened to the grain."

"I listened to everyone and everyone seems to be hiding something."

"What do you mean?"

"Look at Macro. He had stories about your father and less than pleasant things to say about Sura, but he skirted your questions about the grain."

"Go on." Argolicus, now that he was relaxing, felt they were near something.

"Martina, a mistress of surely heard secrets, played the part of being open, but she either didn't know or kept back who might hold a grudge. Donicus didn't so much hold back as not know. He seems like a fool who is incapable of his job."

"Yes, but I think we'll straighten out those grain totals with Proba's help."

"True," Nikolaos said as he patted the earth around the roots of a small plant. Then he straightened up and came to the bench across from Argolicus. "And, that Magistrate, Vespasianus. He supported you in public, but at the funeral, he did everything but order you to pull back."

"Yes, he makes the appearance of wanting to solve the grain shortage, but doesn't want me to probe. How will I learn anything without asking questions, especially of important people?"

"Think of Rome. Even though you held a powerful position, you met resistance because you were an outsider, some appointee of the king from the south. Now, here you are back home, but you are meeting resistance because you have been gone and because you are probing."

"Nikolaos! You've made the distinction. Now we need to discover which resistance applies. Politics. Always politics. If we can narrow it down to who is resisting the probe, we'll be on our way to uncovering why there is a grain shortage."

❀

Outside Quintinus' house people milled in the street chanting, "What about us?" and "Here's the grain merchant." Eboric and Kunimund cleared a way to the front door. The crowd thinned as the dark and forbidding Kunimund and Eboric who looked ready for a fight at the slightest provocation, took their places by the door with their weapons.

A slave led Argolicus and Nikolaos to the study, where Proba sat with two ledgers. One was the book borrowed from Donicus and the other a financial record from Quintinus' library.

"Argolicus," Proba said with a weary smile.

"How are you? The house seems quiet."

"It is quiet. Mother has gone to stay with a friend. She's afraid of the street mobs. I can concentrate on this," she gestured toward the ledgers. "So far, everything seems to tally. I'm doing the totals as I go."

"You've found nothing?"

"Only that Donicus is lazy," she said, grinning. "Methodical but lazy. He enters the numbers but does not do sums or correlate."

Argolicus felt out of his depth with numbers. "What do you mean?"

"He records each transaction but doesn't tally the sums or

correlate them to the warehouses. I have that information here. I don't know how he reports to the *curia*. He has nothing to report. I guess he could drone on about this transaction and that transaction."

"Yes, at the last meeting, that's what he did. I wasn't paying that much attention. I was thinking about talking to Quintinus and what I would ask him."

"Why don't you ask me?"

Argolicus smiled. "Now that you've thought about it, do you have any idea how the grain supply for the town could be short?"

"I don't know." Proba stopped to stare into the middle distance. Then she looked down at the ledger from Donicus. "I haven't finished checking this."

She ran a finger down the columns in the ledger. "It's like dots without connection. Each entry relates to nothing else." She looked up at Argolicus. "The hard part is I'm afraid I'll find something wrong in my father's books. I don't want him to be the one who did this. He was my father."

"Are you afraid your marriage prospects will diminish?"

Proba laughed. Her dark eyes sparkled. "I needed that. Father's death, the funeral, Mother's frantic wailings, and this. I've been in a somber mode."

Argolicus said. "Everyone needs laughter, especially during dark times."

Nikolaos shuffled in the corner and nodded his head.

Proba stood up. "I need a break from this. Let's have some refreshment and talk as friends."

She led them to the *peristylum* where they sat on a bench. Soon slaves arrived with a small table, herbed cheese and bread, and a pitcher of honeyed wine with two glasses.

Proba settled her small body on the bench and lifted her dark eyes. "I don't know what to think. My world centered on Father's work. Now he's gone. You've hinted that he may be the reason for the grain shortage. I don't want to believe that. So far, I've found nothing. And, if it's true, then why didn't I notice?"

"You trusted your father. "

"I did. But, don't worry. If I find that he tricked the entire city, I won't hide it. My father..." A tear ran down her cheek as she blinked back more tears.

"Proba," Argolicus said and picked up her hand and held it. He felt her cool fingers in the summer's warm air. "You are not giving yourself time to grieve."

"I don't want to be like my mother, crying and wailing and scurrying around accomplishing nothing. She didn't even like my father. What she cares about is what will happen to her." She pulled her hand away from his. "Father, why did you go on that trip?"

Argolicus put his arm around her shoulder. She leaned into him and cried. Her sobs pushed against his chest in a rhythm of grief. They sat together for a few minutes until her crying subsided. Through the open space above the *peristylum*, angry cries from the street filtered down. Argolicus wondered if this was what it was like to have a sister, someone to whom you felt warm and protective.

Nikolaos roamed among the plants nodding approval and sporadically stooping down to inspect a flower.

Argolicus untangled from Proba and poured two glasses of honeyed wine. He offered one to Proba. "Here, sip this."

She took the proffered glass and sipped.

Argolicus said, "If asking you to help has put pressure on you, you can stop."

"No, no," Proba said and then sipped her wine again. "This gives me something to do. Without it, I think I would be as lost as Mother, but in a different way. My days were filled with helping father." She paused and then said, "I need to conclude all of his work. It should be simple. The harvest is over, so there aren't many open transactions. I need to check scheduled shipments for grain still in the warehouses."

"I still have principals to see and…"

Louder shouts from the street. Argolicus heard Eboric's voice shouting, "Stay back." Voices shouted back. "The grain merchant. Here!"

Proba's doorman hurried in. "Mistress!"

Argolicus took Proba's hand again. "Stay here. I'll see what's going on. The bodyguards are outside. Nikolaos, leave the plants." They followed the doorman toward the front of the house.

The doorman opened the door to Kunimund and Eboric shouting at a crowd. A horse turd landed at the doorman's foot. Argolicus stepped back, then forward.

Eboric turned, his red hair flashing, as he drew his sword. "They're out of control."

"You can't harm them," Argolicus said. "They are unarmed."

"Romans!" Eboric said with disgust, keeping his sword in his hand. Kunimund stood stalwart, his hand on his sword hilt.

The crowd's chants "What about us! What about us!" silenced as hoofbeats clattered on the street pavings.

Ebrimuth rode up with six supporters. They turned their horses in circles waving swords and shouting, "Disperse. Disperse."

Soon the street was empty, except for Ebrimuth and his men. He tossed his wide shoulders and grinned at Argolicus. "Here you are at the center of trouble. What are you doing here?" He leaped off his horse, nodded at Kunimund and Eboric, and strode up to Argolicus at the door.

"This is the house of the grain merchant, Quintinus," Argolicus answered. "I'm here trying to get to the root of the shortage that's causing this unrest."

"I hope you discover that root soon. But, more importantly, get grain back to Squillace. Unrest can turn at any minute into riots. And food is a basic need. You weren't here when the religious riots happened. It was unsafe to go outside. A bishop was murdered. As fervent as people are about the natures of Christ, food is even more elemental."

Argolicus laughed. "That's the longest speech I've heard you deliver."

Ebrimuth's blue eyes flashed. "Well, I'm in charge now. Wherever the Roman peacekeepers are," he looked around the empty street, "if you can resolve this shortage, we'll all be relieved." He looked at the open door to the large domus. "So, the grain merchant lives here?"

"Lived," Argolicus said. "That's another problem. He was murdered. I'm looking for his killer."

Ebrimuth tossed his blond mane and rolled his shoulders. "Do you think they're connected, the shortage and the murder?"

"I don't know. Finding the killer will be hard. We may find the root of the grain shortage. That's why I'm here."

Ebrimuth gave another toss of his head and smiled. "If anyone can do both, it's you. I'm off." He jumped back on his horse, nodded at the two bodyguards, and led his men away.

Back inside, Argolicus spoke to Proba. "The people think your father is the cause of the shortage. That's what all that was about."

Proba looked at him. She was shaking. "Those people were attacking my home?"

"Shouting and throwing garbage." Argolicus put his arm around her. "I think you should leave, like your mother did, until this is settled."

"Leave? Where would I go? This place is what I know."

Her body trembled against his shoulder.

"What would it take for you to feel safe?"

"A secure place. And... someplace that isn't my father's. If they found this house, they will find the estate in the hills."

"Come to our estate. You'll be safe there with my mother."

"The one who wanted us to marry?" The corners around her brown eyes crinkled in a smile.

"The very one."

## ❧ 14 ❧

The next day while Proba was packing ledgers getting ready to leave, Argolicus decided to visit Pennus, the minor grain dealer who had spoken at the council. He idly thumbed through one of his father's journals waiting for Nikolaos to return from arranging a visit.

As he read the journal entries, he found his father noted details. His father jotted things down, but Argolicus relied on Nikolaos and his constant scribbling. While he might see new plants in a garden, Nikolaos would know the name of each plant. He could not see himself keeping a journal.

Nikolaos came into the study. "He can see you now."

Argolicus closed the journal and stopped his musings. He smiled at Nikolaos, "Let's go."

❦

Pennus lived not far from Quintinus' house. The building was old, large, and well-kept. The man was well-dressed in a fine linen tunic with colorful embroidery. His dark hair, almost black, dark eyes, and chiseled features reflected Greek ancestry common in this area far south of Rome.

Pennus gestured toward a bench by the pool in the atrium. "Come, come. Let's sit here by the pool." He settled his angular body on the bench. "You caused quite a stir at the council the other day, I must say. First Bartholomaeus. Then you. It was quite a day."

The *atrium* was spacious. The mosaics on the floor combined an array of colorful geometric patterns. The wall frescoes of grapes and vineyards were interspersed between colorfully painted panels. Nikolaos stood in a corner by the entrance to the study.

"Bartholomaeus and I have a history. I won't comment. But I stepped in because my work in Rome as *praefectus* required me to solve many complaints."

"Ah, yes," Pennus said. The light cast shadows on his angular face. "Bartholomaeus irritates everyone, even that bishop he claims to support. Rome. Do you miss it?"

"No. Not at all. I am back and I want to contribute. That's why I volunteered."

"But, you didn't know Quintinus?"

"No. But you did. You mentioned that at the council. How well did you know him?"

"We did business together from time to time." Pennus gestured at the frescoes. "My main trade is wine. We often combined shipments to fill a ship—my wine, his grain. That saved money for each of us. And we controlled the destinations."

"These combinations. Are they how you knew Quintinus sent more grain to the north?"

"Ah, you were listening," Pennus said, shifting his scrawny body on the bench.

Argolicus decided he did remember some details, even without Nikolaos.

"Yes. You stood up when Quintinus didn't appear at the council. How well did you know him?"

"I'm not certain anyone knew him," Pennus said, echoing what Argolicus had heard from everyone he'd spoken with so far. "We were social."

"Oh?" Argolicus paid attention. From what he'd heard, Quintinus was not social. And now, here was someone who claimed a social connection.

The light from overhead reflected a blue sky on the pool at their feet.

"Not in the way most people think. We didn't exchange dinner parties. But, we sometimes met at the baths and talked. Sometimes we followed that with a lunch somewhere to continue our conversation. But the conversations weren't personal. It was always about business. How we could profit together. At times, he suggested taking over my grain deals."

"You broker grain, as well as wine?" Someone had mentioned Pennus before. Argolicus could not remember who it was.

"I work with small estates or estates that have smaller grain fields. I've been to your estate."

Ah, now he remembered. Lucius, the overseer, had mentioned Pennus. And what had he said?

Pennus was still talking. "Quintinus didn't want to bother with smaller supplies. That meant he had to combine several to meet an order." He shrugged his bony shoulders. "But when he got greedy... I hope you don't mind my speaking so of the dead... he talked about taking over my grain accounts, so I could grow the wine business."

"That's how he presented it?" Argolicus glimpsed Nikolaos take out his stylus and scribble a note.

"Yes, he would take those smaller accounts. I could grow my wine accounts. There is only so much time." Pennus waved a skinny wrist to suggest encompassing time.

"And it was in one of these private conversations that he mentioned almost all the grain going to the north because of the question about grain from Egypt?" Argolicus was remembering details.

"Yes. Yes, we were eating together. I remember. It was just as the harvest was concluding. He was buying grain from everywhere. That's why he suggested taking over my accounts." Pennus leaned forward, resting his elbows on his narrow thighs, lost in thought.

Argolicus waited. And he was rewarded.

"Greed." Pennus sat back up. "With Quintinus, it wasn't so much greed as an enthusiasm for making money. It was like a game to him. He loved bargaining. But once he made a bargain he kept his word. I think that's why he wanted my small accounts. Not to best me, but to add to his deals with the north."

"So, you turned down his offer?"

"Well, yes, and no."

"Yes and no?"

"We worked out an arrangement. I kept my accounts. But instead of finding buyers in the north, I sold the grain directly to Quintinus." Pennus chuckled. "At my price, of course. So I made out. He was desperate to fill his promises to northern buyers. He barely balked at my prices."

Argolicus nodded. "So next year, you will still have those small accounts?"

"Yes, I think it worked out well."

"Do you know how much grain he had promised?"

"No. He just said it was much more than usual."

"Do you have any idea how the town was shorted? Did he tell you he took from the town stores?"

Pennus shook his head. "No, no mention of that. Just that he had promised more than usual to the north."

"Did he say where he would get this extra grain?"

"No. I've told you all I know. I stood up at the council because he wasn't there. Now we know why."

"Yes, we do. Do you know of any enemies he might have had? Did he ever mention anyone in one of your conversations?"

The sun reflected in a corner of the pool. A bright light on the glistening water.

"No. He didn't gossip. He never mentioned names. He might describe a particular good bargain he'd made... but without mentioning names. It was always quantities with him."

Martina, the mistress, had told Argolicus the same thing. Almost the same words.

"What about you?" Argolicus prompted. "Can you think of anyone who carried a grudge, hated him? Justly or unjustly?"

Pennus set his face, accentuating the chiseled angles. He sat still for a moment before answering. "Quintinus was a powerful man. He was powerful because he had money, but that was only a means to power. He made private loans. You know how it is. Everyone has difficulties from time to time. Quintinus heard rumors, and then made offers before someone came to him. At the time, he seemed like the best recourse. He gave the appearance of being sensitive and discreet."

Argolicus had heard almost the same words before. "Yes," he said, encouraging Pennus to continue.

"But it was part of his game. He liked to think he knew about others' hardships, and he took advantage. I can't name you a specific individual, but I know many, many people owed him."

"I've heard this," Argolicus prompted. It was as though Quintinus had secretly supported the entire council membership. If he had deliberately shorted the town on grain, no one would say.

"During the harvest," Pennus continued, "Quintinus met frequently with two different men. He thought he was unobserved, but I saw him." Pennus looked at Argolicus. His dark brown eyes pleading that he was not an eavesdropper. "Do you know Vopiscus Aurius Macro?"

"We've met," Argolicus answered, waiting for a new picture of the kindly treasurer.

"Well...he..." Pennus gave the same pleading look again. "I saw them together twice, Macro and Quintinus, right around the time of the harvest. I don't want you to think..."

Argolicus nodded reassurance. "You just happened to see."

"Yes. Yes. I was walking by and saw them in the same place where Quintinus and I often have lunch. Both times they were talking with their heads bent close. I didn't hear what they said. I just saw them together. I didn't know they were friends. Well, maybe not friends. I have no idea why they met."

Argolicus thought of Macro's estate. The walls that needed patching. The unkempt appearance. Maybe the old man was worse off than he let on. "I see. You mentioned another. There were two men?"

Pennus traced the lines of a pattern on the mosaic floor with the toe of his shoe. "You know Caeso Rabirius Donicus. He was at the council."

"Yes." Another revelation. This town was equal to Rome in secret goings-on and rumor. Now the ineffectual administrator, the *curator civitatis*.

"I saw them together three times. But, that's all I know. Donicus takes care of the city provisions, but maybe he needed a loan. It might be by chance. He must have talked to Quintinus regularly. He is in charge of the town's markets, the finances, and administration. We've suffered."

"I met with him. He gathers information."

"Yes, as administrator, he needs to know where things are and how commodities like grain flow. I'm not saying he's incompetent..."

He pictured Donicus squinting at his ledger columns without any totals.

Pennus went on. "He just doesn't have control over what he

knows. As I said, an appointment that didn't go well for our town."

"He has another year?" Argolicus asked.

"Yes. I hope we don't suffer too much. In my opinion, Vespasianus needs to prompt him to attention. He is a strong leader and the town needs his leadership... especially with a situation like Donicus."

"Then, we are fortunate to have Vespasianus this year. But, back to Quintinus. I don't see either of those men, Donicus or Macro, physically harming anyone. It doesn't seem in their nature, whatever other failings they might have. Can you think of anyone else?"

Pennus struck his stone face again and stared into the pool. The sun's reflection had traveled to the middle of the pool, spreading light glints in every direction.

"I can't think of anyone specific. It could be so many people. I don't know to whom Quintinus offered his loan assistance. He based it on rumor. As I said, everyone in business has difficult times and shortfalls occasionally."

This man had told him enough. Argolicus was ready to leave. He wanted to digest what he had learned. Maybe Nikolaos had noticed an overlooked detail.

"Pennus, you have helped me in my inquiries."

"Yes, but everything is hearsay. I'm not sure if I've helped you at all."

"I have a better picture. Not just of the grain this year and how it was handled but of how Quintinus went about his dealings with other men."

"You've taken on what no one else in this town would do. I am glad you returned. And glad you decided to actively work in the council. I think everyone appreciates your efforts."

"So far they are only efforts. I have one other question. I'm hoping you can help me."

"Certainly, if I can."

"I've been looking at your frescoes. The frescoes at my town house need refreshing. Yours look recent. I'm wondering if you could tell me the name of the painter?"

"Gladly." Pennus beamed with pride.

## ❦ 15 ❦

In the morning light, Proba looked small and fragile. Her confidence was replaced with nervous energy. She paced back and forth in front of the house. Rufus and Ezio organized their vegetables and dishes in the shops. The cart that had carried Quintinus' body back to town stood filled with Proba's ledgers and belongings for her stay at the estate.

"I'll ride in the cart with my maid," Proba said.

"As you wish," Argolicus said. "Don't worry. My mother is not formidable. You will like her."

Proba arched an eyebrow.

"She might pressure me, and she has. But she will welcome you to the estate."

Eboric turned to lead the extra horse back to the stable. In the street, slaves were out to buy household goods. It seemed like a normal morning. The rabble-rousers were not visible. But Argolicus noticed a slave hurrying down the street. The man eyed the group gathered in front of the house. Stopped, looked at the house. And then went up to the door and knocked.

The doorman, Boden, opened, his massive frame filling the

space. The slave spoke. Boden nodded his head toward the group in the street. "There," he said.

The slave turned and eyed the group. "Gaius Vitellius Argolicus."

Argolicus gestured.

"Your Sublimity, Marcus Vipsanius Vespasianus wishes to speak with you."

Argolicus sighed. "Nikolaos, take Proba inside. Kunimund, you and Eboric guard the cart. Keep the content safe."

The silent, dark bodyguard nodded and labored out the words in Latin. "One of us go with you. Wait for Eboric."

⚜

Minerva gazed with bland unconcern on the luxurious *atrium* as if centuries of Christianity had no effect on wisdom. The collection of marble statues and the glinting gold leaf struck Argolicus as beyond opulent. It was as if Vespasianus couldn't trust his authority without this display.

The large slave greeted Argolicus at the door and led him not to the study, but left him waiting by the pool in the *atrium*. Argolicus eyed the brightly painted statues—Minerva, the satyr, the nymph, and the unknown god—and wondered if Vespasianus was a secret worshipper of the old gods, a crime, or merely admired the old Rome. One was a faith issue, one political. Either way, they were best kept hidden, even though they were far away from King Theoderic in the North. What he did know was that keeping him waiting after summoning him, was a move by Vespasianus to show his power.

Argolicus glimpsed a corner of the study where more gold leaf gleamed on a large box.

"Ah, Argolicus, I need to speak to you," Vespasianus said, striding in from the rear of the house. The gold embroidery on his tunic, intertwined with red and blue, was more elaborate than the last time they had met. His sandals were adorned with tiny pearls. "Let's sit," he said, gesturing toward two chairs by the pool.

"Vespasianus, your slave reached me just in time for a talk. I was ready to leave."

"Oh? Off to interview more principals?" He sat in a chair, crossed his arms over his chest, and gave Argolicus a flinty glare.

"No, off to my estate in the hills."

"Ah, good. No more meddling for a few days, then?"

"Meddling? I've been searching for the cause of the grain shortage."

Vespasianus fiddled with the neck of his tunic, then ran his fingers lightly over the embroidered stripe that ran down from his shoulder. "Yes. I hear you have been talking to more people. But... when we talked before, I asked you to be more discreet, to question gently without probing. I don't know you. Your actions speak well, but I have to protect the town. Perhaps, as you tell me more, I will begin to trust your actions."

Argolicus ran over his conversations with Macro and Pennus in his mind. He couldn't remember anything that had seemed uncomfortable to either man. But, one of them, if not both, had registered a complaint with Vespasianus. Wouldn't members of the *curia* want to know what happened to the grain?

"What is the complaint?" Argolicus asked. "Our community is suffering. Magistrates and principals would want to solve this problem. Just yesterday, there was an incident at Quintinus' house. People were shouting, throwing dung. His daughter was terrified."

"Yes, I heard about that, too," Vespasianus answered, fingering his embroidery. "A new *comes civitatus* broke up the crowd."

"Yes, I know him. I've known him since childhood. We are distantly related."

"Ah, yes. At times, I forget about your mother. What is he like?"

Argolicus pondered how to describe Ebrimuth. "Strong-minded, but fair. Where is our peace warden? I haven't seen a peace warden since all this started."

Vespasianus stopped fingering the embroidery and visibly winced. "Our peace warden has a fondness for wine. I'm afraid he's not up to this situation. This is more than a fight between drunken youth or a family dispute."

"Then Cassiodorus made a timely decision."

"Cassiodorus? I thought the king..." Vespasianus sat back, considering the implications.

"Yes, the king signs, but Cassiodorus is his advisor."

"How did he know?" He gave Argolicus a significant look. "We all know that Cassiodorus is your friend. He got you that appointment in Rome."

Argolicus shrugged. "Perhaps Venantius, our governor, sent a letter. He wouldn't want an uprising to reflect on his name. I've been busy with the grain shortage."

Vespasianus shifted in his seat. "Cassiodorus is your friend, and you know this new *comes civitatus*?"

Argolicus smiled to himself. He felt Vespasianus backing down. "Yes, we were playmates in childhood, the three of us."

"Playmates? All this is based on games?"

"No, on friendship. Strong ties last. This is a small town. I've known Sura since I was a child, but we weren't playmates." Why was Vespasianus diverting the conversation?

"Ebrimuth, the new *comes civitatus*, is a frequent visitor at the estate, and now that I'm in town, I'm sure he'll visit me here. There aren't that many of The People here in the south."

"I see," Vespasianus said, caution in his voice. "You are all connected."

"Yes, by friendship. But I don't see how that bears on the grain shortage or my investigating what happened to all the grain from our good harvest."

"It may be that I overreacted," Vespasianus said, shifting again in his seat. "What have you discovered?"

Argolicus detailed his talks with Donicus, Macro, and Pennus explaining how they all said the same thing. None of them had real information on why the town had a grain shortage.

"The best possibility, now," he continued, "is matching the tallies of Donicus with Quintinus' records."

A flicker of something crossed Vespasianus' face. "You have access to Quintinus' records?"

"Yes, his daughter, Proba, kept his accounts. She is working now on matching the numbers with the civil records." Argolicus was sure he had told Vespasianus before. He had. At the funeral. "If she finds discrepancies, we may be able to make restitution."

Vespasianus rolled his head, lost in his thoughts. "Proba... a beautiful woman."

"Yes, she is," Argolicus agreed. "She is also educated, smart, and facile with numbers. Quintinus relied on her record-keeping." He had no reason to tell Vespasianus about the marriage arrangement that didn't happen.

"I..." Vespasianus hesitated. "At one time, I thought about marrying her."

Argolicus tried to imagine the union. He could not picture Proba with Vespasianus and his luxury of things. He waited.

Vespasianus blew out a breath. His eyes flashed. "But it came to nothing. Quintinus said he had other plans for her."

Argolicus didn't need Nikolaos scribbling notes to see the wisdom of not mentioning his failed marriage arrangement; the disappointment on Vespasianus' face was enough.

"Because of the disturbance yesterday, Proba will be staying at my estate. We are taking this year's ledgers for Quintinus and the book Donicus gave me. I hope we find the discrepancy soon."

"To your estate? But, why not her father's estate?" Vespasianus couldn't keep the curiosity out of his voice.

"If they found his house in town, they could find his estate as well. For all I know they are already there."

"I see. It makes some kind of sense. But, why you?"

"We are working together on this grain problem. You are right, it does make sense."

Vespasianus gazed at the satyr. "So, you are taking this year's ledgers? Not all of his ledgers?"

"Yes, just this year. That's the current problem. We don't need historical background. I'm sure there's an accounting detail we've missed. Perhaps the grain is in a warehouse. We just need to discover what happened."

"In a warehouse?" The doubt was back in the magistrate's voice, as if Argolicus were not up to the task.

"Yes. Proba kept full accounting for her father—the transactions, the amount of grain, the money paid, the storage, and the ultimate destination. Her record keeping is a critical part of tracking down the missing grain."

"Yes, yes," Vespasianus agreed, his voice back to normal. "If you find the grain we can restore equilibrium here in town. Your inquiry is a great service, especially since Quintinus is not here to answer for his actions." He smoothed his tunic over his thighs.

"I continue the search," Argolicus said.

"And the search for his killer as well?"

"That, too. But, I have no direction for that. It could be anyone. I'm hoping the slave that was with him can tell me what happened. For now, he can't remember his name. Do you have any thoughts?"

"None," the magistrate answered.

"I'm retreating from questioning more principals at the moment. I may have questions once we finish comparing the ledgers. For now, that is the next step. Is there anything else you wanted to talk about?"

Vespasianus rose. "No, keep me informed, try not to upset any other principals. Remember, I am the magistrate and I aim for tranquility in our town. That was all."

"I'll let you know what we discover with the books." Argolicus rose, anxious to leave the magistrate and his preemptive interference.

## TESSERA - SAFFRON

"Adofo, you are wrong. Christ was both man and God." Basil thrust the shovel deep into the pile of earth and threw it into the grave. "A woman, the blessed Mary, gave him birth. How can you think that he was only God? His dual nature is part of the mystery."

Adofo threw a shovelful of earth into the grave and shook his head. "That's where you are misguided, my friend in Christ. In Alexandria, even the lowliest man, a fellow like me who came to Italy for a better life, knows and reveres the sanctity of Our Lord as truly divine." He wiped his brow before scooping another shovelful of earth. "To believe that Christ was man trivializes his sanctity."

"You must be careful here to spout such stuff. This one nature of Christ you espouse is not popular here. You could get into trouble. The church here believes in the Trinity. If you start saying things like that, you'll get in a fight. People are touchy about their beliefs."

Adofo slammed his shovel into the pile of earth. "There's so much to learn here. So, you, in your heart believe that Christ was both man and God? That doesn't make any sense. It's as if you are irreverent. I am delighted to know that we are both friends in Christ, but I feel you are misguided in your understanding."

Basil shook his head. "Just be careful. Although Christ taught us to love others, not everyone who says they are a Christian is loving."

"Ah, this much I know," Adofo said. "But look, an angel approaches."

A small woman with dark eyes walked toward the gravesite. She gestured to her maid who approached Adofo and Basil.

"My mistress appreciates the care you are taking with her father's grave." She smiled and handed a small sack to Adofo. Then she turned and headed away with her mistress.

Adofo opened the sack. "Ah, truly we have been blessed by an angel." He poured coins into Basil's outstretched hand.

A rgolicus watched the water play in the fountain. Amalina had whisked Proba away to show her around the house. Slaves were unloading the ledgers from the cart and carrying them to the study so Proba could work.

"I know I've moved, but this place feels like home," he said to Nikolaos who was collecting cuttings of herbs and placing them in a damp cloth. It was more than home. His body relaxed for the first time in days.

"Master, you haven't had time to settle in. All this searching for answers has kept you moving. The house will feel like home."

"All the searching, but no answers. I'm not sure what I know. Let's make some notes."

Nikolaos hurried off with his cuttings. Argolicus continued to watch the fountain splashing in the summer sunlight. Nikolaos returned with a small table, vellum sheets, and pen and ink.

Argolicus pulled out two sheets and placed them side by side. "Two inquiries. I feel as though they are related, but I don't see it. Perhaps the only relationship is Quintinus." He wrote *Quintinus* at the top of one sheet. "And because he was the main grain merchant here, I'm sure the grain shortage has something to do with his manipulations." He wrote *Grain* at the top of the second sheet. He stared at both sheets, then pulled the Quintinus sheet toward him. "I'll start with what I don't know."

He wrote *destination*. "Even Proba doesn't know where he was going. But from the location by the stream, I'd say it was somewhere in the hills." He wrote *hills?*

"Any news of the slave?" Nikolaos asked.

"None. Proba says he may never recover according to the doctor."

"So, did the killer know where he was going? Or did he follow him?"

The fountain played joyfully as he sank into somber thoughts. "To knock him off the horse and strike a heavy blow, I think the killer was a man, and a large man." He wrote nothing. Then, agreeing with himself, he wrote *large man*.

"A wealthy, large man," Nikolaos added.

"Yes, that gold bead." He added *wealthy*. "No vagrants or petty thieves would have adornments on their clothes. That doesn't narrow it down much. There are over a hundred members of the *curia*. And, from what we've heard, many owed money or favors to Quintinus." He paused. "But, if the killer was wealthy, perhaps it was something personal, not about money."

"Personal is usually the reason for murder, even if it is about money," Nikolaos added.

"Yes, that's the problem. We don't know. We have no information. You'd think that women's gossip would help but neither Martina, the mistress, nor his wife seem to know anything about his personal life. They both stressed that he didn't really have a personal life. It was all about business transactions."

"What was business to him, might be personal to someone else."

"Good point." He wrote *personal*.

They sat in silence. Then Argolicus pushed the sheet away and pulled the other sheet forward.

"I think we're stymied with his murder at this point. We need more information. We have more about the grain shortage. The main question is, where did the grain go? And the second question is why? Why was the grain oversold?"

He wrote *destination* and *why* on the empty sheet.

"Where did all that extra grain go?"

"Master," Nikolaos said. "I've been thinking."

"Yes?"

"About the grain. Where was it here in town before it left?"

"What do you mean? Wouldn't it be in the warehouse?"

"Yes. That's exactly what I mean. Has anyone other than Quintinus checked the warehouse? And didn't he have more than one?"

Argolicus slapped the table. "Good questions. We'll need to ask Proba. She must know where all the grain was stored. Then, when we get back to town, we'll visit the warehouses."

"For all we know, the grain is still here."

"That would solve the problem. But it seems too good to be true."

"Always verify," Nikolaos said in his tutor voice.

"There you are," Amalina said as she led Proba into the *peristylum*.

"Oh," Proba said. "The fountain." She went up to the fountain and held out her finger in the flow of water. "What a lovely sound." Then she turned around to face them all, her brown eyes shining. "It's lovely here. Argolicus, how could you leave?"

For a moment, the only sound was the fountain burbling.

Argolicus smiled. "I was just wondering the same thing. It's so peaceful here. But, I made a decision. My best talents are working in the public. The best place for me is in town and working with the *curia*. I did learn how to navigate those dangerous political waters in Rome."

Proba smiled and ran her finger through the water again. "I'm glad you'll be in town. I'll have a friend."

Argolicus glimpsed an expectant light in Amalina's eyes. He ignored her hopeful look.

"So will I."

They heard a commotion at the front door. Ebrimuth strode in, long knife and sword at his side. He beamed at Argolicus. "I heard you were here." He turned to Amalina, "Cousin."

"Welcome," she said. "We were just about to have lunch. Will you join us?" Then she gestured toward Proba, "Argolicus' new friend, Quintinus Cocceia Proba."

Proba looked up from the fountain and turned her delicate body toward the imposing man. She stood mute for a moment and then smiled.

"Ebrimuth," the big man spluttered. "I..."

Amalina interrupted the moment. "Let's have lunch." She turned and headed toward the entertainment room.

Argolicus was lost. What had just happened? Only his mother seemed to know. Not just Amalina, but Nikolaos was also smiling.

❦

After lunch, Argolicus went to his old study with Nikolaos. The table was covered with ledgers. Boxes of ledgers stood against one wall. He was anxious to get answers to his questions about the grain, but Proba had gone off for a walk with Ebrimuth.

"I don't understand," he said.

"What?" Nikolaos asked.

"Proba. Ebrimuth. That brute and... She's so sweet."

Nikolaos arched an eyebrow.

Amalina came in from the *atrium*. "The thunderbolt," she said. "It's simple."

Argolicus was mystified. The sky was clear. The sun blazing outside. "Thunderbolt?"

Amalina laughed. "Yes, it happened when I met your father."

"You mean Proba and Ebrimuth...?"

"Yes. Proba and Ebrimuth. I have to give up any hopes of your marriage there." She smiled. "Your two friends, an old one and a new one."

Argolicus felt as if Nikolaos had just landed one of his punches. Ebrimuth. He was always alone. All those years of their friendship. And, Proba... He felt as if he didn't know her. That he'd missed something. She was so straightforward and logical. And now she was off on a walk instead of poring over the ledgers waiting here for her in his study.

Amalina laughed again. "Look at your face. You know about maneuvering through politics, and think you are in touch with the world, but you are knocked sideways by one of the most basic human emotions."

"Mother, I..."

Proba came in, her cheeks flushed. Argolicus couldn't tell if it was from the heat or something else. She marched to the table, put her hand on her father's ledger, and looked up at Argolicus.

"Your friend is not like you," she said. Her dark eyes were unreadable as she opened the ledger.

"No," Argolicus said. "We've been different since childhood. I think that's why our friendship lasts."

Proba smiled. "You are cousins?"

"Somehow distantly related, on my mother's side." He glanced at Amalina.

"Our family ties come from way back. He's a good man," Amalina said.

Proba smiled. "Still, the two of you are like oil and water. Separate."

"Indeed," Argolicus agreed, wondering if this was a problem for Proba.

"It's time for me to be available," Amalina said, turning to leave.

"Available?" Proba asked, watching Amalina head toward the kitchen.

"After lunch every day, she makes herself available to everyone here for healing or to talk about problems."

"Your family. You are all so kind," Proba said. She ran her finger up and down the open page of the ledger. "My mother is not like that." She paused as if she had something else to say, but remained lost in a thought. Then she looked down at the ledger and the others stacked on the table. "I am pleased to have met all of you. And, I am pleased to help you solve this mystery of the missing grain."

She sat down in the chair and pulled the ledger closer.

"Proba, have you ever been to the warehouses?" Argolicus asked.

She shook her head. "No, I had nothing to do with the grain itself. My father did that. I kept track of the numbers."

"Do you know where all the storage is your father used?"

"He kept a ledger. It's not here. It's in town."

Of course, now they were here above town. He couldn't take her back until things had calmed down. But the key to discovering what happened to the grain was what they needed.

"I brought you here to keep you safe. Would you consider going back to town to look at that ledger? I have a feeling we are missing the physical evidence. We could go tomorrow."

Proba flushed and lowered her eyes. "In the afternoon." Then she smiled. "I'm meeting Ebrimuth in the morning."

"Oh." Argolicus tried to hide his disappointment. He had to adjust to Ebrimuth and Proba and the thunderbolt. Didn't she see the urgency? But maybe the urgency was his pride. He had stood in front of the entire council and pledged he would find the solution. She hadn't been there. And she was helping him. He couldn't demand she work in his time frame.

"The afternoon, then," he said.

Proba smiled again, her eyes warm and bright. "Yes, the afternoon. Maybe he can go with us. But now, you need to leave me alone to check these ledgers. I want to clear my father's name and this seems the best way to do it."

"Good," Nikolaos said. "We can catch up on our practice."

Argolicus laughed. "For an unarmed Roman, I have more sword skills than I could possibly need."

"Perhaps," Nikolaos said. "Nevertheless..." He nodded toward the *atrium*.

Proba laughed. "You are the only man I know who practices with arms."

"Every day," Nikolaos said with pride.

"Go on then," Proba said as she pulled a ledger in front of her and opened it to a marked page.

## ❧ 17 ❧

After a vigorous session with Nikolaos, Argolicus rested by the fountain. The afternoon sun dappled the water. Nikolaos came from the kitchen, trailed by Severa and a kitchen slave carrying a tray of light refreshments.

"Severa," Argolicus said. The girl looked like a different person from the child he'd found on the streets. She looked healthy. But most of all, contentment shone in her eyes.

"Argolicus, my protector," she said. "I'm so glad you are here. Your mother is kind, I like it here. But having you here is like a treat because I can see you with my eyes and remember your kindness. And, you talked to my parents. I never want to see them again." Her eyes flashed in anger. Then the anger left as she poured honeyed wine into a glass. "This is for you. I saw you come in from your practice. I knew you would want something." She handed him the glass. "And Nikolaos, what a fine tutor. Here is yours," she said, filling another glass. Then she looked at Argolicus. "I could live here forever."

"You may change your mind when you are older," Argolicus said, taking her hand. "But, you are welcome here for as long as you need. I'm here for just a short while. In fact, I'm going back to town tomorrow."

Severa's face collapsed.

"Just for the day. I'll be back."

Her face lit up again. "I'm helping your mother with the kitchen. There's so much to learn." Then, like the child she was, she slipped her hand from his and left almost skipping in anticipation.

"A good thing you did," Nikolaos said.

"A small thing. Her parents," he shook his head. "That was an unpleasant experience."

They sat by the fountain, quietly eating cheese, bread, and apricots cooked with spices.

"The *curia*," Argolicus said, interrupting the silence.

"Yes?"

"I think the interconnections, the principals. There's more that I don't see. It's as if I've been dropped in a basket with cats. They seem calm but at any moment I could feel claws."

"Why do you think that? Has anyone threatened you?"

"No, it's a sense I have. I see the surface but not the connections. Everyone seems relieved that I've taken on the search for the missing grain, but no one has any answers. I feel like I'm not asking the right questions."

"What questions?"

"That's the problem. I don't know. My life here before Rome... I was insulated. I read and studied. All that time, I could have been participating. I would understand more. I had the privilege without responsibility. Then Cassiodorus called me to Rome, paying homage to our childhood friendship, I suppose. But, you remember," he glanced at Nikolaos. "I was plunged into politics. All those Senators, with their backhanded plotting."

"Yes, it was an extreme initiation into politics."

"That's just it. I'm sure the same thing happens here on a smaller scale and I don't know who controls whom or what threads lead to someone's appointment. I know all those cats have claws. I just haven't seen them."

"Start with what you know," Nikolaos said, seeing Argolicus struggle.

"That's the challenging part. The principals elect their officials, but the elected officials are not really accountable to anyone. They are above the law and exempt from prosecution. From the outside, and I feel I am an outsider, there is no transparency to the organization. It's all politics, and I'm not privy to the secrets."

He stopped to break off a piece of bread and cut off a chunk of cheese. He gestured toward Nikolaos.

"Eat. You always forget to eat."

Nikolaos broke off a piece of bread.

"Is it like the Senate? Do they elect the magistrates?"

"Yes and no. It's a small group. I think about all the empty seats in that council room. I was one of those empty seats when I was away in Rome. No doubt some matters are voted on by the *curia*, but the members would be swayed by the opinion of the principals. Like I was, they don't want to be involved."

"But there are elections?"

"Of course, but they are guided by that inner circle of principals. They decide among themselves who will hold an office. And often it's just a matter of favors. I'm thinking of Donicus. The grain shortage is partly his responsibility for not planning for the city's needs. He feels outside pressure from the *curial* members and principals, and personal pressure for his shortcomings. He had no idea of the responsibilities involved in his honorary title. And that's the problem, it's an honorary title."

He sipped the wine and watched the sunlight play on the fountain.

"And it could be the same for Macro. He's the town treasurer. He had stories to tell to divert the conversation from the grain crisis." He scowled as he shifted. "And Sura, you remember him."

Nikolaos nodded. "Unpleasant as a youth and still unpleasant."

"Exactly. He invited me to the council, but I think he considers it a mistake. When I see him, he has some nasty dig. Sometimes I think he invited me just so he could be close enough to cause trouble."

Nikolaos asked, "Will you stay? You spent all those years before with no involvement."

"I gave my word about the grain crisis. I will see it through. On the one hand, the council needs guidance and wisdom. On the other, I was relieved to come back from Rome. While I was here at the estate, everything seemed peaceful. But, I was right to move to town and participate. The council needs a voice of reason." He paused. "I wonder if that's what Father thought, why he was involved. One thing is consistent, everyone treasures his wisdom."

"And so do you."

"I do. I wish he were here now to help me with this. I can't seem to progress beyond the surface."

"Your main block with the principals seems to be someone you haven't mentioned."

"Ah, yes, Vespasianus. He was approving at the council, but when I meet with him, it's as though he doesn't want me to find an answer. Baffling."

Nikolaos got up and wandered to the herbs planted around the edges. "Who will take care of these now?" He started plucking tips from the stems. He pulled out a cloth and tucked his trimmings into the cloth.

Severa came in and started clearing away the dishes. "What are you doing?" she asked Nikolaos.

"Put those down and come here. I'll show you." Soon he and the girl were huddled over one plant and then another, talking softly, and trimming stems.

Argolicus was left to think about his predicament on his own. The fountain played in the slanted sunlight of late afternoon.

Vespasianus puzzled him. As the leading magistrate of the

year, he must want the grain shortage repaired. Reparations would stop the civil unrest. Everywhere they went men snarled and cast threatening looks on anyone who looked like a principal. And they had threatened Proba's home, even though Quintinus was dead. A resolution would solve problems for Vespasianus during his term. Unless grain was found, he would be remembered as the magistrate who couldn't take care of the town.

Severa returned to clear the dishes. Then she headed toward the kitchen with Nikolaos chatting about the herbs. Nikolaos' herbs had found a new caretaker.

Argolicus returned to his musings. Even if Proba found the discrepancy as she compared the numbers in the ledgers, that still left the town without sufficient grain. It didn't make sense. Unless they found a supply of grain, the unrest would continue, and people would go hungry. Tomorrow. Tomorrow they would go to the warehouses and search for the grain.

Power and grain. They must be connected. Quintinus liked the power of making a deal. Somehow he had grabbed too much. Whether power or grain or both he was the key. And somehow his murder was tied to the shortage.

Marcus Aurelius came to mind. A loaf of bread to a starving man did far more good than a philosophical discourse. And that was it. Pondering about the principals and their hidden power struggles was a waste of time. Far better to search for grain. If he could find a source of grain, no matter what caused the original shortage, he could bring peace to the town.

If Proba found a discrepancy, that might illustrate the source of the problem. But it was more important, more immediate to find the actual grain. By this time tomorrow after they examined the warehouses, he might have solved the grain shortage.

But he still had to grapple with Quintinus' murder. The same stone walls kept him from knowing more. More! Knowing anything. Proba didn't know where her father had been going or why. All the connections about her father led him to the same principals that knew nothing about the grain shortage.

It was as though the two unsolvable questions were related. Would solving one help him solve the other? Or did they just seem connected because the same people circled around each issue? Was Quintinus really at the heart of the grain shortage? Or did it just seem so because he was the leading grain merchant?

From what he had learned, Quintinus was not a particularly pleasant man. But that was not a cause for murder. He seemed to have no burning passions that would lead to jealousy. The murder must be about business and his business was grain. He drove a hard bargain, but that was not a reason for murder either.

If they found no clues to the missing grain in the warehouses, he would be stumped. Perhaps he could swallow his pride and see Vespasianus to tell him he had found nothing.

Even if he did, that still left him with his promise to Proba.

And then there she was, her eyes somber. "Argolicus, I've found nothing yet."

She sat down next to him in front of the fountain. "This is so confounding." She twisted her hands together. "I can't believe Father would make such a gross error. It must be someone else. Someone who made a large purchase or several smaller purchases that add up to the amount missing. The public accounts and father's records match."

Argolicus took her hand. "You may be right. I've been sitting here thinking and my thoughts have been going in circles. What you say may be true. Your help is immeasurable. I can't thank you enough for checking those records and working in your time of grief."

"I feel better now that I know our records are correct. It was so hard to think of Father cheating the whole town. Now I feel free to mourn him and mourn him nobly."

She squeezed his hand. "You were right to check the records. We've redeemed Father's reputation. I feel such relief."

They sat together in silence, each lost in their thoughts. They heard sounds from the kitchen as dinner preparation was underway. Nikolaos was still gone and the two of them were left alone.

"I've been thinking," Proba said. "About my request."

"About finding who killed your father?"

"Yes. I think I imposed on our new friendship."

"Proba, it was our friendship that made you ask for help. It's our friendship that spurred me to agree. Don't worry about that request. I haven't discovered much, but I will."

It was as though all the questions that had been swirling in his head needed a new prompt. He didn't know where he would find it, but he would keep pursuing the answer.

"Thank you. I had a feeling you would say something like that. I wanted to make sure you were truly willing. Otherwise, I would feel as though I asked too much."

Proba squeezed his hand and then released her hand and stood. "I'm going to pack all those ledgers away and set my attention to enjoying your hospitality."

"Excellent," Nikolaos said as Argolicus parried a dagger thrust with the tip of his sword. He deflected the thrust but didn't knock it out of his tutor's hands.

"We're finished for today," the tutor said.

"Sometimes I question the efficacy of doing this. It's not as though I'm going to end up in a street fight."

"It's about physical discipline, not fighting per se. Many men your age are already showing signs of diminished capacity. You stay fit and alert. Those are benefits above actual fighting."

"So I should think of it like declining Greek verbs?" Argolicus parried with words this time.

"We've been doing both since you were five years old. There's still room for improvement." Nikolaos thrust back.

They both laughed. Argolicus patted his tutor on the shoulder. "Now for breakfast."

They met Amalina and Proba over small pancakes covered with dates and honey, small scoops of melon, and honeyed milk. Amalina had set up a table near the fountain, so they could eat in the relative cool of early morning.

Proba looked refreshed. Her cheeks glowed with color and her dark eyes seemed to be smiling. She wore a green *tunica* that complimented her skin and hair. It was as if...

"Good morning to you all," Ebrimuth said as he strode across the *peristylum*.

"Join us," Amalina said, moving on the bench to make room for him.

Ebrimuth brushed back his flowing hair as he sat. "Proba, good morning."

Proba smiled as her cheeks flushed a deeper rose. Ah, the hair, the *tunica* on Proba, and Ebrimuth looked just as fresh as his massive shoulders leaned toward the table to reach for some melon.

Neither of the two ate much, and then they were gone.

Amalina smiled. "Never thought I would see Ebrimuth in such a fluster."

"Nor I," Argolicus answered. His assured friend treated Proba as if she could break at any moment. "I need to change my thinking to encompass this new aspect."

Amalina almost choked on her milk. "My son, you will."

Outside Pup started barking. Severa flew past them out of the kitchen to find the white dog.

Moments later, the doorman appeared. "Caius Larcius Sura for the master."

Stunned, Argolicus left with the doorman to meet Sura in the *atrium*.

"Sura, good morning," he said as he approached the perfume and silks waiting for him by the pool. "What brings you here, and so early in the day?"

"Rumors. Good morning. I've come here at the request of Bishop Braga."

Now Argolicus was more confused. Sura for the bishop? Two people who disliked him had formed some sort of alignment? What could they want?

"If we could talk?" Sura said with his contemptuous smile.

Argolicus led him into the study. He was relieved Proba had cleared away all the ledgers. The expansive worktable was empty. He gestured toward a chair by the table. "What is it you want to talk about?"

"I hear you have a girl."

Severa. But what could that matter to Sura or the bishop?

"Yes, what about her?"

"Her parents have been bragging about you at the market. Servants talk," Sura said, insinuating some affront to the public good.

"Bragging? I don't understand."

"It seems you paid them money."

"Yes. That's a private matter between them and me."

"The way the story goes her parents were going to sell her to a slave master. Then the girl ran away."

"Yes. I found her in an alley, starving and dirty. Why would this concern the bishop?"

"Ah, you see. That is why I am here."

Argolicus waited.

Sura continued, his silks rustling as he gesticulated for emphasis. "You have disrupted the slave trade."

"I don't understand."

"The church is the largest slave trader in Squillace. In fact, the church controls the slave market. Prices are set. Others, considerably smaller, follow suit."

"Yes, but this girl never reached a slave trader."

"That's the point," Sura continued smoothly. "What if every runaway slave were harbored by a private citizen? There are laws about returning slaves."

"She is not a slave. She was not sold to a slave trader. She was never a slave. She is free to leave whenever she wants."

"But, surely you see that if runaway children are harbored, it disrupts the slave trade."

"No, I don't see."

"You and your so-called goodness," Sura said, now genuinely sneering, "are setting an example for other members of the *curia*. If we all dealt directly with parents, the slave trade would diminish. It's a major source of income for the church."

Argolicus thought about Bishop Braga and his hoard of goods in the name of the church. They had locked horns before when his friend Marcus had been murdered and an icon lost. He rose.

"Sura, neither Braga nor you can control my private dealings. If the parents want to brag, they can. One child does not disrupt the flow of money to the church. You can report back to Braga and tell him the church cannot interfere in my private concerns. Coming here pretending to chastise me based on servant gossip will not sway my actions. Our conversation is at an end."

Sura rose in a huff. He swirled his silks as he headed toward the door. "This conversation is over. But there will be more to come."

Argolicus sagged back in the chair. Sura had been annoying when they were boys, and now he was still a small-minded bully. He would have to take care with that man.

What a strange morning. His old friend and new friend had bonded in a way he didn't understand. The bishop was trying to threaten him, but probably at Sura's encouragement. Since all of his books were now at his home in town, he began searching through his father's library looking for something to read to calm down.

He found the Meditations of Marcus Aurelius. Just what he needed to put everything in a balanced perspective. He opened the book to a random page. We must not chafe and fret at that which happens. Exactly. He kept reading. But just as he was considering those who try to stand in your way when you are proceeding to right reason, Eboric clamored in breathless, his red hair flowing around his shoulders.

"Ebrimuth. Where is he?" he blurted in Their Language.

Argolicus looked up from his book at the bodyguard. "What is it? In Latin, please. What's the matter?"

Eboric continued in Latin, "Kunimund is out gathering all the slaves. He is bringing the women to the house and trying to arm the men."

"Eboric, slow down. What is it?"

"A crowd is marching up the hill toward the estate. Where is Ebrimuth? We need him here."

"He went for a walk with the Lady Proba."

Eboric arched an eyebrow.

"Yes, we all must adjust. They mentioned going toward the hill across the wheat fields."

"You must prepare everyone in the house. The crowd looks angry, dangerous, and bent on a fight." Then he was gone, off to disrupt the lovers' tryst.

Argolicus heard horse hooves galloping away as he went out the door. Eboric was leading two horses toward the fields as fast as they could go. Argolicus looked down the hill and saw a shabby group of men, maybe fifty, marching up the road, shouting "What about us?" over and over, their expressions mean and determined.

He ran back inside to find Amalina in the kitchen. "Mother, get everyone in the house. Gather in the *peristylum*. There's a crowd coming, and they mean to do harm. Kunimund is gathering the field workers to help defend the estate."

"What?"

"Don't question. Just get everyone together."

Amalina nodded, alarm in her eyes. Severa stood by her side. She said, "I'll be right back." Then ran out of the kitchen.

Nikolaos froze as he was standing over his herb cuttings.

Lucius, the overseer, ran in. "Kunimund, I don't understand him. What is happening?"

"Lucius, come with me," Argolicus said. "A group of ruffians is coming toward the estate. We need to organize all the men. Kunimund is bringing them here. Once everyone is here, we'll follow Eboric's directions. I'm sure we will surround the estate. Ebrimuth will be here soon."

He felt his pulse quicken and at the same time felt as though his thoughts were garbled.

"Do you understand?"

"I do," Lucius said. "I'm going out now. The men will follow my orders. I'll listen to Eboric. I'm sure he has a plan."

"He went to find Ebrimuth. He may not be back yet. Listen to Kunimund. Do what he says. If you don't understand him, ask him to repeat his instructions. That group is getting close."

"Master," Nikolaos said. "What can I do?"

"Come with me."

Amalina took all the servants in the kitchen out to the *peristylum* except one. She sent that one to fetch the other house servants.

Nikolaos and Lucius followed Argolicus down the hallway to the side door. He barred the door and went to the main door. To the doorman he said, "Bar the door behind us then go to the *peristylum* to help my mother. The only person to let in is our guest, Quintina Proba. Then bar the door again."

Outside the summer heat was intense. Argolicus felt it on his skin. Then he realized he didn't know what to do. All the hand-to-hand practice with Nikolaos had not prepared him for an assault on his home. Men were coming in from the fields and the barns. He couldn't see Kunimund. He looked back toward the fields for Eboric and Ebrimuth and saw nothing. He took in a breath and faced the slaves, his little army.

"Men, we are being threatened. Do you hear that chanting? A group, maybe fifty men, is headed straight here. We will defend the estate and the people here. Soon Ebrimuth will be here, and he will have a plan."

Heads nodded. Argolicus had no idea what the plan would be. These men weren't armed. He spied Kunimund leading women and children toward the house. Argolicus realized they would have to open the door again. He had given the right instructions, but his timing had been off. He went to the door and banged. "Let in the women and children." He banged again. Soon the door opened a crack. "Let them in."

The door opened and the women and children, some in tears, all looking terrified, streamed into the house. He heard the bar fall in place behind the closed door.

Kunimund strode up following the last of the women and children. "I saw them," he said. "We have more men."

Argolicus knew he was right. But he still didn't have a plan. Then he heard horses galloping and turned to see Ebrimuth and Proba followed by Eboric. As they neared the house, Argolicus could see the fear in Proba's face.

Ebrimuth leaped off his horse and instantly stood by Proba's horse. He reached for her trembling hand and helped her dismount. Then the big man bent down, kissed her, and led her toward the house.

Kunimund and Lucius organized the men into groups. Two groups at the front of the house and three more groups to defend each side.

Eboric began exhorting the men in front.

Argolicus felt useless as he watched his friend and the two bodyguards mount the horses. Without any words, Kunimund and Eboric circled the house. Ebrimuth rode up to Argolicus.

"They will be gone soon. We'll take care of it." He reached down and patted Argolicus' shoulder with his large hand. Then he pointed to the horse Proba had ridden. "Mount."

Argolicus wasn't sure about the crowd leaving with nothing, but he mounted the snorting horse and rode beside his friend.

## TESSARA - CRIMSON

Matho's stomach growled. He'd grown over the summer. His mother had made him a new tunic, but the light wool made his skin itch in the heat. "It will be good enough soon," she said.

He heard his father come home from working at the warehouses. And sure enough, he said the same thing he always said, "What a day." Then he plodded into the kitchen. That was Matho's cue to join the family to eat.

The family sat around a wooden table in the kitchen. No triclinium here, just a good table. His two brothers and his sister were already there. All of them were waiting for him.

They bowed heads as Father blessed the food. "In the name of the Father, the Son, and the Holy Spirit."

"Amen," the family responded.

Mother laid out lamb stew, turnips in honey, boiled eggs, and half a loaf of bread. Father looked at the meal and shook his head. They ate in silence. Finally, Father spoke.

"I met with some of the men today. It's bad. The grain is gone. Soon there will be no bread." He looked at the plate where the bread had been. "What did the baker say?"

Mother shook her head. "One more round of baking and then

his supply runs out. I went to another baker, and he said the same."

"That's why we met. We must do something. The patricians have grain from their estates. They don't understand how regular people will suffer. We're good Romans. This shouldn't happen." He banged his fist on the table. "That saying that's been going around, it's true. What about us?"

Mother glanced at the girls and said, "Don't do anything foolish. We need you."

"All well and good, but we need bread. Everyone needs bread." Mother frowned. They all sat in silence again.

Matho decided whatever Mother thought, he would join the cry for bread. Tomorrow he would go out and paint graffiti in town. Yes, he would cover the council building.

## ❧ 19 ❧

As the unruly crowd advanced, Argolicus saw torches among the men. The crowd was larger than he first thought, or maybe more had joined. His horse pawed the ground and snorted. All of his training with Nikolaos was hand-to-hand and one-on-one. His knowledge of military tactics was limited. Without Ebrimuth he would be at a loss. No time for thinking. The crowd was coming to the crest of the hill.

Ebrimuth sat astride a prancing horse looking every inch the king's count and ready to create civil order. He turned to flash a smile at Argolicus, moved his shoulders to loosen them, and signaled the two bodyguards. Their small cavalry was ready to fend off the ragtag infantry. Because the three men were armed, the crowd moved back, but only a little.

Ebrimuth rode toward the crowd, calling "Disperse!" Rocks flew through the air. Men yelled and waved sticks and clubs. Moving back was not the same as leaving.

Kunimund and Eboric rode up from the sides and called, "Disperse!"

The cries of "What about us?" changed to roars and shouts.

"The principals owe us bread." "We want what is here." "Give us grain."

Argolicus felt he should say something to quell the crowd. He was the one looking for the grain. But he hadn't found it. He could not promise anything, much less grain. These people were hungry and angry. Ebrimuth couldn't stop them from being hungry even if he could make them go away.

Ebrimuth and the two bodyguards stopped shouting, "Disperse." The crowd responded by clustering together. Somehow, the lack of confrontation left them confused. Men muttered and murmured. They stopped throwing rocks. They had come in anger but without a plan.

Argolicus heard shouting far away on the hill. A similar crowd must be up at Bartholomeus' villa. Hunger and frustration were driving unrest here in the hills, not just in town. Without warning, a man stepped forward from the group in front of Argolicus, bringing his attention back to the crowd here not up the hill.

The sun beat mercilessly. Argolicus felt sweat roll down his back. Ebrimuth's horse pranced and blew out air from his nostrils. The seasoned horse anticipated action.

"What can you give us?" the man shouted. "We need bread."

Ebrimuth turned in his saddle toward Argolicus.

Argolicus nudged his horse toward the front next to Ebrimuth. Kunimund and Eboric frowned. Ebrimuth raised an eyebrow.

"We have failed you," Argolicus said. The crowed stopped moving. "Our government supplied bread for everyone. Somehow in Bruttium, the grain was sent north..." Mumbling in the crowd. "...and the grain supply here is short. No one knows how this happened. Squillace's main grain merchant has been murdered. Whatever reason you chose to come to this villa, you have come to the right place for answers. Not grain. Not bread. Answers. I have recently joined the council. At the last meeting, just days ago, I spoke with the council and stepped forward to get to the bottom of why there is no grain here."

The crowd relaxed. All faces were turned toward Argolicus.

"I know you are hungry for bread. It is the staple of life. I see on the walls and hear shouts of 'What about us?' You come to my home because you think the principals are hiding something from you. That's not true. None of us knew this shortage was coming. None of us planned for it. We all know you are suffering." Nods and murmurs of agreement in the group.

"So now, we must find grain for all of us. By we, I mean the principals who maintain and safeguard the community. We all wonder the same way you do, why isn't there enough grain when the harvest was good?"

"Yes," men cried, faces now expectant with hope.

"I don't know. The principals don't know. What I vow to you, is what I promised to the council. I will keep searching until I discover what happened. I promised you answers, so here is what I am doing."

"We must eat."

"A promise won't feed us now."

"I agree, a promise is not food. I am working now to unearth what happened. I am reviewing the records. Furthermore, I have spoken with Caeso Rabirius Donicus who regulates the markets, and have his records. I have spoken with Sextus Gabinius Pennus and have just finished comparing his records with those of Pompeius Severus Quintinus. On paper, all the grain is accounted for. And..."

The crowd started moving, shouting "Paper!" and "Paper is not food."

"You are right. Paper is not food. Grain is the problem. I will find the grain."

"When?"

"We are hungry now."

Argolicus felt the sweat pouring down his back and under his arms. The heat was like a fire burning his skin.

"Results require action. You may scoff at paper, but records are the first step in discovering missing grain. Tomorrow I return to Squillace and will physically explore the warehouses. The grain must be somewhere. And I will write to the governor and the king. If we cannot find grain here, we will ask the king to send grain. Now, I ask you to return to your homes. Have faith in the system."

Vague grumbling and foot shuffling in the crowd.

"Today, I ask you to return to your homes. Tell your families what I have told you. This cannot go on forever. The king will send grain if we cannot find grain here. I know that will be weeks away, but no one here, not the principals nor the leaders of Bruttium, knows what happened. So, when you ask, 'What about us?' My answer is bread is coming... but I don't know when."

Silence.

"Go home. Tell the others, we have not forgotten you. Tell them bread is coming."

One man turned and walked away. Then three. They were followed by small groups. As Argolicus sat astride his horse in the summer heat, the crowd dissipated.

"You turned them away," Ebrimuth said. "My friend, you did what I could never do. This town needs you."

"Let's go inside and tell everyone they are gone," Argolicus said. He dismounted and handed the reins to Kunimund. Ebrimuth did the same.

"Tell the men," Argolicus gestured to the men guarding the villa, turning toward Eboric, "they deserve a rest."

Ebrimuth clapped him on the shoulder as they walked to the front door and knocked.

In the *atrium*, Nikolaos and Amalina stood surrounded by the household. They both gazed with questions.

"What happened?" Amalina spoke first.

"They are gone," Argolicus said, and relief fell on the expectant faces.

Proba ran to Ebrimuth. The large man enveloped her in his arms. "It was Argolicus," he said. "Amazing man."

"We all know that," Amalina said. "What did you do?"

Before Argolicus could answer, Ebrimuth spoke, shaking his head in wonder.

"He did it with words. No arms. No threats. Words."

"Words," Nikolaos said. "No wonder they left."

Amalina smiled. Ebrimuth chuckled.

Amalina said, "Really, what did you say? How did you get them to leave? We were frightened."

"I was, too," Argolicus said. "Ebrimuth and the bodyguards were calling for them to disperse. They were getting angrier."

"He was powerful," a small voice called from the back of the room. "I heard him."

"Severa?" Argolicus called.

"Yes," the girl said as she urged her way through the crowd of slaves and servants. "I was there, waiting to strike." She emerged holding up a leather sling. "I would have hit their leader."

"Severa," Argolicus said, more warmth in his voice. "Come here."

The girl stood in front of Argolicus, the sling in her hands.

"You were very brave," Argolicus said.

She smiled and raised her shoulders.

"But, you were also foolish."

Severa hung her head, as her shoulders slumped.

"It's how I kept thieves and stray dogs away," she said. "I have a good aim."

"We had many men to do that. I'm sure you would have helped if it had come to a fight... but it didn't."

"I was ready," she whispered.

"Yes, you were ready. But, you disobeyed."

"Disobeyed?"

"Yes, everyone was to stay here in the villa, indoors."

Her face fell.

"In times of crisis, when everything can turn to chaos, it's important for everyone to follow instructions. That way, everyone has a role, and we keep chaos at bay. Do you understand?"

Severa nodded and stood mute, then she looked up at Argolicus, tears brimming.

"May I stay?" she asked.

For a second, Argolicus was startled. Then he reached out his arms and put them around the girl's shoulders. Amalina smiled. Ebrimuth nodded.

"Severa," Argolicus said. "This is your home as long as you want to be here. Of course you may stay."

She sobbed in his arms. Then she whispered, "Thank you."

Amalina came up beside them. "Come," she said to Severa. She took the girl's hand. "You are always welcome here. Do you want a new job?"

"Yes," Severa said, her eyes lighting.

"Alright, then. Go and sing to Pup. He needs calming after all the excitement."

Severa smiled and ran to the side door of the villa.

"Two resolutions in one day," Amalina said, crossing her arms across her chest. "I think we all need a refreshment."

Argolicus smiled and then looked at the surrounding crowd of householders, the slaves and servants. "Yes, refreshments for everyone. Then back to duties."

"Everyone to the *peristylum*," Amalina said, ushering the people toward the rear of the villa.

As the servants and slaves flowed out, Ebrimuth and Proba remained behind with Nikolaos and Argolicus.

"You must teach me your method," Ebrimuth said. "Now that

I am the king's representative, I need more subtlety. Words." He shook his head.

"They are what I know," Argolicus said. He glanced at Nikolaos. "In spite of my ardent tutoring in arms. But, they were spontaneous. That was not a prepared speech."

"Yes, well..." Ebrimuth said. "But, if I could calm an angry crowd like that..."

"There would be no reason for them to be angry, if we could find the missing grain."

Proba looked up from her place next to Ebrimuth. "Are we still going back to town to look at the warehouses?"

"Yes," Argolicus said. "It's even more urgent. Today's crowd showed us how important it is to find grain and get it to people."

"You're leaving?" Ebrimuth asked, looking at Proba with alarm.

"Oh, yes," she said. She reached to squeeze his hand. "I owe it to my father's memory."

Argolicus had never seen his friend look so forlorn.

"You have the rest of the day. She is here for now."

They both smiled at him, and then they were smiling at each other.

"I wish I had been there to hear you," Nikolaos said as the lovers retreated to a corner.

"I don't know how the words came to me," Argolicus admitted. "The crowd was there, angry and threatening. I've never been in a situation like that."

"It's not the words," Nikolaos said. "It's the thinking. Whatever you said made sense to them."

"Yes... but I made them promises I'm not sure if I can keep."

"Ah, you always want to make things right. But, sometimes without thinking."

"There wasn't time to think."

Nikolaos chuckled. "Must have been very uncomfortable."

"I don't need your jibes right now."

Argolicus gazed silently at the sunlight on the pond in the almost empty *atrium*.

"Ah, grumpy. Time for some food. Let's join the others," Nikolaos said, waving in the direction of the *peristylum* where faint sounds of laughter floated over good food.

The next morning, after training with Nikolaos, Argolicus sat in the *peristylum* of the town house. The sounds of the street—horse hooves on the pavement, muffled voices—filtered through the open roof.

Nikolaos crouched at one of the beds planting herbs he'd brought from the estate. He dug a hole in the earth, pulled a plant from a mound at his feet, placed it in the hole, and patted the soil above the roots.

Argolicus thought about Proba, how they'd moved to friendship in a matter of days. Now his other friend had disturbed that friendship.

When they came back to town, Ebrimuth had come with them and continued to Proba's home, "to safeguard her stay." Argolicus shook his head. He wondered if he would ever experience a thunderbolt. It seemed unlikely.

"I've been looking at Quintinus through Proba's eyes. She sees numbers. But that wasn't his life. It was her work. His life was people and the grain. The grain in the warehouses and transported on the ships. I want to see the warehouses. I think the answer is there. Not in numbers, or journals. In empty warehouses and hidden grain."

Nikolaos nodded, intent on his planting.

"Quintinus did something. Something Proba didn't see. It's as though he lied to his daughter by not telling her everything."

"Nobody tells someone else everything," Nikolaos said. "It's unrealistic to think he shared all of his secrets. If he was underhanded, why would he tell the person who idolized him?"

"You are right. There's something I'm not seeing."

"Maybe it's someone you're not seeing in the right light."

"It could be someone I don't know about. He knew so many people. Lucius knew him. Proba didn't mention him. There must be many people he dealt with. Maybe it's not about grain but some personal grievance. How would I know? Everyone I've spoken with so far said his life was about business. About dealing. About making the most from every transaction."

"From what you say, he wasn't likable, just efficient." Nikolaos' mound was diminishing as the plants each found a place in the soil.

"So, his efficiency made someone angry? That doesn't make sense. Except..."

"Yes?"

"From another perspective, efficiency could be viewed as obdurate. If he refused to yield? No. That can't be right. A man doesn't get murdered because he is stubborn."

"It depends," Nikolaos said, as he patted the soil around the last transplant. "Think of it from the other side. If there was something you wanted or something you didn't want known, and someone like Quintinus full of their righteous efficiency refused to budge, that would make someone angry."

"Yes. And it could be about anything, not necessarily grain. But what else was in that man's life? Proba, his wife, his mistress, Lucius, the principals, all say the same thing. His life revolved around dealing. And most of the dealings he had were probably with men like Lucius, overseers, not the owners."

"If that's the case, then the owners who had direct transactions with him would be more likely suspects."

"Ah. There you have a point." Argolicus thought about the men he'd seen. Donicus. That old man, squinting at numbers and life. He seemed an unlikely killer.

"Yes, a point. I'm going to get water for the plants," Nikolas said, interrupting his thoughts. He trotted off.

Then there was Macro. He had good words to say about Argolicus' father but not much about Quintinus. And he didn't mention any particular dealings with Quintinus, mostly hearsay. His fortunes seemed to be declining and that seemed even less of a reason for him to deal with the grain merchant directly.

"Here we are," Nikolaos said, toting a large jug of water and a cup. He knelt before his transplants and poured water into the cup. He waved the cup in the air. "A man like Quintinus took every bit he could. That seems to be one consistent message you heard."

"Indeed. I was thinking of Macro. I couldn't find a way that Quintinus would take from him."

"Maybe a loan? His estate looked in need of repairs."

"I'll ask Proba again. She didn't mention him. That fellow Pennus. He seems capable of underhanded dealings. He's a wine merchant. His grain supply would be about the same as our estate. Certainly nothing to impact the grain shortage or stand as the ground for murder."

"That fellow Sura?" Nikolaos asked, starting another round of water for the plants. "He seems like just the kind of person who would bear grudges and make a mountain out of some small pebble."

"No, not Sura. He is petty. You are right about the small pebble. He finds them. But I don't think he knows how to make a mountain. And think of where Quintinus was killed. A creek bank, a steep incline, boulders, mud. He wouldn't want to get his clothes dirty."

Nikolaos chuckled. He capped the water jug with the cup and stood up. He motioned to a slave passing through to the kitchen to remove the jug. "Who else, then?" he said as he came over to sit by Argolicus.

"I don't know all the principals. It could be anyone. Of the people I've met, there's Pennus. But he's old, and more to the point, he's physically weak. A bony, weak man. Not Pennus. He's also doesn't have much moral fiber. He makes excuses for himself. I don't see it."

They sat on the bench pondering. After a moment, Nikolaos shifted.

"Master, there's something you are not addressing."

"What? Do you have an idea?"

"It's not about Quintinus or the grain shortage."

"What then?" Argolicus pursed his lips. "Whenever you talk like that I know some advice is coming."

"Proba. You are acting as if you have no feelings about her."

"Of course I have feelings. We're friends. We enjoy each other's company." He crossed his arms.

Nikolaos nodded his head at the crossed arms. "That," he said. "You are not confronting your feelings."

"What feelings? I like her."

"Yes, you like her. You've been spending time with her. You are working together on both problems—her father's death and the grain shortage."

"Yes, she is companionable and smart."

"And in less than an hour, you'll meet with her to go to the warehouses. Perhaps you will even discover the root of the grain shortage. But when you meet, will you talk about Ebrimuth? He may be there."

Argolicus uncrossed his arms. "You're right. There is something." He turned to look at his tutor. "It's not about Proba and

Ebrimuth. They are both my friends. One for a short time, one for most of my life."

"So, you are not jealous?"

"Jealous, no. That's not it. I don't understand the thunderbolt. How can two reasonable people... I don't know how to say it. How can they just know? Like that? In an instant?"

"You pride yourself on understanding people. It's how you get to the root of problems. But, somehow, you put what happens between men and women out of your mind."

"No, I see men and women all the time. They form allegiances, they quarrel, they protect each other, they expose each other. I've seen men and women in all sorts of situations."

"Yes, that's true. But, I'm talking about you. There's Proba, a perfectly lovely woman. Beautiful. Smart. And the first thing you do is decline marriage. Why?"

"I... I don't know. I knew that I didn't want to marry her."

"Marry her or marry?"

Nikolaos knew him better than anyone, even his mother.

"I'm not against marriage, though Mother thinks that. It's that I want to find the right woman."

"What was wrong with Proba... before the thunderbolt happened with Ebrimuth?"

"I didn't feel drawn. She's everything you say. I didn't feel anything more than appreciation."

"Are you waiting for the thunderbolt?"

"I didn't think of it like that. There are some women who are physically attractive. Some very physically attractive. I can't ignore that. My body responds."

Nikolaos smiled.

"But," Argolicus continued, "that attraction doesn't mean I want to marry them." He paused, thinking.

Nikolaos waited.

"I don't know what would make me think about marrying. The idea of marriage, the right marriage, is appealing. Julia was a good wife as far as the world was concerned. Our marriage was arranged. We got along for the most part. But, you know, that was all. You asked me about my feelings. I think I'm waiting for feelings to consider marriage again."

Nikolaos nodded and smiled. "I am happy to hear that."

"I remember Mother and Father before his death. There was smiling and laughter and... something... a sense of peace. I don't know how that happens. Mother says it was the thunderbolt. It must be more than a moment of lightning because it lasted for years."

"It's a knowing and trust."

"Yes, a trust. I have seen men and women together in many situations. Marriage, most marriages I've seen, are not like that. The two come to some arrangement within their marriage, but that trust and what you call *knowing* isn't there. I don't want that. Can we put the idea of marriage aside?"

"Yes, yes. It wasn't so much thinking of marriage, although I did ask. Let's go back to your feelings about your friends."

"I've never seen Ebrimuth pay attention to any woman. Now he's off on walks and escorting her home. He didn't need to come with us back to town. I've known him all my life, and now he's acting like a smitten youth. How do I feel? There's more to my friend than I imagined."

"And?"

"As long as he stays his exuberant self and Proba doesn't hurt him... If something happens between the two of them, as much as I like Proba, Ebrimuth holds my concern. I would be angry if Proba hurt him. You think I hold back about women, but this is Ebrimuth's first 'love.' He is not experienced, even theoretically. Ask him about hunting, or arms, or fighting, and he is in his element. This is something new for him."

Nikolaos nodded toward the herbs. "So he is like a transplant, needing nurturing in a new garden."

"Yes. But we must all find our own way. Whatever happens, he is my friend."

They sat in quiet again, both looking at the new transplants.

"What weighs on my mind is not Proba and Ebrimuth, it's finding what happened to Quintinus. I'm making no progress. Everyone seems to agree that he wasn't likable, but that's not a reason for what happened. I have a feeling, speaking of feelings, that it's tied to grain, but only because that was his focus. It must be something personal. But everyone speaks only of his business dealings."

"This morning you are looking at the grain warehouses. Maybe that will head you in a new direction."

"The warehouses are about the shortage. Without Proba's help I would have nothing. She's the one who checked the ledger numbers. She's the one who searched for the discrepancy. And she's the one who has access to the warehouses."

"Will you find an answer there?"

"I don't know. Whatever happened, whether it was Quintinus or something else, the town is suffering. I made a promise to the principals thinking I would talk to Quintinus and everything would be resolved. Instead, I have two problems I cannot solve."

"You will."

"Both seem unanswerable right now." He made a sweeping gesture with his arm. "And here I am in my father's house. Talk about feelings. I feel as though I haven't settled in at all. I've been out trying to solve problems."

"I'll call the bodyguards, and we'll be off. The house will still be here."

# ❧ 21 ❧

The sun beat down as they stood at the main gate. They were in front of a tall wall surrounding the complex of warehouses. Storage facilities spread out in every direction. The warehouse area was the heart of commerce for the town, holding goods until they traveled north. Shouts and cries came from the other complexes as men loaded carts to carry stores to the harbor.

Proba carried a large iron ring with many large keys. Eboric and Kunimund hovered around her. Argolicus was sure Ebrimuth had given them special instructions. They might be bodyguards for Argolicus, but if Proba was there, she was part of their watchful concern. Nikolaos blinked in the sunlight as Proba knocked on the wooden door in the massive stone wall.

A slave opened the door. "Mistress! We were expecting you. I am so sorry for your loss."

Proba nodded at the slave who closed the door behind them as they entered the courtyard paved with large, flat stones, radiating heat from the sunlight. Three lines of warehouses stretched out beyond the courtyard. Here and there slaves walked between the buildings, but activity was low. Most of the grain had left and the warehouses would stay empty until next year. There should be a warehouse filled with grain for Squillace.

Argolicus asked, "Which building holds the grain for the town?"

Proba pointed down one of the alleys between the warehouses. "Down there. We keep the grain that gets shipped away in the nearest facilities."

Argolicus said, "Let's go there first. I want to see what is there. Are they truly empty?"

Proba didn't answer but led them down the alleyway. The bodyguards' leather creaked as they walked. The slave trailed behind them. The tall buildings shaded the alleyway giving them respite from the heat.

The space was vast. Once again Argolicus understood he knew next to nothing about local commerce, especially how much grain was produced locally. Just a few weeks ago, these immense, stone buildings had been filled with grain. Now there was nothing.

Proba's sandal caught on a crevice between the paving stones. She cried, "Oh," in surprise. Before Argolicus realized she was falling, Kunimund's dark form clasped her torso, pulling her upright.

"Thank you," Proba said, looking up at the silent, dark man. He nodded and resumed his place next to her.

When they reached the first civic storehouse, Proba handed the ring of keys to the slave with one key extended. The slave inserted it into the lock at the bottom of the door holding a massive transverse beam in place. When the lock freed the beam, he slid it to an upright position and opened the door.

Inside the stone walls, the space was cool. Pieces of a broken amphora lay scattered on the floor in a corner. Otherwise, the expansive, dark room was empty.

"Let's look at the next one," Argolicus said, as they walked back out into the bright morning.

Proba gave him a sideways glance and shrugged her shoulders.

"According to the ledgers, they will all be empty." She gestured around the complex. "Everything is gone."

"Let's look at another," Argolicus said.

The slave locked up the storehouse and ran ahead to the next one. He stood at the door and waited for Proba to hand him the correct key.

Argolicus noticed that most of the keys on the ring looked almost identical except for about ten which all varied in size and shape.

The slave opened the door. The next warehouse was empty—not even broken shards on the floor. Nothing.

"What are those other keys?" Argolicus asked, pointing to the ring.

"These?" Proba fingered the oddly shaped keys. "These open storage warehouses rented by others. My father bought grain directly for the most part, but some growers wanted to do their own transactions. They rent storehouses from Father." She was still struggling with verb tenses after Quintinus' death. "Father still made money, just not as much."

"And, you know what is in those storehouses?"

"The space is rented. What goes in the space is not recorded."

"But you have keys for those spaces?"

"Yes, that's part of the agreement, in case something happens to the man who rents the space."

"Where are these warehouses?"

"On the far side, over there." Proba pointed diagonally across the expanse of warehouses.

"Let's look," Argolicus said.

"But, those belong to the renters."

"You own the space. You have keys."

Proba's brown eyes widened. "Do you really think there's grain hidden away? Why would someone keep grain and not sell it? It doesn't make sense."

"Maybe they knew this shortage would happen and wanted to be prepared."

"But that's wrong," Proba said, alarmed.

"It is. Let's look."

The late morning sun was hot. The paving stones seemed to throw back the heat as they trudged past warehouse after warehouse to get to the other side.

At last, Proba stopped and gestured to a row of warehouses, each with a stone painted red over the door.

"How do you know who rents the space?" Argolicus asked.

"Do you see the number over the door?" Proba pointed to the red stone which had a number carved in the stone.

Argolicus nodded.

"There's a separate ledger for these spaces. We keep track of the names there. Sometimes two people share a space when they don't have enough goods to fill up an entire storehouse."

"We'll go down the row, starting here," Argolicus said.

They opened the first warehouse. It was filled with amphorae. Argolicus could smell olive oil.

The second warehouse held more olive oil and the third, wine.

The slave opened the fourth warehouse door. Rows and rows of amphorae filled the space. The walls held shelves with amphorae stacked up to the ceiling. And the room was heavy with the scent of the summer grain harvest.

Argolicus bent down examining the floor. He touched his index finger to the floor and brought it back up to look at the tiny grains stuck to his fingertip. "Grain. A warehouse full of grain." He turned to Proba. "We don't know who rents this?"

"Not without checking the ledger."

"Alright, this is number four. Let's look at the next one."

Five held more olive oil. Six was filled with olive oil, wine, and some cheese.

Seven was the same as four, filled with grain.

Eight and nine held more olive oil and ten was empty.

Proba was crying. Eboric looked grim. Kunimund hovered closer. But she stepped to Argolicus and buried her head in his chest. "How could someone do this?" she said, sobbing. "The whole city... The people... Under my father's eye. Were we responsible? Do I have to answer to the council?"

Argolicus put his arm around her, thinking the same questions.

❦

The surprise was Ebrimuth waiting for Proba at her home.

"I'm taking her back to your mother as soon as you've finished here," he said to Argolicus. He put his arm around Proba. She looked up at his rugged face, her eyes dry.

"Good," Argolicus said. "Let's find the rental ledger."

Proba led them to her father's study. They gathered around the large table while she ran a finger across ledgers on a shelf.

'Here," she said, pulling a volume from the shelf. She brought it over to the table and opened the pages. Then ran her finger down a page.

"Four, Caeso Rabirius Donicus."

"Donicus?" Argolicus lifted an eyebrow in surprise. That old man. What was he doing?

Proba continued, "Seven, Caeso Rabirius Donicus."

Proba sank into her father's chair. "I don't understand. The *curator civitatis*. He is in charge of the markets, finance, and administration for the town. Isn't his role to provide for the city?"

"Not so much to provide as keep track and monitor," Argolicus said.

"I don't understand the Roman ways," Ebrimuth said, shaking his mane over his broad shoulders. "This couldn't happen with Our People. A man who did such a thing would be dead."

"That's swift retribution," Argolicus said, "but that's not how

Roman law works. Disgraced and shamed. He'll end up living impoverished. No one will have anything to do with him."

"And the grain will go to the town?" Proba asked.

"I will make that happen." A wave of relief flooded his body. He would keep the promise he made to the mob yesterday.

"How?" Proba asked.

"First I will go to Vespasianus. He is the magistrate. He may call a town meeting, or he may simply make a public announcement. And, then, we'll start distributing grain. Vespasianus will be pleased. The unrest will vanish and our town will be peaceful again. Proba, you'll be able to return here to your home."

She cast a glance at Ebrimuth.

"For now," Ebrimuth said, "until this is resolved, I'm taking her back to your mother. The crowds know nothing of this, yet." He shook his head. "Romans."

"Right," Argolicus said. "Proba, can I take the ledger with me to show Vespasianus?"

"Of course."

She placed a scrap of vellum in the ledger as a marker, closed the book, and handed it to Argolicus. She stared at the table and then raised her eyes to Argolicus.

"This means my father was not at fault. He rented the space but couldn't know how it was used." She smiled in relief.

Argolicus nodded. "Perhaps."

Her smile faded. "Perhaps? What do you mean, perhaps?" Tears welled in her eyes.

"We may never know. But, surely your father would notice cartloads of grain coming to the warehouse. I'm sorry to be harsh, but your father knew more about the comings and goings of grain than anyone else. It's hard to believe he didn't know."

"He wouldn't. He couldn't," she said as the tears started down her cheeks. She ran to Ebrimuth who took her in his arms and leaned his chin onto the top of her head.

Argolicus handed the ledger to Nikolaos. "Keep that safe." The book disappeared into the folds of his tunic.

Argolicus turned to Proba and put his hand on her shoulder. She turned from Ebrimuth's chest.

"Proba, you've done a great service to the town. Give me the keys to the two warehouses. I will take them to the magistrate Vespasianus. He will be in charge of distribution."

She fumbled with the ring, removed the two keys and handed them to Argolicus.

"Without your help," he continued, "we wouldn't have grain for the people. You are not at fault. You wrote down what Quintinus told you. The city owes you a debt of gratitude. I will tell Vespasianus we wouldn't have found the grain except for you."

She shook her head. "But my father."

"We don't know. We've found grain, but many questions are unanswered. Go with Ebrimuth. He and my mother will take care of you. You are grieving. All this searching, comparison, and review of records has kept you from grieving. The estate is a safe place. You are welcome to stay there for as long as you need."

Ebrimuth nodded.

"I have much to do. I don't need your help with the next steps. I will be busy with council business, talking to Vespasianus, deciding what to do about Donicus. I'll talk to him, too. We'll get to the bottom of this. Your father may or may not have anything to do with this. Leave this to me. As soon as this is resolved, I'll come to the estate and tell you everything."

He leaned down and kissed her cheek. Then patted Ebrimuth's solid shoulder. "Thank you."

Ebrimuth smiled and shrugged. "I will keep her safe."

"I'll see you at the estate as soon as I know something." He turned and headed across the *atrium* toward the front door. Nikolaos followed with the ledger secreted in his folds.

# TESSERA - SEPIA

Bene and his followers hunkered in a small clearing hidden in the woods. His tunic was bleached white on the shoulders from the sun, but smeared with dirt and stains from his life in the woods. The surrounding men all had the same look—bronzed by the sun, smudged and streaked from living in the woods.

"I know the man, Argolicus. I met him once before. He is fair. We must wait."

A rumpled man of indeterminate years said, "We don't know him. How can he promise something he doesn't know how he'll resolve? I think he said those things just to get the crowd away from his family estate."

The group murmured assent. "Yes, we don't know."

"Who can trust a promise from a patrician?"

Bene said, "When I met him, he was taking care of a slave, a field worker. He treats all equally. He keeps his word."

"So we do nothing?" the rough man asked.

"We do nothing about the grain, for the moment."

Shoulders sagged. Heads shook.

Bene looked at the group. He had to come up with something that would take their minds off the grain.

"I've heard there's a horse trader bringing thirty horses to ship to Ravenna. What do you say to thinning the herd?"

At once, their faces changed from disappointment to glee.

"Where are they now?" the rough man asked.

## ❧ 2 2 ❧

**B**y the time they reached Vespasianus' house, the morning was almost over. Shops were closing for the midday break and the sun beat down on the paving stones.

Before Argolicus could knock on the door, Nikolaos said, "Master, what do you know about Vespasianus other than that he is a magistrate?"

"He is the magistrate. Telling him about Donicus' secret hoard is the next step. Then it's up to him and the principals to make a decision."

"Remember Rome. Don't take him at face value. You tend to do that."

"I remember Rome. Power is its own reward. People are people in Rome and here." On the stones next to the door graffiti proclaimed, "What about us?" Argolicus knocked on the door.

The door swung open and the neatly dressed doorman raised an eyebrow. "The morning is over. The master has retired."

"Gaius Vitellius Argolicus," Nikolaos announced.

"With important news," Argolicus said.

The doorman motioned them toward the *atrium*.

Argolicus stood contemplating the statues of the nymph,

satyr, Minerva, and the unknown ancient god. The gold leaf on the bench facing the pool glinted in the sunlight shining down through the opening in the roof above the pool. The colors on the brightly painted statues echoed on the walls in large swaths of color. On the mosaic floor, bright colors in the *tesserae* arranged in repetitive geometric shapes, added to the dizzying color palette. The most public room in the house was designed to impress.

"Argolicus, what is so important it can't wait until tomorrow?" Vespasianus strode in frowning.

"Apologies for the late arrival. I have news that cannot wait. Important and good news for the town."

"What is it?"

Nikolaos handed the ledger to Argolicus.

"I've been working with Quintinus' daughter to discover why we are missing grain. Following the information written in ledgers, comparing the town records with Quintinus' accounts led us nowhere. That's why I haven't come to speak with you."

"Yes, yes, and now?" Vespasianus said, deepening his frown.

"This morning we went to Quintinus' warehouse complex and found grain."

"What? Was he holding back from the town? How did he expect to make money, or, more importantly, improve his reputation by hoarding grain?"

"It wasn't Quintinus."

"What do you mean, it wasn't Quintinus? You were at his complex. Who else would it be?" Vespasianus' mouth twisted in scorn. "You interrupt my midday with no answer?"

Argolicus held his temper. The man was so full of himself and his importance. He was accustomed to speaking with disdain.

"We found that a set of storehouses belong to him, but the spaces are rented out to local men for convenience." He opened the ledger to the marked page. "Quintinus kept track of the rentals, but not what was stored there. He kept a set of keys for each unit, and entered the names in this ledger."

He read from the open page. "Four, Caeso Rabirius Donicus. Seven, Caeso Rabirius Donicus. Those were the warehouses we found filled with grain."

"Let me see," Vespasianus said.

He took the book from Argolicus and sat on the bench. His eyes ran down the page, once, twice, three times. "Donicus. Donicus, what would that old man...? It doesn't make sense." He closed his eyes and breathed in.

"Exactly. That's why I came here as soon as we discovered the grain. It's a boon to the city because, small as the store is, it's enough to quell the unrest."

"Yes, but..." Vespasianus rubbed the neck of his tunic.

"Yes, but it brings shame on the principals, the town's leaders, who somehow missed this hidden grain. And a principal who was responsible for the town's welfare, the one who cheated everyone."

"Right," Vespasianus said. He closed his eyes again and took another deep breath. "Donicus doesn't know what you found?"

"No."

"Here's what we'll do. I'll call a meeting of all the principals for tomorrow morning. Not the entire *curia*, just this year's principals. Since Donicus doesn't know about your discovery, he will come. Then we can accuse him in front of his peers, and they can decide on the consequences."

"That is an efficient plan. Since we are the only ones who know about Donicus, except for Quintinus' daughter. He will arrive unprepared for the accusation. He will have to explain to everyone how this travesty is his doing."

"The principals will be relieved about the grain," Vespasianus said. "The town can return to normal. There's one man to blame, and we will decide, together, what must be done."

Vespasianus rose from the bench. "And Quintinus? Do you know anything about his death?"

"Nothing. It happened in a lonely spot by the river. I've found no one who knows anything. Everyone says the same thing. He was committed to his business. At the same time, I haven't found anyone who had a close relationship with him. No one with a personal grudge. The only person who cared about him is his daughter. She was so relieved to find he had nothing to do with the grain hoarding. But no, nothing. We may never know."

"And you are marrying this girl?"

There were no secrets in a town. But this news was outdated. "No. The two of us agreed not to marry."

"Oh? She is a good-looking woman." A flash of something crossed his face. Argolicus remembered he'd wanted to marry her.

"She is, and intelligent. But, we decided not to marry. We're both adults. Our allegiance now is to finding her father's killer."

"I see," Vespasianus said. He stared down at the ledger for a moment. He handed it back to Argolicus and sat down again. "Bring that book with you tomorrow to the meeting. With written evidence and the grain in the warehouses, Donicus will have no defense."

Vespasianus looked at the pool as he fidgeted with the folds of his tunic.

Argolicus said, "Indeed. The challenge will be explaining what happened to the *curia*. Donicus had a trusted position."

"Yes, we must also elect a new *curator civitatis*. Someone has to take charge of the grain distribution to the people. It will be a long and emotional meeting."

Vespasianus continued staring at the pool glimmering in the midday sun.

"We will get through this."

"We will. I heard you spoke to the ruffians when they threatened your estate."

"I did. At the time I had no idea we would find grain."

"But you see what you did. You were just out on the streets. You saw how the unrest has subsided. That's due to your words. What did you say?"

"It wasn't planned, I spoke in the moment. I can barely remember what I said. I promised to look into the grain, which I was doing at the time. I said there would be a resolution. Beyond that, I don't remember the exact words. It was a tense moment."

"I remember your father when the people rebelled against a bishop. I was young. I don't remember what he said, but he had a tone. A tone of reassurance. It was his delivery as much as the words."

Since he had moved to the town, Argolicus kept hearing about his father. Was he like his father? Was his delivery yesterday what had influenced the small mob? He said, "I can't speak for myself. It was a tense and threatening situation. I felt I had to do something, say something that would make them go away. It was as simple as that."

"Perhaps you could speak to the principals tomorrow. Explain the findings. After all, it was you who found the grain. You are new to the meetings, but your voice should be heard. I know the principals will listen. If I speak, it will be hearsay."

"I can speak. It will merely be a telling of the discovery. It won't be long."

"Yes, well... bring the ledger. I must go now and send messages to the principals. You've taken a burden away from the council. Thank you."

Argolicus recognized dismissal. He turned to Nikolaos to hand him the ledger.

"You should reconsider marrying that girl," Vespasianus said as he rose from the bench. "You're here in town, an active member of the council. You say you get along with her. A marriage would solidify your position."

"I've considered. We both decided." He thought of the thunderbolt and Ebrimuth. "Marrying Proba is not something I will do."

"If not her, then someone. Men trust men who are married. It indicates stability."

Argolicus thought about his marriage to Julia. And he considered the many married men he'd met. He shook his head.

"I appreciate your concern for my position in the town. For now, I'll remain as I am."

Vespasianus looked at the pool again. "Your addition to the principals is valuable. So many men are there only because of position. Look at old Pennus, and I would have thought of Donicus before this travesty. It was Sura who invited you to the council meeting, yes?"

Argolicus considered the sequence from Sura in the street, to the council meeting, to his promise to the council, and finally to the grain warehouses.

"It was."

Vespasianus gave him a curt nod and strode to his study, off the *atrium*.

Outside on the street, with the sun beating down, he felt hot, weary, and disgruntled.

"It's time to make the house a home. I moved in, and then I've hardly spent time there."

Nikolaos nodded and said, "We'll get you transplanted with new roots."

The bodyguards followed them down the street toward his father's house.

## 23

"Is it true? Is it true?" Rufus called from his shop as Argolicus approached the house.

"Rufus, what do you mean?"

"Look around. The rowdy crowds are gone. We heard it was you." He nodded toward the other shopkeepers who had stopped their trade with the last morning shoppers and were staring at him in admiration.

"I spoke to a small crowd."

"It was you." Rufus began clapping and the others joined in.

Stunned, Argolicus nodded toward them all. "Since they are gone, let's all return to our lives. Isn't it time to close down for the afternoon siesta?"

"Indeed it is. And we can close in peace," Rufus said. "Here, take some peaches."

He handed three peaches to Argolicus. Suddenly, the others were offering gifts, plates, cups, a tunic.

"But I..." Argolicus felt tears welling.

Eboric and Kunimund gathered the goods.

Somehow they were all inside. The bodyguards distributed the goods to slaves and retired to their rooms.

Argolicus went to his father's study, his study, and collapsed in the chair behind the table.

"Nikolaos, I came here for a quiet life. Alright, perhaps some local politics, but all this. The unrest, a murder, secret grain stores, none of this was in my plan. And now this public acclaim. Shopkeepers applauding."

"You don't know your strengths. I don't mean physical at which you are still not excellent after years of my tutoring. I mean your natural ability to say the right thing. It's a gift."

"I don't think of it like that. I don't want notoriety. It could just as easily be something I'd done wrong."

"Master, you have talents that have nothing to do with what I've taught you over the years."

"Father had to deal with this. He's been gone seventeen years and people still mention him."

"He was a good man."

"What does that mean, Nikolaos? A good man."

"Perhaps we should read Marcus Aurelius tonight. I'm going to water the transplants and leave you to your thoughts."

Weariness overwhelmed Argolicus. He considered a nap. But it wasn't tiredness. He was weary. Marcus Aurelius. Nikolaos would think of that.

He stood and went to the bookshelves. But when he scanned the shelves, he noticed his father's journals. How had his father dealt with the politics of everyday life? The politics of a small town? He pulled one off the shelf at random.

Settled in the chair, he began to read.

*September 9. Amalina made an infusion of herbs for the slaves. Many ill. Unable to work. Macronius came by with the wine receipts.*

*September 10. Household returning to normal. Slaves recovering. Argolicus bullied by that little twit Sura. Talk about bullies. Severinus wants to sell his property in town. What will that mean for the principals?*

*September 11. Anicius wants to enlarge the harbor. Wants support at council. Apple harvest at estate. New overseer competent.*

He paged through the journal, spot reading entries. He found nothing that stood out. What was the point of keeping a journal? Why had his father been so diligent about his daily entries? Should he keep a journal? How would that make him a better man?

He didn't see anything important. Just quotidian notes. Certainly nothing like the thoughts of Marcus Aurelius or other philosophers.

Who were his father's friends? He vaguely remembered dinner gatherings and laughter seeping up to his room as he read with Nikolaos in the evening. Who would he invite to a dinner? He didn't know anyone as a friend. He didn't even know anyone for political alliance either. Wasn't that why he had moved to town? To make his own life?

That plan had been disrupted by the grain disaster. He hadn't started a new life. He'd been swept away in events. And, there was still one more promise to fulfill. Quintinus. He'd made no progress there. He'd found no path to pursue. Everything felt like a dead end. He had no resolution for Proba.

He was thinking in circles. Perhaps he should read Marcus Aurelius as Nikolaos suggested. He closed his father's journal and put it back on the shelf. He found the volume of Meditations and returned to the chair.

He heard the sounds of slaves still cleaning and chatting with each other. He drew in the faint scent of food cooking in the kitchen. He was making a start on his new life. The house sounded like a home. The early afternoon was a time for reflection. He stopped feeling overwhelmed by the swirling thoughts.

He opened the book to a random page.

Short-lived are both the praiser and the praised...

He thought he heard Ebrimuth. No, there was knocking. It was Ebrimuth's voice. As he shook himself awake, he heard Proba. It must be one of those dreams when you dream you are waking.

But when he opened his eyes he still heard both their voices. And then Proba and Ebrimuth stood in front of the table in the study.

Proba's face was pale and her brown eyes seemed huge. Ebrimuth was shaking his head.

"We came to you first," Ebrimuth said.

Argolicus was fully awake.

"What are you doing here?"

Proba said, "I changed my mind. I wanted to talk to Donicus. I was so angry."

"Talk to Donicus? Everything is arranged. There's a council meeting tomorrow."

"I don't care about that," Proba said. "I was angry. Donicus had ruined my father's name. I wanted to confront him." Her voice was tight.

"Proba, that wasn't wise..."

Ebrimuth said, "Donicus is dead."

"That's what I was trying to say," Proba said. "I went to his house. I didn't care if it was siesta time. But when we got to the house, it was full of commotion. No one was resting. A slave took us to his study." Her face contorted. "It was terrible. He was sitting in his chair, but slumped over, and there was blood. Blood all over his chest. Lines of blood running down his front."

"He'd been stabbed," Ebrimuth said.

"Stabbed?" Argolicus asked, fully awake.

"Yes," they both said together.

"The slaves didn't know what to do," Proba said. "I told them we would come to you."

"I can't do anything," Ebrimuth said. "This is a matter for Roman law."

"Why did you come here? Why didn't you send for the cohorts?"

"One death is enough for Proba don't you think?" Ebrimuth put a protective arm around her shoulders.

"None of this is making sense," Argolicus said.

"If I hadn't turned around," Proba said. "We were halfway to your estate. Ebrimuth said no, but I was so angry. I wanted to confront that wicked man myself. I wanted to hear from him how he betrayed the town and ruined my father's reputation. So, we turned around and came back."

"It's not your fault," Ebrimuth said. "You couldn't know he would be dead. But now we have to report this and get out of it. A Roman should report a Roman death. And Proba is in no state to talk to authorities. If you could just come to Donicus' house."

Proba pleaded with her eyes.

"I don't like this," Argolicus said. Donicus hoarding grain was one thing. Murder was another.

"Please," Proba said, pleading again with her eyes.

"Nikolaos," Argolicus called.

His tutor appeared almost instantly.

"Find Eboric and Kunimund. We're going out." He turned to Proba. "You stay here. I agree with Ebrimuth, you don't need to be involved."

"No," she said. "If it weren't for my anger, someone else would have found him. I need to be there. I was the one who found him." She burst into tears.

Eboric and Kunimund stood in the doorway to the study looking from Argolicus to Ebrimuth to Proba.

Ebrimuth held Proba as she sobbed.

Then she lifted her head from his chest. "It's alright. I'm alright." She took a deep breath. "Nothing could be worse than finding my father in the mud. I'm ready."

Outside, the shops were closed. The streets were quiet. They walked in silence.

At the door of Donicus' house, the slave opened the door without a word. Kunimund and Eboric waited by the door.

Ebrimuth led them to the study. At the door, a group of slaves stood silently, all staring in.

The study looked normal. Papers on the table, but nothing disturbed. Donicus sat in the chair, slumped as if he'd fallen asleep over the pages of numbers, except for the dark, sticky blood covering his front.

"There's no knife," Argolicus said. "This wasn't a fight. Look." He gestured around the study. "Everything is in order. A man at his work. He must have known who it was. And whoever it was left with the knife."

He turned to Proba. "What a terrible sight for you. You must feel guilty because of your anger, feeling as if you had caused this. It's gruesome."

She looked into his eyes, grateful, and nodded.

He turned to the slaves, still standing silently in the doorway. "Who is in charge?"

A sturdy man stood forward. "I'm the housemaster."

"Did you see anyone come in?"

"No. I was in the kitchen with the cook."

Argolicus turned to the others. "Did you see anyone?"

They shook their heads, mute.

"Where is the doorman?"

The silent slaves looked at each other. No one spoke.

"Surely the doorman had to let someone in. No one knows where he is?"

The slaves shook their heads.

Argolicus looked at the housemaster. "Go to the cohorts. Report the murder of your master. We will wait here."

"We'll wait in the *atrium*," he said to Ebrimuth and Proba. His peaceful move to town was unreachable.

## 24

The afternoon had faded by the time the cohorts left. At last, Ebrimuth took Proba, and they returned to the estate.

Argolicus trudged along the streets toward Vespasianus' house. He was uncomfortable with unpleasant news and wanted it all to be over. Instead of a peaceful life in town, he seemed embroiled in controversy and death.

He noticed that the graffiti "What about us?" had been cleaned from the wall of the house. The doorman looked at him in surprise when he opened the door.

"Again? What was your name?"

"Gaius Vitellius Argolicus for Marcus Vipsanius Vespasianus," Nikolaos announced as if the doorman had not been impertinent.

Eboric and Kunimund remained by the door as Argolicus and Nikolaos entered.

In the *atrium*, the statues stared stonily in the fading light. The mosaic patterns on the floor felt dizzying, or was it that Argolicus was tired? He took in the rich surroundings and wondered how rich Vespasianus was and if money alone was the reason he was Magistrate. He heard a burst of laughter from the other end of the house.

Vespasianus strode in dressed in finery. He wore another elaborately embroidered tunic and soft, embroidered shoes.

"Argolicus, greetings. I hope this is short. I have guests."

"A few minutes. I have disconcerting news. It impacts the council meeting tomorrow."

Vespasianus sat on the bench by the pool. "If you must." He gestured to the place next to him.

Argolicus joined him on the bench as Nikolaos wandered to a corner.

"It concerns our plan for tomorrow. Donicus was found murdered this afternoon."

"Donicus? Why would...?"

"Whatever the reason why, the fact is the council meeting will have a new tone. We'll still have the grain, but there will be no public accusation, only an announcement."

Vespasianus sat silent for a moment. "Murder seems to follow you. First Quintinus and now Donicus. Didn't you just move to town?"

There was no answer to such an absurd statement.

Vespasianus said, "Tell me more. Who found him? What happened?"

"Quintinus' daughter, Proba, found him. He was stabbed in the chest. I went there. He was bloody and dead in his study, collapsed in his chair."

"What was she doing there, Proba? Why would she visit Donicus?"

"I think she was angry at him, for what he'd done with the grain. She felt it as a personal affront to her father's name. So many people thought Quintinus had cheated the city. His house was besieged by the people."

"And so she wanted to confront him face-to-face?"

"That is my understanding."

"How do you know all this? Why did she ask for you? Why are you here before the cohorts?" Before Argolicus could answer, he added, "Oh, that rumor that you were to marry, is that it?"

"We became friends. She asked me to help find her missing father. I said this before."

"And she was the one who found him dead?"

"Yes."

"Have you considered that she could have killed Donicus? Did you say she was angry? Angry about her father."

"Proba?" Argolicus was astounded. "No, that's not possible. She's not like that."

Vespasianus raised an eyebrow.

Argolicus continued, "I've only known her a short time, but we've become friends. She's not capable."

"Anyone is capable. Surely you know that from your time in Rome."

"Yes, anyone is capable. But in this instance, it's not possible. Someone was with her. The *comes civitatus* Ebrimuth."

"The barbarian! What was she doing with him?"

Argolicus struggled with how to explain the thunderbolt. It was impossible.

"He was protecting her," he managed. "They met at my estate."

"Protecting her? She is a Roman. And how do you know he was 'protecting' her? He has arms. Maybe she hired him to help her kill Donicus?"

What was Vespasianus thinking? Proba and Ebrimuth?

"I've known Ebrimuth all my life," Argolicus said. "He is honest and trustworthy in the extreme. He would not be complicit in an act of murder."

"A barbarian?"

"My mother is a barbarian, as you put it."

Vespasianus pulled back.

"I knew that. So, your considered opinion is that Proba did not kill Donicus?"

"Yes. I know Proba. I know Ebrimuth. The thought is inconceivable."

"Well, you know how a magistrate must think. You dealt with all kinds of cases in Rome. She was there, with no good reason. You said she was angry about her father's reputation. Angry women can be particularly vengeful."

"They can. But, she came to me as soon as she discovered Donicus. She was upset. Ebrimuth corroborated everything. My personal opinion is that going down that path not only will lead nowhere but will keep us from finding the killer."

"I'll think about that, but I can't dismiss it."

"Fair enough," Argolicus said, not thinking it was realistic at all. "Who else knew about the grain? It's been only a few hours since I came here. I haven't spoken to anyone. I was waiting for tomorrow at the council."

"I haven't told anyone in person. I only sent the call for the emergency meeting by couriers, but only that it was about the resolution of the grain shortage. I mentioned no details."

"In that case, maybe it was about something else. Something like that would bring up mud from the bottom of the river. Who could guess what other motive? Did he have enemies?"

Vespasianus snorted. "That old man. As far as I know, he was ineffectual but not offensive. He tracked everything but couldn't make a decision to save his life." He realized what he'd just said and grimaced.

More laughter came from the entertainment room. Vespasianus turned his head toward the sound.

"I need to return to my guests soon. Tomorrow we'll get everything arranged for the grain. Yes, we'll find a new *curator civitatis* and that person will be in charge of the civic duty of grain distribution. The principals will be relieved this struggle is over."

"And you will investigate Donicus' death?" Argolicus

prompted. "You will announce that when you announce his death?"

"I will oversee the cohorts. They are in charge. When they find the killer, I will make a judgment as magistrate. A severe judgment."

"I regret I disturbed your dinner party with this distressing news."

Vespasianus waved his hand. "As magistrate, I needed to hear as soon as possible. I'm sure a cohort will be along soon to verify your news. Coming here was the right thing to do." He brushed his palms against his thighs and said, "Think more about your 'friend' Proba. Perhaps she is angry at you, too, because you rejected the marriage."

"I will think about her," Argolicus said. He knew this was true, just not in the way Vespasianus suggested. "I'll leave you to your guests."

They both rose. Vespasianus turned toward the sound of his guests without another word.

Argolicus and Nikolaos joined the bodyguards outside. The street was mostly empty. Argolicus thought about his promise to the crowd at the estate. Was he following in his father's footsteps? Would he have a reputation as a mediator? He reviewed the day's events and marveled at the highs and lows, longing for the peaceful life he'd envisioned when he moved to town.

# TESSERA - OCHRE

Inside the warehouse, Farid breathed in cool air. The thick stone walls protected the rows of amphorae filled with olive oil. Everything was as it should be. He turned and walked out of the warehouse into the sunlight.

He pulled a tablet covered with vellum from his belt and made a mark with a piece of charcoal. His master, Quintinus, had insisted that he make a mark for every warehouse he checked. It was simple, he didn't have to count, just make a mark. The warehouse overseer tallied his marks. If they equaled the number of warehouses, Farid was done.

He pushed the heavy timber warehouse door until it was closed. He slid the locking timber across the groove in front of the door until the timber rested in a diagonal across the door. Then he bent down to the lock at the bottom and secured it.

His work wasn't hard. All he had to do was be thorough and consistent. What would happen to him, now that Quintinus was dead? Murdered, he'd heard. Would the warehouses sell? Would the new master keep all the slaves? Would everything keep going the way it had?

He trotted along in the sunlight, past the rental warehouses, which weren't his responsibility. No one had come to them since they'd been filled.

The next warehouse on his rounds held last year's wine. It was too early to ship, so the wine would stay there for several more years. He bent down to unlock the clasp to the massive timber. He slid it across the groove, opened the door and walked into the cool room filled with sleeping wine.

## ❧ 25 ❧

The great marble walls of the council hall echoed with the hushed murmurings of the principals. Without the *curia* lining the benches along the walls, the great space felt empty. The principals gathered on the dais and waited with questioning looks for Vespasianus to begin.

The magistrate finally rose to address the group. "When I called you here yesterday, I had good news." He looked around at the expectant faces. "We've found grain to stave off the shortage. Not much, but enough to keep people from starving. They will have food for winter."

Mild cheers rose, and a sprinkling of applause resounded off the high walls.

"But, since then, I have discovered some distressing news. Donicus is dead. He was found murdered in his home, yesterday afternoon."

The room fell silent.

"There are no details," Vespasianus continued, once again turning his regal head to look at everyone there. He hung his head for a moment. "He was stabbed. It seems he died quickly. He was found by Quintinus' daughter, Proba."

Whispers and murmurs.

Vespasianus paused, then began again. "We owe a debt of thanks to Proba because she was the one, along with Argolicus," he nodded toward Argolicus, "who found the grain for the city."

The principals looked at Argolicus and waited for more.

"Argolicus, if you could give us a brief background?" Vespasianus sat down.

Argolicus stood. "As I promised at the last meeting, I've been investigating the grain shortage. After Quintinus' death, without a direct source, I interviewed a number of people. Donicus was one, and he generously loaned the city grain ledgers, so we could compare them with Quintinus' written records."

Every face was turned toward him. Anyone who thought only women loved gossip should have seen their faces.

"Quintinus' daughter, Proba, is gifted with numbers. She kept all the records of her father's transactions. Unfortunately, after comparing the two sets of numbers, we found no discrepancies. At that point, I was baffled and reached for one more possibility. I asked her to show me her father's warehouses. Inadvertently, that's where we found the grain."

"Quintinus, that greedy bastard," someone said. "He was always out to get the most out of anyone, even the town," said another. The marble walls echoed with grumbles and mumblings.

Argolicus raised his hands to quiet the group. "No, it wasn't Quintinus."

He waited for the principals to quiet down.

"Quintinus rented storage space. The grain is in two of those warehouses. When we checked the rental records, we found that Donicus rented those spaces."

Now the voices were angry. "He was supposed to take care of our town."

"No."

"Traitor to us all."

"Yes," Argolicus continued. "He was underhanded and risked

the peace of the city. But we may never know why he kept the grain. That is all I can tell you. Today we're here to restore equilibrium and do what we can for Squillace."

Argolicus sat down.

A man Argolicus didn't recognize stood up.

"Is it true you kept the ruffians from roaming the streets? And that is why the unrest has subsided?"

"A band came to the estate and I spoke to them," Argolicus said. "I told them I was working to find the source of the problem. I promised there would be a resolution. I asked for their patience. In essence, I told them we were working to get them grain."

Nods of approval.

Vespasianus rose from his chair. Once again he turned his head, so his gaze encompassed everyone there, then he spoke.

"Our first step is to appoint a new *curator civitatis*. This person will be in charge of the markets, finance, and administration. And in this unusual situation, he will have the added responsibility of arranging for a smooth distribution of grain to the people. You will be instrumental in restoring peace in our town, and monitoring future transactions for our city."

Quiet whisperings, but no one stood up to volunteer.

Vespasianus waited, casting his noble gaze out over the men. He looked into each man's eyes hoping for a connection.

The whisperings died down as everyone hoped someone else would stand for the position. After several minutes, the man Argolicus didn't know stood up again.

"Gregorius," Vespasianus said. "Does this mean you would accept the position?"

Gregorius wore a linen tunic with no adornments, much like the one Argolicus wore. He was remarkably handsome like a statue in the forum come to life. His brown eyes looked out from his steadfast, chiseled face.

"If the principals would accept," he said.

"Anyone else?" Vespasianus asked. No one else stood.

"May I see a show of hands for Mettius Pullo Gregorius as our new *curator civitatis*?"

Hands rose in unison.

"Very well," Vespasianus said. "We have decided. Thank you, Gregorius, for your contribution to the city."

Universal applause broke out, resounding on the marble walls. The council had chosen.

"There is much to do, but we have accomplished the reason for our extempore gathering. Thank you all for being here today."

"Wait," a voice cried out.

Sura rose, his pomaded hair glistening. "What about Donicus? I have some questions." He stared at Argolicus, then gazed around at the men gathered on the dais. Vespasianus waved his hand at Sura. Those who had prepared to leave settled back in their seats.

"How will we know what happened to Donicus? His murder seems tied to the grain. And the one person who seems to be everywhere in this grain mystery is Argolicus."

Argolicus was stunned. Where was Sura going with this?

"How do we know this isn't a plot for Barbarian subversion? Who has ties to the Barbarians? Who was appointed by the King to work in Rome while the rest of us remained here in Bruttium? There are hardly any Barbarians here, except Argolicus. Yes, he is a Barbarian. His mother is one. His 'friend' is the richest Barbarian in the region. And, he interfered in the town ways by riding around with his men, sending the ruffians off the street. I hear he is also appointed by the king, their own *comes civitatus,* some kind of Barbarian count."

Everyone was staring at Argolicus, not Sura, as he continued his rant.

"And, who else has Barbarian bodyguards? Have you seen him parading on the streets with those two armed brutes? As Romans, we cannot carry arms. He has sidestepped this law with

legally armed men. Argolicus encouraged this Barbarian
Ebrimuth in the streets. Argolicus 'found' the grain. His
Barbarian friend 'found' Donicus. And, then, who goes to
Donicus' house? Who calls the cohorts? Gaius Vitellius Argolicus. I find it suspicious, that one man, one man who is new to
the principals, one man who seems to arise from nowhere, was
involved at the heart of all these matters. I call on Vespasianus,
our Magistrate, to investigate this seditious man. Furthermore, I
believe he is encouraged by the king to disrupt our Roman
ways."

Argolicus felt his anger rise with every word, every aspersion.
What misguided thinking had led Sura down this path? And
where did he get all those details?

Sura glared at Argolicus while the corners of his lips hinted at
a smile.

The men on the dais were stunned. Their eyes went back and
forth between Sura and Argolicus.

Sura must have been one of the guests at the dinner party.
And against his word, Vespasianus, must have mentioned the
details to Sura if not to all the guests. His ears pounded, and he
felt a rush of energy flood his body. He was angry at Sura and felt
betrayed by Vespasianus. Here he was, locked in politics again.
How could he have thought that moving to town was a good idea?

Men who minutes before had looked on with appreciation
now gazed at Argolicus in speculation or downright suspicion.

Before Argolicus could rise to respond, Vespasianus took
charge. "Sura, we have heard your complaint. And, I will, when
this meeting is concluded, meet with Argolicus to begin an
inquiry. You may sit."

Sura sat, then turned his head to Argolicus, gloating.

Argolicus missed the closing of the meeting, as he reeled in
surprise and anger. Why was Sura determined to bring him down?
Sura was the one who had invited him to the council. Had that
invitation been calculated to ruin his reputation? He could not

remember in youth, and certainly not as an adult, affronting Sura. Was Bishop Braga behind this slur? And Sura his instrument?

The hall was empty now except for Argolicus, Vespasianus, and Gregorius the new *curator civitas*.

Argolicus went to the two men.

"Proba has the most recent ledger. She used it to compare against her father's records."

Gregorius said, "I don't know her. Will you set up a meeting?"

Vespasianus said, "Argolicus, Gregorius is the shipping master for the harbor. Everything that goes somewhere else on ships, goes through his management."

Argolicus nodded. In Ostia, it had been the same. Shipping was the power that controlled the goods going in and out of the harbor. Gregorius' classic face read an open welcome.

Vespasianus turned toward Gregorius. "I can help you retrieve the town ledger. I knew Quintinus and I've met his daughter. I am certain it will not be a problem."

"She's not in town," Argolicus said. Still hesitant to explain the thunderbolt and certainly after Sura's accusations, Argolicus said, "She's at my estate, staying with my mother."

Both men looked at him. Finally, Vespasianus said, "I thought you called off the marriage."

"I did. She's been staying at the estate since the uprising." Why did Vespasianus keep asking the same questions? He'd already explained about Proba. Maybe it was for the benefit of Gregorius. "The mob targeted her house because they were angry at Quintinus. And now... things have changed." It was a lame ending, but he could hardly explain the thunderbolt, something he didn't fully understand.

"We'll need the ledger," Vespasianus said.

"I am certain she will meet with Gregorius and give him not just the ledger, but anything else he needs to know about grain."

"I'll meet with all the major brokers," Gregorius said. "Wine, oil, horse breeders, everything that has to do with the town's assets. I spend every day keeping track of ships and their cargo. I have every confidence that I can serve Squillace with finance and administration."

"The other ledgers will be at Donicus' house," Vespasianus said. "I'll have a cohort escort you there at your convenience. You could start there until Proba arrives back in town."

In minutes, Gregorius had left the great hall, leaving Vespasianus and Argolicus alone on the dais.

"As for those accusations," Vespasianus said, sitting back in his chair and gesturing Argolicus to sit. "Sura made points that disturbed the principals. I don't believe a word he said, but he has raised questions that must be answered for the principals and the rest of the *curia*. You know how word travels."

At least not everyone had believed Sura's wild claims. Vespasianus had power. His backing would help put the suspicions to rest.

"I'm grateful for your support," Argolicus said, with due courtesy.

"It's not so much support but a desire to quell unrest of any kind. We've had enough with the missing grain and two murders. Spurious allegations are not what we need right now. Is there some reason I should believe any of it?"

"No," Argolicus said. "Yes, my mother comes from The People, as they call themselves. But she always served my father as a wife of a Roman. She raised me to be a Roman citizen. Ebrimuth has been my friend since childhood. His recent appointment by the king was a result of the unrest here. Considering how very few of The People live here in the south, I would consider it mainly titular. He had no reason to interact with Donicus. He was there only because he was protecting Proba. Proba wanted to clear her father's name. Yes, I know these people. Yes, I have a connection with the king's court through Cassiodorus. But a plot is laughable."

"Let's meet for a formal inquiry," Vespasianus said. "I will come to your house with a secretary to record what is said. That way there will be an official record. I will close the case and make a public announcement. I'm afraid there's nothing I can do about Sura. Do you know why he made the accusations?"

"I'm baffled," Argolicus said. "He was the first person I met when I moved into my father's house. He invited me to come to the council right then at our first meeting. I have some suspicions about why this happened, but they are unfounded. So, I won't air them."

"Understood. I'll come to your house for the inquiry, and we'll hope this dies down."

## ✣ 26 ✣

Argolicus ate the cook's midday meal in the *peristylum*. He broke off a piece of bread and dipped it into the egg salad with bits of cheese, leeks, vinegar, thyme, and coriander. He longed for a fountain, deciding that would be his first change to the house.

Nikolaos tended the transplants, which all stood upright in their new plot. "Soon the cook will have more herbs to add variety to your meals," he said, brushing a leaf.

"This is good as it is," Argolicus said, dipping another piece of bread into the salad.

"Tell me again about Sura," Nikolaos said, rising from his plants and coming to sit beside Argolicus.

"There's nothing to add. I suspect Bishop Braga put him up to it. He wouldn't be so brash without feeling he had some kind of support. He came here with that nonsense about Severa. And that was directly from Braga. I think this is more of the same. Braga wants power. He deals in slaves. I exposed his deacon. And even though the deacon was dismissed, Braga's reputation was damaged."

"This doesn't feel like a theological difference," Nikolaos said, shaking his head.

"Of course not. That is just a tiny thorn. My guess is it's about power. Who knows how many of the principals attend his church? This was about reputation. Remember how Adeodatus suffered from that accusation of rape? That was all about controlling vineyards."

"So, this is about controlling the council?"

"It's about power. Sura is an unknowing pawn. I'm sure he thinks he is protecting the town. Braga, or someone else, put him up to it. The worst part is, now there will always be doubt in the minds of anyone who was there today."

"But you found the grain. You calmed the mob."

"As they say, that was yesterday. He accused me of plotting murder."

They sat each with their own thoughts. Street noises filtered from outside. Argolicus heard Rufus and the other shopkeepers closing up their stalls for the afternoon.

"Do you think I should have dinner parties?"

"Dinner parties?"

"Yes, become part of the town society. I've been thinking how reclusive I've been up at the estate. It was a luxury, reading, spending time with my books. One of the reasons I moved to town was to become more active in society. That's why I went to the council meeting... even if it was at Sura's invitation. In a few more days, I would have gone of my own volition. It just happened that the council meeting was the day after the move."

"And now the Magistrate is coming for a formal inquiry. And that's about your ties to The People, especially in this case, Ebrimuth. Why is he here in the south? Your mother is here because she married, but Ebrimuth and the people on his estate are about the only ones here other than your mother. You'll have to explain that to Vespasianus. Will you tell him you are related?"

"I suppose you could call us distant cousins. But I'm not sure what the relationship is. Mother would know." Argolicus shrugged. "For an inquiry, I should tell Vespasianus. But that's not the reason we're friends. We are friends because we get along. We've always enjoyed each other's company. Maybe it's because we are opposites. His action, my reticence."

"Reticence isn't the word I would use," Nikolaos countered. "Look at how you quelled that mob the other day."

Argolicus laughed. "Well then, not reticence but bookish, restrained. You keep me going with our fighting practice, but without you, I would probably not do it. Ebrimuth lives and breathes action."

They sat in silence, Argolicus still wishing for a fountain.

"Years ago, when Theoderic came to power," Argolicus said finally, "Ebrimuth's grandfather received his three percent tax from a Roman who lived up north but had land here. He gave the land here as his tax to The People. The family story goes that his grandfather was tired of fighting and moved here to retire. But I don't see how that has any bearing on Sura's outrageous charges."

He took another piece of bread and scooped the last remnants of the herbed salad.

"You sent my notes to Ebrimuth and Proba?"

"As soon as you wrote them," Nikolaos said. "They should have arrived a while ago."

"I feel tired but not sleepy. I'm too upset for an afternoon siesta. I'm going to the study to read more of Father's journals. He seems the right model on how to navigate local politics. I always feel out of my depth in these things."

*January 6. The new year celebrations went well. Our small town is full of festivities. Norbius is a credit to organization.*

Now that he thought about it, he wasn't sure his father's journals would help. The entries had names he didn't recognize and notes too brief to give any sense of how his father maneuvered the shoals and channels of politics. He would have to navigate his own path.

His anger came in waves of frustration. He wanted to hit Sura. Hit him hard. But that would accomplish nothing and backfire on the accusations. He couldn't do anything. But he didn't even know what to do.

"Here it is." A voice broke into his thoughts.

Ebrimuth stood in front of the table. His golden hair was tousled as if he had run against a wind that didn't exist on this hot summer day. His outstretched arm presented a key. "And a note of instructions to the household."

He produced a sheet of vellum and slapped it down on the table, followed by the key.

"What key is that?" Argolicus said, recovering from his reverie.

"To Proba's house. She wants you to get the ledger and give it to this Gregorius."

Ebrimuth flexed his shoulders, pacing in front of the table.

"I suggested she not come to town. What is this insanity? Who is this Sura?"

"I don't know. He's concocted some wild story about a plot devised by King Theoderic. It's absurd. I think the only reason the king thinks about us here in the South is because Cassiodorus comes from here." He thought a moment. "And, there's another reason. Our governor, Venantius. He tries to keep money for himself instead of sending it on."

Ebrimuth found a chair in the corner of the study and pulled it in front of the table. He sat. "We must make a plan."

Argolicus was startled to see his friend sit. He never sat. He stood. He paced. He crouched. But he didn't sit. "A plan? You have a plan? I've been sitting here trying to think."

"Ha! That's your problem. You think too much. This insult requires action." He grinned.

"That's just it. I don't know what action to take."

Ebrimuth hopped up out of the chair and paced again.

"This is what I don't understand about Romans. First, no one of The People would act that way. And why? Because he would know that there wouldn't be thinking about it. He would know that he would be dead within minutes."

"Yes, but..."

"No, buts. No thinking. You must confront this man." The long knife on Ebrimuth's belt banged against his thigh. He pulled it out and waved it in the air.

"He says I killed Donicus with this. He didn't just insult you. He insulted me. It's ridiculous. My knife would be covered in blood. I would be covered in blood. The cohorts would have seen that right away."

"But you are not going to kill him. You see? That's the differ-ence. You have the laws of The People. We have Roman laws. That's how these two cultures live together in one country. That's how the country has had peace and flourished for decades. The king is shrewd. He understands people."

"Ah, so, you are aligned with the king."

Argolicus was puzzled until another broad smile broke out on Ebrimuth's face.

"You see. That's how Sura twists everything good about you."

Ebrimuth sat again.

Argolicus looked his friend in the eye. "I must abide by the law. I uphold the law. That's what I did in Rome. That's what Vespasianus does for the town. This is not about the laws of The People." He paused. "I want a plan and if you have suggestions other than killing Sura, I'm ready to listen. But, let's have a cup of wine while we talk."

Ebrimuth slapped his thigh. "Ah, better. Good idea."

Soon a tray arrived with two cups and a pitcher of wine.

Ebrimuth leaned forward. "You are right. I was angry, and that doesn't solve anything especially in your world of Roman law. But a man's reputation is sacred. Take that away, and you are left with nothing."

"That's how I feel. Powerless against the accusations. Donicus is dead. There's no way to consult him. The cohorts keep the streets relatively peaceful. Everything Sura said twisted what is known into dark hints at unknown."

"So, you need to come up with more known details. Isn't that what you always do?"

Argolicus smiled at his friend.

"Yes." He paused. "Usually I'm looking to uncover facts that already exist but are hidden. This is different."

Ebrimuth frowned. "How?"

"None of what Sura said is a fact. He made it up. It's hard to prove or disprove something that isn't there. That is what is so frustrating. I don't know how to go about refuting his allegations. It's like arguing with nothing."

"Isn't that what Nikolaos teaches you? Logic?"

They sipped their wine. And, as if on call, Nikolaos appeared in the doorway.

"Nikolaos," Ebrimuth said. "We need your thinking skills."

Argolicus looked up from his wine cup. "Ebrimuth says logic is the best way to refute Sura. But there is no logic to his claims."

"I've been thinking about that," Nikolaos said, coming up to the table.

"Aha, you see," Ebrimuth said. "The very thing."

"Refuting the claims," Nikolaos said, "doesn't prove anything. In fact, it will remind everyone of the claims and possibly strengthen them in people's minds. They heard them once, and now they hear them again as you try to counter."

Argolicus pressed his fists against his cheeks. "Yes. I feel boxed in. And it wasn't just me, he accused Ebrimuth of murder."

Nikolaos nodded. "So, the best way to counter the allegations isn't to refute them."

Argolicus and Ebrimuth both waited for the tutor to continue.

"You need to provide an alternate solution. That way you will persuade people to revise their beliefs and reject those falsehoods. You must explain what actually happened instead of bolstering those negative claims."

"But," Argolicus countered, frustrated with his tutor's suggestion. "We don't know what actually happened."

"So, you must be patient. Without bringing the false claims to attention, do what you do in any investigation. Find the facts. Dig for the truth."

Argolicus started to protest, but Nikolaos went on.

"You want to make those claims disappear overnight. You want them gone right now."

Argolicus and Ebrimuth said in unison, "Yes!"

"Don't you counsel other people to be patient while you investigate the facts? Isn't that what you told Proba about her father? Now you must take your own counsel. Be patient. Focus on discovering facts. You just found the missing grain. You can and will discover what happened with Donicus and Quintinus."

"And all that time, however long it takes, men will think ill of me."

"That is their choice. There's nothing you can do about suspicion... except, find the truth."

## 27

Argolicus spent a restless night. He kept waking up trying to make a connection between Quintinus and Donicus. Or, feeling that he liked Ebrimuth's approach and wanting to fight Sura. Then realizing that a fight would only exacerbate the false claims.

By the time Vespasianus arrived with his recording secretaries, Argolicus was enervated, weary with conflicting thoughts. Now he had to gather mental strength and answer the claims.

Slaves brought chairs into the study. The secretaries sat at each end of the table with their writing implements. Vespasianus, dressed in another finely embroidered tunic, sat across from Argolicus.

Now that Vespasianus was here, Argolicus felt the inquiry was unfair. He shouldn't have to disprove false statements. At the council hall, Vespasianus' suggestion of an inquiry to clear the air had felt supportive. Now it seemed a verification of Sura's claims. Argolicus had no facts. Whatever he said, it was still his word against Sura's.

The secretaries finished arranging their writing tools. Vespasianus smiled.

"This procedure is official. Your words will be recorded. And, think of this, Sura's are not recorded, so what you say here today will bear more weight than his accusations."

"Let's begin," Argolicus said, mentally readying for a fight. "But first I need to clarify my position. Extraordinary claims like those of Sura demand proof. He made these claims out of thin air. There is nothing to back them up. He takes birth and association and implies they are in themselves insidious. It is true that nobody can disclaim their birth heritage. Nor can they contradict familial relationships like mine to Ebrimuth. That we are also friends does not in any way prove that we are plotting against the local laws."

Vespasianus listened, nodded in agreement, and asked, "Are you ready?"

"I am."

"You Gaius Vitellius Argolicus have been accused of sedition against the town of Squillace."

The secretaries' pens scratched across the vellum sheets.

"We are here today to hear your responses to each of the claims rendered by Caius Larcius Sura another principal, stated at the principal's meeting in a public forum."

Argolicus didn't know if it was the sleepless night or the strength of Sura's spite, he felt anger surge through his body, tightening his muscles as if for a fight. That it had come to a formal inquiry, galled his sense of honor. But Vespasianus was attempting to resolve it. Argolicus was grateful. This session was keeping him from a physical confrontation that would further ruin his honor and accomplish nothing.

"As I see it," Vespasianus said, "there were two main accusations. One, you participate in activities and associations that subvert the Roman law. And, two, as part of this subversion you were complicit, if not instrumental, in Donicus' death."

Argolicus spent the morning answering questions, watching the secretaries write down his words. Yes, his mother was one of

The People. His tutor had prepared him for life in the public world as a Roman citizen. Yes, he knew Ebrimuth and had since childhood. They were distantly related. They were friends. He had nothing to do with his appointment as *comes civitatus*. He hadn't known Proba and Ebrimuth would visit Donicus. She made the decision on her own. Neither Ebrimuth nor Proba were likely to have killed Donicus. Surely the cohorts had not suspected them when they arrived at the scene. He had never met the king. He had correspondence from the king, but it was by way of Cassiodorus about his role as *praefectus urbi* in Rome. A pause while Argolicus searched for the letter.

Nikolaos found the letter which Argolicus handed to Vespasianus. He read through and then raised his head.

"And who were these brothers? Why were you reluctant to settle their claim?" Vespasianus said, suddenly interested.

"It's a shameful tale," Argolicus said. "They cheated me in a game, and I was angry."

Vespasianus waited for more.

"I was naive. That's the short version. I believed them to be honest. They cheated me. It had nothing to do with subverting Roman law. I didn't want to meet with them. They were scoundrels. We finally met. I verified their claim to property. That was the end of it. No conspiracy."

"And, so, nothing more from the king? No following letters?"

"No. Except for the complaining brothers, I performed my role to the best of my ability."

"And you didn't return to Bruttium to cause trouble or subvert our way of life?"

"Not at all. I came here to retire from public service."

"If you retired to your estate, why did you reopen the town house?"

Argolicus wasn't sure why this question applied to the accusations, but he answered.

"I wanted to live my own life. And, as I said, the first day here was when Sura invited me to the council. When I considered his invitation, I felt it was my public duty to attend."

There were more questions and more scribbling by the secretaries.

"One incident I want to clear, that might make it seem you were counter to our governance."

Argolicus sighed inwardly and nodded. It was as if his whole life was under scrutiny.

Vespasianus continued, "Soon after you arrived, there was an incident with the governor, Venantius. Something about an old man and wine. But the governor was angry."

"Ah," Argolicus said. "Adeodatus. Similar to now in that his reputation was at stake. There was a false accusation. The governor was complicit. He wrote a complaint to the king. It was messy. The one who suffered the most was the old man." He paused, looking at Vespasianus. "As you know, not everyone is fair. Not all complications come to a clean end."

"I think that is enough to close the inquiry," Vespasianus said, watching the secretaries until they finished writing.

"Thank you for your support and quick resolution at the council meeting," Argolicus said. "If this process helps to counter Sura's claims, then I am grateful."

"It will be the official record," Vespasianus said, nodding at the secretaries. "But nothing can stop rumors."

"Nevertheless, I am grateful." Argolicus knew that now he had to find the facts, the details that would clear his name. "When you make the results public, I will do my best to help you find Donicus' killer."

Soon Vespasianus and the secretaries left. But for Argolicus, all the questions about Sura, Donicus, and Quintinus still remained.

Nikolaos materialized at the doorway. "I was in the *atrium*. I heard most of what transpired."

"It's official. A public record," Argolicus said, soul-weary. "But until we find who killed Donicus, the rumor will be alive. And, although Quintinus' reputation has been restored, we haven't found his killer either."

"There's nothing for it but to keep looking."

"I'm sure the two murders are related, and related to the grain, but I don't have any idea how. First, we need to conclude my part in the grain supply. Find the bodyguards, and we'll go to Proba's house to retrieve the ledger."

❧

When Gregorius arrived to retrieve the ledger, Argolicus was struck again by his good looks. But he knew that looks were not the measure of a man.

They met in the *atrium*. The afternoon light slanted on the pool's water surface. They sat on the bench facing the pool. Nikolaos took an inconspicuous stand in a corner.

Argolicus handed the weighty book to Gregorius. "Here are Donicus' records. When Quintinus' daughter checked the numbers, they agreed with his records. One of Donicus' strengths was keeping tabs on numbers. But my understanding was he had trouble using the information to make good decisions for the town. You have work to do. He recorded the amounts but totaled nothing."

Gregorius smiled. Even his teeth were perfect, white, and evenly aligned. "I keep track of ships, their cargoes, and their destinations. The harbor is relatively small, so I make decisions every day about which ships come to the dock to load or unload and when. I volunteered because decision-making is second nature to me."

A man who knew his strengths and did not pretend to false modesty.

"Let me offer you some refreshment, and we can talk about the town and its recent hardships. Do you have time?"

Gregorius smiled and this smile was less toothy but more genuine.

"I'd be delighted."

Nikolaos disappeared. Soon slaves arrived with small tables, with wine cups, bowls of almonds, apricots, bread, and white cheese.

Gregorius nibbled on an apricot and then sipped the wine.

"How did you find the grain? The story of how you turned around the mob is impressive. I can't imagine speaking to an angry mob."

"I don't know. The words just came out. I wanted to save the estate. I can't remember anything I said," Argolicus said, grinning. "And for the grain, I'd made a promise to the council. I just kept digging, with the help of Quintinus' daughter, until we found the warehouses."

"I heard you at the council. I didn't know who you were before then. You'd been gone in Rome, I hear."

"Yes, and I am glad to be back."

Argolicus broke off a piece of cheese and placed it on a morsel of bread. Gregorius did the same.

"I knew Quintinus. He sent shipments north on many vessels. Last month was busy. I must say he was a difficult man."

"Oh?"

"He haggled over everything."

Argolicus nodded in agreement. That was one consistent message about Quintinus.

"And he interfered. To be truthful, I didn't like him."

"Interfered?"

"Yes, he gave contradictory orders to the harbormaster, like trying to change loading order of ships. He was out of his element, but tried to act like he was in charge. He consumed my time with incidents like that. Then I had to calm down the harbormaster and assure him the original schedule was correct.

It's not just ships in the harbor, but loading times, and tide flows. Things he didn't comprehend."

"Did you admonish him?"

Gregorius smiled again. "Not admonish, but certainly caution. I explained how attempting to alter the schedule was not in his best interest. It wasn't really about the schedule. It was his desire to control."

"I never met him." Was Proba so amenable because her father was controlling? He tried to picture the two of them together. But Gregorius had asked him a question.

"I'm sorry. I was lost in thought."

Now Gregorius laughed. A good hearty laugh. "That happens to me all the time. I asked, Will his daughter take over the business? I understand she is the only heir."

"I find that unlikely. I suppose next year one of the minor grain merchants will emerge as the main source here."

"I have another question, but it's more personal."

"Go ahead."

"What will you do about the outrageous accusations?"

"I don't know—yet. I have a strategy for countering the untruths. I don't know what the tactics are yet."

"Strategy and tactics," Gregorius said. "Battle planning."

Gregorius broke off more cheese and bread.

"Your house," he continued, "has a warm feel. How did you manage that when you've been here such a short time?"

"The echoes of my family. We spent time here when I was young. My father died seventeen years ago. My mother moved to the estate after his death. Moving here was mainly a matter of cleaning and refreshing the paint."

"Whatever you did, I like it. It feels lived in. So many people now try to create a show and there's no warmth."

"Yes, it seems to be a trend. But, of course, in Rome, it's a style. Like house braggadocio."

"If you'd like to know about the harbor, I can show you around. I'll show you what it's like there."

"I would like that."

"Come the day after tomorrow. It will be a slow day. I'll have time to show you around."

Argolicus was curious about the harbor. But what he liked right now was the feeling he was starting a friendship.

# TESSERA - AZURE

The transport ship backed away from the quay, its imposing curved bow reaching up as the ship settled low in the water line filled with goods.

Qasim watched as a smaller ship headed for the quay. He signaled to the livestock handlers to bring the cattle. They bellowed as the herdsmen guided them down to the quay, bringing their stench with them.

Unlike amphorae filled with oil or wine or grain, livestock were unpredictable. That's why Qasim liked to be present to make the loading as smooth as possible. Even if the herd leader was manageable, any animal could bolt causing a catastrophe. Worse was when they ran into the water. Qasim liked to time the arrival of the ship and the animals to coincide, so there was no delay.

There were only ten head of cattle, so this should be smooth. The linesmen were securing the ship, as the cattle arrived.

Above the lowing, he heard an angry voice. Now was not a time to spook the animals. He turned his head to see two men gesticulating at the harbor's accountant.

Qasim signaled to the lead herdsman. "Load them as quickly as possible. I'm going to see what the ruckus is."

"The horses," the herdsman said, as Qasim strode down the quay.

"It's not our fault," one of the shouters cried.

The accountant, a tall, handsome man, said, "Whatever happened, you will only be paid for the horses you deliver, not the whole sum."

"Damned bandits," the man said, scowling. "Who will find the missing stock?"

"You need to report the theft to the cohorts," the accountant said. "I'll pay you for the animals you delivered, once they are loaded on the ship."

"We came all the way from Tarentum," the man grumbled.

"For now, get the horses ready."

## 28

Three days later, Argolicus still had no tactics in place. He'd visited the harbor with Gregorius and watched the ships load and unload. Nikolaos had his martial practice sessions back each morning and reading in the evening. He'd heard nothing from Proba or Ebrimuth. Most of all, he had no idea how to look for Quintinus' murderer.

Unlike a magistrate like Vespasianus, he had no authority. People would have to meet with him out of their good will. And, that wasn't the biggest challenge. He didn't know where to go or whom to meet to find more.

He looked at his list: Donicus, Pennus, Macro, Martina, Vespasianus, Sura, Fabia, Proba. He was about to cross out Donicus' name and stopped.

What did he know about Donicus? So much had happened since he met with the old administrator. He remembered the table strewn with papers. At the time Argolicus had been focused on the grain and numbers. The man hadn't totaled the numbers. The ledger was accurate but a shambles for information.

Now, he tried to remember the man's aspect. Squinty eyes, a whine. Had Donicus cringed when Argolicus mentioned

Vespasianus? Was he ashamed of his lack of attention? Was he afraid of rebukes from the principals?

The man was spineless. That was about all he knew. Did he use his position to bully people? Weak men often tried to use their position to manipulate others. He tried to imagine Donicus whimpering in the face of Quintinus' controlling methods. But there was no transaction involved. They'd merely exchanged tallies. Quintinus reported, Donicus recorded.

What was it that tied the two men together? He pounded his fist on the table. He stood up and began pacing.

Who had helped him? His first tactic would be to go back to the people who had given him information without hesitation. When he thought about those he'd talked to he came up with two names, Martina and Macro.

"Nikolaos."

His tutor came into the study.

"Get the bodyguards. We're going out."

Once again, red hair gleaming, Eboric knocked on the door of the house nestled among those of prosperous merchants. The large doorman let in Argolicus and Nikolaos. And once again Martina was there immediately. This time her lush body was draped in linen but not as transparent. Her eyes shaded by the long lashes, opened in surprise.

"You are back, Your Supreme Excellency." Her soft voice lilted an invitation. "I'm hoping this is a personal visit. Perhaps your slave could wait here in the *atrium*. Or the kitchen? He looks as though he could use a visit to the kitchen." Her brown eyes sparkled in amusement.

"No, I'm here to ask you more questions."

Martina pouted her full lips. "In that case, let us sit here by the pool."

She moved to a bench by the pool, her hips swaying under the linen. "Come. Sit. Ask me your questions."

Argolicus sat and the same inviting floral scent made him feel as though he were enclosed in her presence. How could one woman be so provocative? He understood how Quintinus managed time in his organized business life to visit her.

"When I was here before, you mentioned how Quintinus complained about people who owed him money."

The upturned corners of her mouth broke into a smile.

"Yes, he did. But I can't tell you anything more than I did then." She shifted causing her breasts to sway. "Can I offer you wine?"

"No, no, thank you. I'm trying to understand Quintinus. That's why I am here."

"Quintinus is dead," she said, in a matter-of-fact tone, losing her seductive voice for a moment.

"He is. As I told you, I promised his daughter I would try to find his murderer."

"Ah, the noble promise. You are a man of principles. So fascinating in this world of transactions and business and politics. Very appealing. It makes you more attractive."

"Martina, stop. That is not why I am here."

"Oh, I know. But I would be delighted if it were otherwise," she purred.

"I know you told me he gave you no names. But tell me about the loans."

She parted her lips. She couldn't help herself. Once again, he found her temptation hard to resist.

"A loan is a loan. Sometimes men couldn't meet obligations, and sometimes they just needed money." A faint frown appeared. "The last time he was here, he was angry at someone. Someone important. I could tell by the way he talked about him. The man was in over his head. Desperate."

"How?"

Martina shifted again moving a little closer.

"Quintinus had no pity. He just complained. I told you that before. For him, it was all about transactions, money and power. He was proud of his control over people. It was as if he was boasting about this man's desperation. That he could bring the man, whoever he was, to ruin."

Proba's filter of her father through a loving daughter's eyes was a kinder portrait. But now Argolicus had a direction, a desperate man. But most men thought they had power and that financial problems would bring them to ruin. It wasn't much to point to someone.

"He gave no hint of whom it could be?" Argolicus swept his arm in a broad arc. "Someone who lived in this area of town?"

Martina's skin was smooth and creamy, like an invitation to touch. The corners of her lips turned up in the perpetual almost smile.

"For a smart man, you don't listen well. No. No names. No position. No reference to anything that would identify him. You are asking me for more than I can tell. Are you sure I can't offer you some refreshment?" She smiled again, tilting her head and shading her eyes with her extraordinarily long lashes.

❧

The afternoon sun exposed every chip and crack in Macro's villa. Here was a man with position whose financial circumstances had deteriorated. Argolicus considered their last conversation full of fond reminiscence but not much about Quintinus.

This time Kunimund knocked on the door, but it was Eboric whose Latin was better that announced Argolicus.

Macro ushered Argolicus, followed by Nikolaos, into the *peristylum*. And here was another fountain, burbling in the sunlight. Shrubs and flowers bloomed in the beds around the courtyard.

The old man might have been less wealthy than before, but he lived in comfort.

"I received your note. I don't know what else I can tell you. But I prepared some refreshment." Macro gestured toward small tables with wine, fruit, olives, bread, and cheese. "It's a warm day to be traveling on the road."

Argolicus sipped from the cup of honeyed wine.

"You know the principals better than I do. Do you know anyone who is suffering financially? I discovered Quintinus had loaned money to someone. Someone who couldn't pay him back."

The old man shook his head and then smiled. "Just like your father, right to the heart of the matter. But to answer your question, no. Men of position rarely talk about their financial trials. To talk about them would immediately lessen their esteem and ability to conduct business. I remember a man, Petri, I think his name was. This was before you were born. He splurged on finery, hosted lavish parties—I never attended—invested in dubious schemes. Everyone thought he was one of the leading men of the town. But then his dubious investments fell through. He lost everything except a small house in town that he kept for his mistress. He moved in. She moved out. Well, of course, he no longer had any money. Everyone was shocked. He seemed so well off. And then, overnight, he was ruined. It does happen."

Macro shook his head again. He looked around the *peristylum* and then swept his arm. "My financial position is not as strong as it was. But I'm nowhere near ruin. The estate brings in money from crops. I have enough, well, not quite enough, but I don't need much. My wife Julia—wasn't that the name of your wife? So sad—is gone. There's only me. I don't entertain. I have no lavish interests. I'm an old man enjoying his solitude."

He turned toward Argolicus.

"You. You should get married. You are young."

Here it was again.

"I've been thinking of it. For now, it is a concept. I haven't met anyone..."

"Well, good," Macro said. "The right woman will complement your happiness."

Argolicus wasn't sure what that meant, but he nodded politely.

"You are in town. You know the principals. Supposedly the man in question is powerful."

Macro shook his head again. "I'm rarely in town. I go to the council, but those meetings are infrequent. Except for the latest grain problem. You've resolved that."

Argolicus interrupted before Macro could go off on another story.

"You haven't heard anything? No one has come to you in confidence?"

"Why would they come to me? I have nothing to loan, no way to help someone in financial distress. Quintinus was the right person. Everyone knew he supplied private loans."

"It was general knowledge?"

"Oh, yes. A ship that hadn't come in or was lost at sea. Bad crop year. A little overextended on expenses. Quintinus had no qualms. Was it morally right? No. But he focused on transactions that brought him money. A grain harvest, a loan, it made no difference."

"When his daughter speaks of him, she uses kindlier terms."

"Yes, she colors him with filial admiration. But out in the world of commerce, he was... well... ruthless. I know what you are trying to do. You want to find his killer. But men don't talk about their financial hardships. Petri is a good example. No one knew until it was too late. If Quintinus was driving someone to extremes, you'll have a hard time identifying who it is."

Argolicus nodded. Every man in the town could be a suspect. Not everyone. Martina had said he was important. But important could be in the fellow's head or in Quintinus' head. It was a jumble.

Macro reached out his scrawny arm and patted Argolicus on the shoulder.

"Try the cheese, it's soft and fresh. A good cook makes a household."

Argolicus took a piece of cheese and broke off a bit of bread.

"It does. I have a new cook at the house in town. Nikolaos organized an excellent staff."

"You need a wife. That would be the finishing touch to a home."

Argolicus laughed. Everyone was intent on seeing him married.

"First, I will solve this puzzle."

"I heard something about an arrangement with Quintinus' daughter." Macro raised an eyebrow.

"Yes, our mothers. But we both decided it wasn't right. However, we became good friends."

"My Julia was a lifelong friend. If I can be bold, perhaps you should reconsider."

"It was a mutual decision. And our friendship grew as we worked together to solve the grain crisis."

"You saved the town from pain and social disruption. That is quite an accomplishment. I was shocked, yes, shocked, when Sura brought up those accusations at the council."

He patted Argolicus' shoulder again. "No one believes his wild claims."

"Perhaps. I saw faces filled with doubt. For some, those claims, false as they are, will color their perception."

"Keep being who you are. Many were skeptical of your father Maximinus when he returned from the war with your mother. But he soon overcame the skepticism by continuing to be a wise and honorable member of our society. You can do the same."

"Live a good life, that's what I aim to do."

"You do. Whether you find Quintinus' killer or not, what

you've done for the town in the brief time you've been back from Rome will uphold your honor for some time."

"Macro, you know that reputation can turn in an instant."

Macro nodded. They both sat watching the light play on the fountain.

## ❧ 29 ❧

**W**as Macro an artful liar? One of the hardest parts of an investigation was holding things close. Argolicus remembered Pennus telling him that he'd seen Quintinus and Macro meeting several times. This knowledge was in the back of his head while he talked to Macro.

Each time he had talked to Macro, he didn't mention meeting with Quintinus before his death. Pennus, the old wine merchant, had insisted that he saw Quintinus with Macro. But, Macro had seemed so open when they talked.

Pennus had mentioned seeing Donicus with Quintinus as well as with Macro. These meetings seemed suspicious because both men were now dead, killed at someone's hand. But it was only the word of one man. A man who seemed to relish spying on others. So much had happened since his talk.

He thought about going back to Pennus and prodding him for more secrets, especially about loans. Pennus had elaborated on loans that Martina had merely hinted at. Donicus had mentioned nothing about loans.

Argolicus stared at the mosaic lozenge patterns on the floor of his study. Each small *tessera* fit with others to form a pattern. He felt he had the tiny pieces, but they weren't forming a pattern. Somehow he had to realign the pieces. And then he had to find the missing piece.

He heard voices at the door and soon Proba and Ebrimuth were in the study. Both of them were smiling. Proba's small body leaned into his large frame.

"I thought you were staying at the estate," Argolicus said to Proba.

"I was... I am... but I decided it was time to put my father's estate in order. There are so many papers. I need to find someone to take over his business. It certainly isn't me. And I will be moving out of the house." She beamed at Argolicus and then Ebrimuth.

"Moving? Are you going to the estate to join your mother?"

Her smile flickered. "No, I won't be joining my mother. Our lives... they are different. But I will be moving." She beamed again.

"With me," Ebrimuth said. And Argolicus couldn't believe it, but Ebrimuth was beaming too. More thunderbolt.

Argolicus briefly wondered again what it would be like. To instantly know. He couldn't imagine. Argolicus stood. "My two friends, I am happy for you."

Ebrimuth grabbed him in a tight hug. "I knew you would understand. Amalina assured us that these plans would not harm our friendships."

"As always, she is right." Argolicus chuckled.

"So," Proba continued, "I will spend some weeks organizing my father's business for transfer and finding the right person to take over the business. And, as I'm doing that, I will be readying the house to close it."

"This all seems so abrupt," Argolicus said.

"It is," the two said in unison.

"And the period of mourning, for your father?"

Proba's brown eyes looked at the floor briefly, then up at

Argolicus. "I believe I am the only person mourning my father's death. You saw everyone at the funeral. It was a social obligation. Did you see anyone mourning?"

"No."

"So I will mourn my father in my heart. But my heart is full of something else, too. I will follow the new fullness." She smiled at Ebrimuth.

"And you still want my help?"

"Oh, yes. I don't want vengeance, I want..." she paused to think as the smile faded. "I want to know who did this merciless crime. There is no justice. But, it would bring the mystery of his death to a conclusion."

"Murder is a public matter. If... when I find who killed him, he will be at your mercy." Proba's small frame stood straight. "I know. I will take full responsibility. I've talked with Ebrimuth about what to do."

Argolicus was puzzled. Ebrimuth's solution would be to kill the murderer, or at least ask for some life payment. "That is all an imposing *if* for now. Let's go to the entertainment room. You can tell me more about your decision to close the house. I have to say I will miss your presence in town. We'll drink some wine, and I'm sure the cook has something delicious to add to this impromptu celebration."

Ebrimuth's blue eyes twinkled, and then he gave Argolicus a crushing hug.

There was a loud knock at the door.

All three turned toward the front of the house.

"Now what?" Argolicus said.

"Nikolaos go tell the cook, we'll be in the entertainment room."

Nikolaos was about to leave when Boden, the doorman, came holding a long leather tube. He pulled off the leather cap and pulled out a scroll with a large seal.

"Master, from the governor."

Argolicus took the scroll and broke the seal.

Ebrimuth hovered. Proba looked perplexed.

"The messenger is waiting for a reply," Boden said.

Argolicus began reading the flowery beginning. He skimmed. *And because I have received this inquiry relating to serious charges against you, I command your appearance to answer these charges again, in my presence...*

Argolicus tossed the scroll onto the floor.

"What is it?" Ebrimuth asked, his hand on the hilt of his sword.

Argolicus didn't answer. Instead, he said, "Nikolaos, come. We must write a reply."

At once, they were all back in the study where Argolicus dictated a polite reply. Ebrimuth and Proba stood in silence as they listened to the dictation. Proba's face turned pale. Ebrimuth began pacing.

Nikolaos finished writing and took the reply to Boden waiting in the *atrium*. The doorman opened the tube, rolled the reply, and slid it into the tube. He nodded at Argolicus and headed for the door.

"I don't understand you Romans," Ebrimuth said, shaking his mane and frowning. "All this back and forth, and inquiry and now another inquiry. Why must you go to say the same things again to the governor?"

"Think of it as power, not legality," Argolicus said. "I'm sure Sura didn't think of this on his own. I'm sure the Bishop Braga is behind all of this. He holds a grudge from before when I exposed his deacon. He tried to cause trouble about the girl Severa and that message was delivered by Sura."

"And Venantius, the governor?" Proba asked. "Does the bishop hold power over him? That doesn't make sense."

Argolicus shook his head. "Anyone can make a claim to the Governor Venantius. He can take up the claim or dismiss it. In this case, he adopted the complaint."

Ebrimuth flexed his shoulders and tossed back his hair. "Well, if you are going to see Venantius to counter these claims, I am going with you."

"But..."

"So am I," Proba said. "We discovered Donicus. We will support you and your actions." Her brown eyes glowed fierce.

"You both are kind, but the summons is for me," Argolicus said. "I am the one to answer to Venantius."

Ebrimuth said, "He needs to see that you are not alone. This nonsense is about a Barbarian plot. I am one of The People. I will look him in the eye and deny this claim." He paced back and forth by the pool in the *atrium*, leather creaking as his boots slapped the mosaic tiles of the floor.

"Yes," Proba said. "We will show him you are not alone. I am a woman of stature. I was there, too. Whether you can 'handle' Venantius is not the point. The Governor needs to hear how baseless these claims are." Her tiny hands formed fists. "He must see. This has to stop."

Argolicus smiled at his friends. "Friends," he said, shaking his head as his anger dissipated.

Nikolaos said, "They are right. No need to go alone."

"I concede," Argolicus said. "Venantius is devious. He wants everything to focus on his glorious self, as he sees it. If you come with me, be prepared for odd questions and let me speak first. Whatever you do, don't interrupt him." As soon as he spoke, he considered Ebrimuth's temper and direct approach. He looked at Ebrimuth. "Agreed?"

Ebrimuth stopped pacing.

"Agreed. But I don't like it." He crossed his powerful arms over his chest. "I don't like it at all. But you need support. Who else knows you as well as I do? I am the right person to be by your side."

"That's the problem," Argolicus said. "Our friendship is the basis for these claims. Sura has turned our friendship into a political barb. Do you see how he turned everything around to make our friendship a threat to the local powers?"

"But it is nonsense!" Ebrimuth stomped his foot. "There is no real substance to the claim."

Nikolaos waved his arms to stop Ebrimuth. "His strength is his weakness."

"What do you mean?" Ebrimuth asked, towering over the small tutor.

Nikolaos looked up at the face above him. "We fought him with words before, we can do it again. He may be the governor, but he is so vain he is unable to make decisions. Everything is about him."

"Words!" Ebrimuth said, shaking his head. "There you go again, my friend. This will be a battle of words. I hope you do as well with Venantius as you did with the mob."

Argolicus tried to imagine Ebrimuth blustering and threatening in the Roman Senate. He couldn't. Venantius was the focus of the vicissitudes of Rome in southern Italy.

"The best way to counter rumor, is with facts. When I met with Vespasianus for the formal inquiry, I thought we were done. He as much as hinted that the inquiry would put it to rest. The papers would be filed and the rumor would die down. Of course, he sent a copy to Venantius. What baffles me is why Venantius, out of the copious papers he receives from all over, would choose this one to investigate. Something else is happening behind the scenes. Something we don't know. Something someone has flagged for investigation."

"What do you mean?" Proba asked. "I've never met Venantius. I work in numbers, not politics."

Argolicus frowned. "Normally, an inquiry that was closed would be put to rest. A copy is sent to the governor and filed away, never to be seen again. Much less examined or called to question. For Venantius to single out this document and open his own inquiry doesn't make sense. Someone must have called it to his attention. But why?"

"We may never know," Nikolaos said. "Asking why is speculation. Venantius himself holds a grudge. He could have seen your name and decided to be vindictive."

Argolicus nodded in agreement. "Speculation will further nothing. Whatever Venantius has in store, we must all answer with facts. And," he looked at Ebrimuth, "without emotion, just the facts."

Proba came up to him, smiled, and took his hand. "You can rely on our support."

"We will leave early in the morning to meet Venantius. But now, weren't we going to celebrate before this happened? Nikolaos, go see the cook. Come," he said to his friends, "celebration before inquiry."

He smiled and held his arm out gesturing toward the *peristylum*. He put his arm around Ebrimuth's wide shoulders and took Proba's hand.

🙌 30 🙌

In the morning dark, it was as if the sun had never set. The heat was oppressive as Argolicus, Nikolaos, Eboric, and Kunimund waited for Ebrimuth and Proba. The eastern sky was turning gray as the two rode up.

Nikolaos spoke to a house slave as Argolicus greeted his friends.

"We should get there before the governor's morning has gone too late. In four hours he should be ready for an audience. And, by his note, he is expecting me, but not you."

Ebrimuth answered, "Since we are implicated in the accusation, it is only right for us to be there."

Proba shook her head as if waking up. She wore a broad straw hat against the sun that would soon rise over the hills. "This all seems so invented. It's as though someone deliberately wanted to cause you trouble, but we don't know who it is."

Argolicus ran a hand through his hair, pushing back curls. "We don't know. We can only guess from Sura's accusation. He is mean-spirited, but not an instigator. Perhaps Venantius will reveal some hint. But maybe not." He turned his horse toward the road.

"Master, wait," Nikolaos said.

"For what?" Argolicus said. "It's time to go."

The slave ran out carrying a large straw hat.

Nikolaos gestured toward Argolicus. "This," the tutor said. "It's already hot. Protect yourself from the sun."

Argolicus grunted, irritated and grateful, as he placed the hat on his head. Nikolaos was right to guard him against the heat, but he was embarrassed to show a weakness in front of his friends. He thought about it for another moment and knew that fainting from the heat would be more humiliating.

He nodded his thanks at Nikolaos, adjusted the hat, and led them all out onto the road.

They rode in silence up to the hills north of town.

Argolicus' red rage that erupted yesterday when the message arrived had turned to cold speculation. Someone wanted him discredited, and he would discover who. But only when he knew why. And Venantius had his own reasons for discrediting him. Argolicus was the cause of a chastising letter from King Theoderic after the cruel treatment of his old friend Adeodatus. After only a few months, the wound would open again when Argolicus stood in front of the arrogant young man. Spoiled and self-centered as the governor was, he would harbor deep resentments for anything that tainted his power.

As the sun rose, every eastern slope felt warmer than the next. Argolicus was grateful for the wide straw hat. Ebrimuth and the bodyguards appeared unfazed by the heat. Proba seemed lost in thought, still with the faraway look she'd had when they started.

At last, they went down the farthest slope. The governor's estate spread out before them.

Argolicus looked out over the expansive estate—villa, barns, stables, outbuildings, and fields, which covered the opposite hill. Horses grazed in various pastures or stood in small groups under trees. As far as he could see, everything was neat, well-ordered, and in good health—animals, plants, fields, trees.

The bodyguards remained outside the villa. Ebrimuth had to

relinquish his sword and knife, which made him frown. And then, at last, the four of them stood before the young governor seated on a dais in a large, ornately carved chair.

Venantius wore a silk toga woven in an intricate and colorful eastern pattern; an echo of the Emperor in Constantinople. He was much younger than Argolicus, perhaps twenty, and gleamed with youth and beauty. His hair was cut so that his brown curls tumbled about his head heedless of the smooth fashion in Rome. His eyes narrowed as they glanced from the document in his hands to Argolicus and back. His lips pressed together into a white slash. He glanced at Ebrimuth, towering over everyone, his blond hair flowing over his shoulders and then at tiny Proba silent with defiance glowing in her dark eyes. An eyebrow twitched. Clearly, he hadn't expected an entourage.

A scattering of courtiers stood around in silence. Sycophants ready to agree with whatever Venantius said.

He started with pomp about the indictment coming to his attention through regular reporting channels from the city of Squillace. Then he looked directly at Argolicus. "What do you have to say?"

"What I have to say is written there," Argolicus said, pointing at the papers. "What are your questions?" He still did not understand why he had been summoned. And, he was uncomfortable because, as Nikolaos had counseled for facts, he didn't have them yet. And, refutation without facts was meaningless.

"The matter of your birth," Venantius said. "When you were here before, I had no idea about your mother."

"I, like many Roman citizens, have a mixed birth. It's a fact. As you know, my patriarchy makes me a citizen. And your father, Liberius, and my father were friends. His marriage and subsequently my birth, were not issues in their friendship. I am a citizen by Roman law."

Venantius blinked at the mention of his father, a man who had been just and fair.

"Well, that is true," Venantius said, waving his hand. "But what about your current alliance with this man," he paused and shuffled the sheets, "Ebrimuth, a known man of The People? How did you influence his appointment as a count?"

Ebrimuth twitched his shoulders.

"The answers are there," Argolicus said, pointing again to the papers. "I had no knowledge of his appointment until I met him in the street. We've known each other since childhood. It's all there."

"And the bodyguards? Why do you have those bodyguards? I hear they came with you today."

Ebrimuth spoke before Argolicus could answer. "They are at my insistence."

"And who are you?" Venantius said, shifting in the throne-like chair.

Argolicus' nostrils flared. He was the one getting angry, not Ebrimuth. Venantius knew who they were. They had all been announced when they entered.

"Ebrimuth, *comes civitatus* of this area, recently appointed by the king. And," he nodded his shaggy head toward Argolicus, "he had nothing to do with my appointment."

"So it says here," Venantius said, glancing down at the sheets again.

"And because of the riots and disturbances," Ebrimuth continued, "I thought bodyguards who could carry arms in public would protect my friend. It was a personal favor. He," Ebrimuth nodded his head toward Argolicus again, "tried to refuse. I insisted."

"But, you killed the *curator civitatis* . It says here in the statement..."

"My answer is in the statement," Argolicus interrupted. "I did not know Ebrimuth would visit Donicus. Ebrimuth happened to be with Quintina Proba. She wanted to visit him to ask him a question about the grain shortage."

"Exactly," Proba said, her dark eyes flashing. "I was helping

Argolicus discover the missing grain for the city of Squillace. My father was the largest grain merchant. Surely, you know about my father. And, you know about the grain shortage." She crossed her arms and glared at Venantius.

Venantius frowned. "So you went to the house of Donicus and found his body?"

"Yes, it was shocking... it was horrible," Proba blinked back tears. "He was... blood." She sniffed and continued. "Ebrimuth was with me. He was escorting me to town. He didn't know Donicus. Not only that, but he had no reason to kill him. I was the angry one. I felt Donicus had held back information or... stupidly omitted information. Certainly, no reason to kill him."

Surprised at her tears, Argolicus looked at Proba. His heart swelled with gratitude toward his friends. At the same time, his anger grew. Why were they here? Why hadn't the indictment been filed away? Why was Venantius keen on... what? He didn't understand why they were here.

Venantius sorted through the sheets on his lap, then smoothed them.

Then Proba spoke as if she had read Argolicus' thoughts. "Why are we here? What failing do you see? Not what was accused by Sura, but in reality? What do you want to accomplish today? Why is this important?" Her small body vibrated with emotion.

All the while, Argolicus had feared Ebrimuth would lose his temper. But, no, Proba charged the governor, hinting at incompetence.

The two young people, Proba and the Governor, glared at each other. Venantius, looked down at the document again. He pulled out one vellum sheet and read.

The entire room was silent, courtiers stood mute. Proba continued to glare at the governor.

"I have a note," Venantius said, gesturing toward the sheet he was reading. "It was attached, calling my attention to the inquiry record."

Ah, he was putting the blame on someone else. It wasn't his idea. He would keep the person a secret. But who would have sent the note? Vespasianus? But why? He'd left the inquiry as if it was closed.

"It is my considered judgment," Venantius continued, looking at Argolicus and ignoring Proba, "that you should refrain from participating in the Council of Squillace for six months."

Silence.

"Think of it as a protection," Venantius said, straightening the sheets. "No one will notice your absence," he said with disdain. "Let your resolution of the grain shortage bolster your reputation."

Argolicus stood mute with rage. The courtiers began whispering. Something leather creaked on Ebrimuth as his shoulders moved.

"No!"

Proba's cry filled the room.

"No, no! He hasn't done anything wrong. He saved the town from an uprising and found the missing grain. This is backwards! This should not be happening!" Her tiny body trembled again, her glare fiercer.

"My dearest Proba," Venantius said. "You are suffering from grief. This is not a matter for a woman. These are affairs of state. They do not pertain to you. You should be with your grieving mother. I have spoken. So, it shall be."

Venantius rose from the chair, silks rustling, handed the documents to a subordinate, and strode out of the room.

"You can't! You can't!" Proba cried. She looked after the retreating governor.

"He did," Argolicus said. "Come, let's leave this place."

He put his arm around Proba's shoulders and ushered her toward the door.

Argolicus, Nikolaos, and Proba waited outside the villa's door while Ebrimuth retrieved his sword and long knife.

"It's unspeakable. It's unfair," Proba said, the sun evaporating the tears on her cheeks.

Ebrimuth burst out the door, sheathing his long knife. "What a despicable man. So much for your Roman law."

Argolicus said, "He has power. He wields it unwisely. He doesn't like me. It was an excuse to punish me. Not for any legal reasons, but for personal spite."

"But," Proba looked up.

"You see, Proba, you are right and so is Ebrimuth. I haven't done anything wrong. He had no recourse but power."

"This would not happen with The People," Ebrimuth said. "First he tried to imply that you are not a Roman. That would place you under my jurisdiction. But he was wrong. He knew it. The only way he could hamper you was with his power. The man is disgusting."

"Let's save our personal remarks until we are away," Argolicus said, gesturing toward the guards at the door.

Eboric arrived with the horses. Ebrimuth held Proba until her crying subsided and then lifted her into the saddle.

Nikolaos came up to Argolicus, his face set. "Master, your hat."

# TESSERA - AMBER

The stall in the forum shaded Muco as he worked the leather. As far back as anyone could remember, his family, his father, his father's father, and beyond, had sold leather goods in the forum.

He threaded a needle, placed the strap of the bag against the wall of the bag, and pushed the needle through with help from the leather padding on the palm of his hand. Others might punch holes and tie with leather strips, but stitching lasted longer and was secure.

He listened as he stitched. He learned more from listening than from any public announcements. Patricians ignored his presence and spoke as if no one was there. Take these two, standing in front of his stall.

"...and I heard he went before the governor today."

"It's hard to know what to believe. Sura causes trouble just to cause trouble. Then our noble Vespasianus went to his home. Who knows what was said? But, the governor..."

"That's just it. Could it all be as Sura said? Why would the governor call him when Vespasianus already questioned him? Something more must have shown up." The speaker shook his head.

Muco knew that principals and magistrates came and went, but everyone needed leather goods. Belts, bags, shoes. No accusations. No hearings. No public shaming. Just solid wares for good prices.

Soon his wife would bring a small lunch. She stayed just long enough to gather the morning gossip. Today he'd be sure to give her a playful kiss, thankful that their life was simple and good.

I n the evening, Nikolaos said, "You are tired. Why not make the reading easy tonight? No Greek. We'll read from the book Boethius gave you. What is it called?"

"Aristotle's *Categories*."

"Ah, yes. It's in Latin. It will be a light read."

They went to the library and settled down.

Argolicus held the small leather book in his hand. His mind flooded with memories of Rome. Boethius and his noble coterie. His own countless sessions resolving disputes. The two brothers who tricked him. How they had seemed friendly, inviting him to a party. And then got him drunk—his one and only time—and fleeced him at dice. How, he, in a small-minded way had delayed the settling of their estate claim.

"I'm not as noble as Proba and Ebrimuth think I am," he said.

"You are human," Nikolaos said. "Wasn't it Christ who said we all have sin? Who, besides you, will be let down if you are absent from the council? You've been absent most of your life. A few weeks are nothing in the span of a life."

"Now I must go to Vespasianus, and tell him the governor's decision."

"Yes?"

"He was sympathetic and expedient after Sura's accusations. He listened. His scribes wrote. He left with reassurances."

"Wasn't he the one who wrote the note to the governor? I would think he was. Who else had access to the copy that went to the Governor? I think it was his note that brought the documents to Venantius' attention."

It was as if Nikolaos had pushed something from the back of Argolicus' mind.

"That makes sense. But why? It doesn't fit with my experience of him."

"I don't know," Nikolaos said. "Why don't you read? Sometimes reading helps thinking."

Argolicus opened the small leather book at random and began reading aloud. He kept at it for a while, but his mind kept wandering. When he came to, *There are six kinds of change: generation, destruction, increase, diminution, alteration, change of place,* he stopped.

"What type of change brought Quintinus to his death?"

"What?" Nikolaos replied, jerked from a mental reverie.

"Quintinus. Now that I am relieved of anything to do with the council, I can focus on Quintinus. I promised Proba. What happened that caused someone to kill him?"

"Everyone you asked had no answer."

"I'm aware of that. So, now I need a fact. Something that triggered anger. You saw the body. That was deliberate... and provoked by anger. So, let's use Aristotle to find an answer."

"Somewhere," Argolicus continued, "there's something. Some *thing* that's evidence of something Quintinus did. He could have started something new. Did he make a new transaction? Was he on his way to make a new transaction? That would be generation."

"If it was a verbal agreement without documentation, you won't find it."

"Yes, that's what makes me think it was possibly something new. Something Proba hadn't recorded, yet."

"But, we don't know if he arrived at his destination."

"Could the creekside have been his destination? They met there and Quintinus said or did something that angered the other person."

"Possible, but not likely." Argolicus nodded his head. "You're right. People didn't like his negotiations, but they were always conducted in a business-like manner. There were written agreements. I don't see him meeting in the open by a creek, with writing equipment. What about destruction?"

"A document? A reputation? A business? Do you mean he was bringing someone to destruction?"

"Probably not a document. But a reputation or a business. That would certainly trigger anger. Fear and anger. But how would we know?"

Nikolaos shook his head. "We don't know. That's the problem. What's next?"

Argolicus looked down at the book. "Increase. That was Quintinus' stock-in-trade. He increased his wealth by making deals with others. That's not much help. We already know that about him."

"Next?"

"Diminution. Whatever Aristotle thought, in this case, it's similar to destruction, only not complete destruction. The motive would be the same. Who was threatened by Quintinus' power? Did someone owe money he couldn't pay? That would be a motivation. They would lose their reputation and their standing. Diminished to nothing."

"But, who fits? How would we know?"

"And that question leads us to Donicus. Proba went to see him, to question him. I would go now to question him. And, somehow, his death is tied to Quintinus."

"And what is the next change?" Nikolaos asked with a raised eyebrow.

"You know."

"Yes, I was listening," Nikolaos said, smiling.

"Alteration. Isn't that what happened with the grain? Donicus kept that grain in his own warehouses altering the supply."

"Before his death, Donicus would have been a likely candidate. We'll never know what he was doing with those grain stores or what he hoped to accomplish. And, we won't know if Quintinus knew the grain was there or if they had a scheme together to manipulate prices. You can't move large quantities of grain into warehouses without somebody noticing. Whatever is on Proba's records, it's highly likely that Quintinus knew what was happening on his property. He owned the complex."

"Who is tied to the two of them?" Nikolaos asked.

"Anyone. All the principals. They know each other. They gossip. I feel like we're thinking in circles. There's a puzzle within the puzzle of Quintinus' death."

Argolicus closed the book, sat back, and sighed. When he glanced at Nikolaos, he found his tutor waiting.

"Something is on your mind," Argolicus said.

"Venantius. You haven't mentioned him."

"Just months ago I exposed his plan to take over a vineyard and destroy an old man. As heartless and greedy as that was, he feels wronged. As Proba said, I didn't do anything wrong. But he had an opportunity for revenge. Keeping me from the council isn't much of a punishment. I've been involved for less than a month. Will it damage my reputation? Perhaps, especially coming right after the grain restoration."

"That's all very rational," Nikolaos said. "How does it make you feel?"

Argolicus sat in silence for a minute, then answered, "Angry, resentful, and frustrated."

"Ah," Nikolaos said. "Tomorrow we'll have a good practice session in the morning and read Marcus Aurelius in the evening."

The next morning, after a rigorous sword session with Nikolaos and a light breakfast, Argolicus went to see Vespasianus. Still angry and resentful toward the governor, he felt a responsibility to speak with Vespasianus personally, and thank him for his equanimity during the inquiry.

The gilt statues in the *atrium* gleamed in the morning light through the roof. Vespasianus entered carrying a sheet of rolled vellum.

"Argolicus, welcome. Venantius sent me this," he held out the rolled vellum.

Argolicus wondered if the man ever relaxed. Vespasianus wore another elaborately embroidered tunic with beads and multi-colored threads in geometric designs. The leather in his black shoes was cut in intricate patterns. Argolicus felt plain in his tunic with red patterned medallions near the hem and brown walking shoes.

"I came to tell you myself. Since you already know, I'm after the fact."

"We all know Venantius is arbitrary, to say the least," Vespasianus said, smiling.

For a moment Argolicus thought he would pat his shoulder. "Yes, but I also wanted to thank you."

"Thank me?"

"For the way you conducted your inquiry. It was fair and honest. You recorded the entire proceeding. And, I felt a certain sympathy."

"Yes, sometimes members of the council get carried away. Sura's outburst was an example. It's up to me to smooth the waters, so we can act on the decisions at hand. Disruptions keep us from making reasoned decisions."

"Just so with the Senate in Rome," Argolicus said. "I am thankful to you for saving us from civil disruption."

Vespasianus shook his head. "We'll never know what Donicus was thinking. What could he possibly have been planning? Why didn't he release that hoarded grain?"

"I've been thinking about Donicus... and Quintinus. You knew Quintinus."

Vespasianus nodded. "I did."

"How could someone as shrewd as Quintinus not know the grain was in warehouses on his property? Although I never met him, my sense is that he liked to be in control. How could he miss something like that?"

"You are right, he relished control." Vespasianus sat on the bench by the pool. "Come sit. Let's talk for a minute."

Argolicus joined him on the ornate bench, waiting for an answer.

Vespasianus arranged his tunic over his thighs, careful to smooth out the fine linen.

"How could he miss it? He could have been traveling north, or merely out of town for a day or two. I'm sure his daughter told you he didn't keep track of what was in the rented warehouses. He only kept track of the rent."

A plausible explanation.

"You don't think the two of them had some scheme?"

"No. You met Donicus. He was a man of small thoughts. For all I know, he wanted to charge the town some exorbitant price. If he did, that he let it go so long with the roads and streets in near-riot would be a truly scandalous action against the town." He paused, then said, "Unlike the assertions made by Sura against you which were personal."

What the town magistrate said made sense. But, Argolicus had another question. "Somebody must have known. However foolish or shortsighted Donicus was, someone killed him. The murder was deliberate. Why kill a bumbling man who failed at his attempts to wheedle the town? It doesn't make sense."

Vespasianus smoothed his tunic again as he thought.

"What bothers me," Argolicus continued, before Vespasianus could answer, "is two murders. Quintinus and Donicus. I don't see the connection, but I'm sure they are related. You know the town history. Do you have any ideas?"

This time Argolicus waited as the magistrate fussed with his linen and pulled at an invisible thread.

"I don't. You've been so involved in finding and exposing the grain shortage, perhaps the murders have nothing to do with grain. The murders and the grain shortage just coincided in time."

"Of course, you are right," Argolicus said. "From what I've learned, Quintinus was involved in many transactions, not just grain. But the records available, the ones now with Gregorius, all relate to grain. I have no trail to follow."

Vespasianus sat back, his gaze wandering over the bright frescoes on the walls. His hands stopped fidgeting with his tunic and rested in his lap, fingers loosely clasped. "I hear various rumors," he said. "You still have your bodyguards?"

"Yes, they're outside your door."

"And I hear Quintinus' daughter is making preparations to close the house."

"Yes, she is making a change." Either Vespasianus had heard of the real reason, or he hadn't.

"What will happen to the business? To Quintinus' records? Surely he had other records beside the grain."

"I believe she plans to sell the business. What there is of it. Grain is an annual phenomenon. But Quintinus is known throughout Italy. I don't know, I'm speculating."

Vespasianus brought his gaze back from the frescoes and looked at Argolicus. "So that will be the end of that grain merchant?"

"So it seems."

Argolicus had no other questions. Vespasianus seemed distracted.

Argolicus continued, "Thank you for your time this morning. I appreciate your understanding. I won't be seeing you for months now."

They both rose from the bench.

The sun cleared the opening above and the pool reflection lit up the room.

"You made a difference," Vespasianus said. "We will all welcome you back after your... penance. What will you do now?"

"I promised Quintinus' daughter I would find his killer. I don't know how. I don't know how long it will take. After that, I don't know."

## ❧ 32 ❧

The best way to keep his promise to Proba now that he was free of municipal responsibilities was to start again tracking people who had done business with Quintinus. Now he wanted to go farther than grain, he wanted the personal business relationships.

At Proba's home, Kunimund and Eboric were as watchful as though the streets were filled with rioters. But, the morning was peaceful. Shopkeepers sold their wares, men chatted in small groups, slaves bustled on errands. It was as if the town had not experienced disruption.

"Argolicus," Proba cried, grasping his hands in hers. She gushed, "You look better than you did yesterday. Venantius was abhorrent. I'm sorry I lost my temper. That session should have been between him and you. But, I'm not sorry because..."

"Proba," Argolicus said, squeezing her hands and then releasing them. "You were noble."

"Tears are noble?"

"Yes, your support was noble. I would have lost my temper and probably made things worse. Venantius would have welcomed that. He didn't know what to do with your tears."

"I'm so glad you are here. Come in. Come in." She led him into her father's study. Empty spaces on the shelves attested to the transfer of ledgers to Gregorius.

"I need your help."

Her brown eyes sparkled. "Again?"

Argolicus smiled. "Yes, again. It's about your father."

Her eyes lit up and then darkened. "His murder."

"Yes, I'm still looking. Looking for the person who killed him."

"Good," Proba said, resolute. "It was wrong. I want to know who killed him. At this point I don't care why, just who."

"But I must look for the why," Argolicus said. "When I find it, I will know."

"I've told you everything I know. How could I help you?"

"I've been spending time browsing through my father's journals. They are filled with what seems like trivia—daily actions, people he met, prices of goods. But every once in a while he comments on a person. He even has a note about Sura when we were children. Did your father keep a journal?"

"Not as such," Proba said. "He had a small notebook. He jotted notes to himself. As long as I can remember, just before dinner, he would jot notes. But maybe two minutes' worth. A word. Someone's name. I've looked. They made sense only to him."

"Could I read them? Borrow them to read?"

"Of course, if you think they will help."

"What about his loan transactions? You said you didn't keep track of those, but now that he is gone, you do, yes?"

"I do. I've been so busy," she paused, "with other things."

From the smile on her face and the faint blush on her cheeks, Argolicus could tell the other things were mostly time with Ebrimuth.

"As his daughter, you would want to know which loans are still outstanding. So would your mother."

Proba crinkled her brow.

"Yes, Mother would want any money owed to him. I should have thought of that."

"You would have in time. Do you have time now to find those documents and go through loans that are outstanding? What I want is a list of the names."

"I can do that. Once done, I can clear out those papers. I am ready to leave this house as soon as my father's estate is cleared. I'm looking forward to my new life."

"Ebrimuth."

"Yes." Now her face was glowing. "A new life. The sooner I can get this house packed up, the sooner I can leave."

"Have you found anyone who is interested in purchasing your father's business, his connections, the warehouses?"

"Not yet. I don't know how to go about it. I wish Mother could help, but she can't. She knew nothing about his contacts or business. It's up to me."

"I'd like to help, but I don't know anyone. Why don't you tell Vespasianus, the magistrate? He could spread the word."

Proba's face clouded.

"He seems intimidating. He looks so... magisterial. So formal."

Argolicus laughed, thinking of his meetings with the magistrate. "He does. But he wants the region to prosper. He would want to help continue a thriving business."

"I hadn't thought of it like that," Proba said. "You're right, that's a good idea. I will." She paused in thought. "First I'll need to memorize a speech."

Argolicus burst out laughing. "No, no speeches. Simply approach him with the information and tell him you are looking for a buyer. Be yourself."

Proba looked doubtful, but she nodded in agreement.

Argolicus took her hands in his. "I am happy for you. Your change, your new life."

"Thank you," she said. "I'm working up the courage to tell

Mother. Ebrimuth was not who she had in mind when she tried to arrange a marriage."

They laughed together as Argolicus dropped her hands.

He said, "Ebrimuth has been my friend all my life. He is a good man. And I'll have two friends to visit when I'm at the estate."

"You're staying here?"

"I am. I thought I had a plan. It's been disrupted, but I'll find something else. Meanwhile, I can focus on helping you find your father's killer."

"I'll gather my father's notebooks and send them over. Five years should be enough, right?"

"Yes. Five years. And the list of outstanding loans."

"I'll send the notebooks today. Then, I'll make the list."

Argolicus left marveling at life's turnarounds. He'd moved to town, he'd passed up a marriage to a good woman. Now he was in some semi-disgrace by following what he thought was a good decision.

⚜

At this point, Pennus, the wine merchant was his only known link to Quintinus. Argolicus decided to visit him again. This time he wouldn't be searching for just any information, he would ask about personal relationships and loans.

One thing about living in town, calling on others took only minutes. Here he was retracing the steps toward the same neighborhood he'd visited this morning to see Vespasianus. If he were still living on the estate in the hills he would have to make two journeys on the same day or schedule the second visit for another day.

Kunimund and Eboric seemed to enjoy these short walks out in the open air. They must miss the hills and freedom. Here in town, they were tied to whatever Argolicus did. If he didn't go anywhere, they were stuck waiting.

"He saw Quintinus with Macro and Donicus," Nikolaos said as they tramped the paving stones. "I read my notes before we left."

"Yes, I remember," Argolicus said. "Anything else?"

"Only that he sold his grain to Quintinus for a good price."

"Ah, yes. Sold the grain but kept the accounts."

When Pennus received him, they went straight to the old man's study, bypassing the *atrium* with the ornate mosaic floor and the colorful frescoes of vineyard scenes.

Nikolaos stood in a corner as Pennus gestured to a chair for Argolicus.

The study was much like his father's. A large table and shelves of scrolls and journals against the walls. The one bare wall was brightly painted in red and green, but no fresco.

Pennus placed two scrawny elbows on the table. "I told you all I could about the grain. That is resolved. Why are you here?"

"You are right, the grain issue is resolved. I'm not here about that. I'm remembering what you told me about Quintinus. I want to find who killed him."

"And Donicus? Do you want to find his killer, too? We were friends."

"I pledged Quintinus' daughter to find his killer. About Donicus I know little."

Pennus held his face closed, the sharp angles of his Greek heritage like a carved facade. Nothing to see behind the facade.

Argolicus continued, "I'm hoping you can help me with more information about Quintinus."

Pennus took his elbows off the table and folded his hands. "I told you everything I know."

"Think back to when you saw Quintinus and Donicus together. You told me you saw them three times. Donicus was the civil administrator. What did you notice the first time you saw them together?"

Something slipped behind the chiseled facade as Pennus' dark brows knit together. "It was a while ago..."

Argolicus kept silent.

Pennus closed his eyes. "They were friendly as if it were a chance meeting. But, I could tell it wasn't by chance."

"How?"

Behind him, Argolicus heard Nikolaos scratching at his notes.

"They met at one of those food stands. I wouldn't have noticed them, except Donicus kept looking around as if he were waiting for someone. He left his food untouched. Then Quintinus arrived. They nodded a greeting. Quintinus ordered his food. Neither of them had servants with them. I thought it was unusual. That's when I watched. I was curious. They put their heads together. I couldn't hear what they said." Pennus opened his eyes. "It was just unusual."

"And that's why you watched? You were curious?"

"Yes. It was like a meeting that wasn't a meeting. Normally if you had business with Quintinus... like I did... you went to his house."

"And the second meeting?"

Pennus closed his eyes again. "In the forum. It seems like a public place, but they were heads together again... and it didn't seem as friendly?"

"How so?"

"I couldn't hear what they said, but they were gesturing. Quintinus scowled. Donicus kept gesturing with his fist as though he were trying to make a point." He opened his eyes and blinked.

"So, from what you saw, they disagreed."

"Yes. That's what made me notice them the third time. That was at another little food stand. I wanted to see if they still disagreed. I wondered what Quintinus was plotting. It had to be Quintinus. Donicus wasn't that creative."

"And were they? Arguing?"

"No. I hope you don't think I'm a nosy spy. It was just that I'd seen them twice before, and I was curious."

Argolicus shook his head. Quintinus with a finger in another pie. The two men had plotted something, but how had that led to their murders? Or was it a separate issue?

Pennus said, "That's all I remember. The two of them, do you think their meetings had something to do with both being killed?" His eyes were wide now with his own revelation.

"I don't know," Argolicus said. "But your remembrances help me form a better picture of their alliance. Do you remember anything else?"

"No. Nothing else." Pennus closed his eyes. "There was one thing. It confirmed my suspicions that they were up to something."

"What was that?" Argolicus said. Maybe this would be a clue that gave him direction.

Pennus opened his eyes. No need to close them to remember. "It was in the forum. Vespasianus strolled by with some others. As soon as Quintinus and Donicus saw him, they stopped their argument. They feigned a casual conversation until the magistrate had strolled on."

"So that verified your idea that the two had a secret."

"Yes, exactly. They obviously disagreed about something, but when they saw Vespasianus, they were both play-acting. Whatever it was they were planning, they wanted to keep it a secret. That play-acting was what made me notice them the third time."

"You were very observant, Pennus. I don't know how that information will help me find a killer, but it's more than I knew before."

"I didn't like Quintinus, but Donicus was a friend. We both cared about the council and civic responsibility. I know he wasn't good at reporting, but he did care. If anything I said helps, I am glad you came back to talk to me."

## ❧ 33 ❧

"I feel like I'm chasing wisps," Argolicus said, sitting in his study. "Instead of a plan, I'm grasping at bits of information trying to make them fit into a picture."

"The picture's not forming?" Nikolaos said.

"Not at all. It's like *tesserae* are spread out in front of me, but there's no design." He looked at the floor, where mosaic pieces fit together in interwoven geometric figures. "There's no pattern, just pieces."

"Ah, like the change of place, in Aristotle's *Categories*. You need the pieces to change places."

"Yes, well, I don't see it." Argolicus sighed.

"It helps to do something else. Something not related that gets your mind off trying. I would work in the garden. If you don't need me, I'm going to do that now."

"Go. I'll think of something else."

Nikolaos left.

Argolicus cast his eyes around the study looking for a distraction.

Boden, the doorman, stood in the archway. In heavily accented Latin, he said, "A package for you."

He entered and placed a bundle wrapped in a scrap of wool on the table.

When he left, Argolicus untied the strings and pulled back the fabric. He uncovered a stack of five small journals with a note on top.

*I can't decipher these. Proba*

He picked up the top journal and opened it to the last page, hoping for an entry that would explain Quintinus' last journey. Right away, he knew what Proba meant. Unlike his father's brief notes, Quintinus wrote in abbreviations of his own internal system. *T with M. To F for V.* Deciphering these notes would take time. Initials and prepositions with no references.

While his father's journals were dated, sometimes skipping days, Quintinus' notes were organized loosely a month at a time without a specific date. He went back a few pages to find the beginning of August, then flipped back to the last page. *E must.* A verb among the prepositions. But must what? And who was E? He needed a reference point or several points.

He went through the pages at random, trying to find something. He noticed that there were no blanks. Quintinus had kept the notes when he was traveling. Maybe Proba could tell him travel dates. That might be a way to correlate something. Did the preposition *to* refer to a destination or someone as a recipient? With only initials, the nouns had no declension. He threw down the notebook.

"Nikolaos," he said.

In a moment, the tutor was there, brushing his hands. "The transplants are looking healthy. What is it?"

"Proba sent her father's notebooks," he gestured toward the stack, "but they are meaningless."

Nikolaos stood waiting, without a response.

"Initials, prepositions, an occasional verb. But I can't tell what the initials stand for. *To F for V.* Was he making a payment in someone's name? Was he going to F, whatever that is, on behalf of someone else? To meet someone else? Father's notes," he gestured toward the shelf full of his father's notebooks, "were brief, but coherent."

"Let's go have a snack. You've been running back and forth without eating," Nikolaos said.

In minutes, food appeared in the *peristylum* as Argolicus and Nikolaos enjoyed the afternoon. All that was missing was a fountain. Herbed cheese, honey, bread, plums, and wine. They sat in silence as Argolicus ate. Finally, he sipped his wine, and said, "Your plants look healthy. You were right. I was hungry. I feel better, but still don't know anything more."

Nikolaos was tending his plants, brushing the leaves, patting soil around the roots. He moved to another planting and patted the soil and asked, "How are you doing with the anger and resentment?"

Argolicus took another sip of wine. "I've been busy."

"That's why I asked."

"I thought I'd settled in to a new life. Here we are in town, refreshing the house. Look, you've started your herb garden. And then I was invited to the council and felt that I'd found a role. As much as I dislike politics, I thought I could do some good."

"You have. You saved the town not just from riots, but the people from starvation."

"It all turned inside out as if overnight. One rant from Sura and my new life exploded. Then it got worse, somehow Venantius noticed. And now that new life is gone. If it weren't for Proba and her father's murder, I would have no purpose."

"Did you have a purpose at the estate? Why should your life be different just because you set up your own home?"

Argolicus felt as though Nikolaos had just dealt one of his martial punches. Did he have his guard down? But no, this wasn't a fight, not even a mock fight.

"I thought I had found it as soon as we arrived. But to answer your question, no, I didn't have a purpose at the estate. Mother tried to get me involved, to work with Lucius and learn more, but all those things didn't hold my interest. You taught me to love books. I do. But books aren't a purpose."

"So you're back to the first day, before you met Sura. That didn't turn out so well. Maybe being on the council isn't your purpose. Do you want to be a merchant? That seems to be what occupies many here."

"No! That wouldn't be a fit. Negotiating, manipulating people for the best bargain. That's definitely not what I want to do."

"Maybe you are trying to rush things. Why don't you start with less noble endeavors? You want a fountain here in the *peristylum*. Start with that."

The fountain. He would like that. He missed the one at the estate.

"That and helping Proba. Isn't that enough for now."

"You are right... again. I don't need to think about Venantius. I already knew he was mean-spirited."

Nikolaos stood and surveyed his plants. "All coming along. Summer is not the best time for transplanting, but they all made it."

He turned around and looked at Argolicus. "Your father was content."

"I believe he was. Reading his journals, I get a sense of a regular life. He had a way with people without being particularly social. He had friends like Macro."

"You see. It doesn't take much. You have Ebrimuth. Good friends."

"Yes, good friends make life full. All the time with Venantius I was worried he would lose his temper. But he didn't." He shook his head. "The surprise was Proba. Challenging that venial man. He could have asked for a fine, but there was nothing to charge."

"I will feel better about our friendship if I find who killed Quintinus." He broke off a piece of bread and grabbed an olive from a bowl. "I'm discouraged. I thought those notebooks would help, but I can't get inside Quintinus' head to understand his shorthand."

"You are approaching this logically. Murder is emotional. Why not try illogical thinking?"

"Illogical?" Was his logic tutor suggesting this?

"Yes. Did Proba have a secret admirer who learned that her parents were arranging a marriage? Maybe he wanted to get rid of Quintinus, so he would have a better chance with Proba."

"That seems farfetched."

"Yes, that's the idea. Think of situations you normally wouldn't."

Argolicus nibbled on another olive and tried to not think logically. After a few moments he said, "Macro seems like a genial old man, a friend of my father's, but he hated Quintinus because..." He stopped at the because.

"You've got the idea. Keep going."

"There was no one behind Sura. He smeared my name because he didn't want me looking into Quintinus' murder. He owed Quintinus and had no way to pay. He wanted to keep me away, destroy trust, so people wouldn't talk to me."

"That's better. A devious sycophant as a killer."

"This seems impossible... The mistress Martina hired someone to kill Quintinus because she hated him. Why did she hate him? Did he slight her in some way? She was pregnant and he had refused help?"

"Was she? Is she?"

"I don't know."

"Continue."

"This seems improbable and unconvincing."

"Yes, but, you found something you didn't know about Martina."

"Who else? Vespasianus hired someone... No, that would make him vulnerable. Vespasianus followed Quintinus and killed him by the creek. He is big enough and strong enough. He likes to be in control and was tired of being manipulated by Quintinus?"

"How was he being manipulated? And Donicus, too?"

"I don't know that either. You asked me to be illogical. Vespasianus wouldn't want to get his fancy clothes dirty. I'm doing my best."

"Stretch your imagination."

Argolicus took another sip of wine. "This is ridiculous."

"Good. Push for dubious thoughts."

"Proba? All this friendship and helpfulness is a smokescreen? She was probably the most manipulated of all."

"She killed Donicus, too?"

Argolicus shook his head. "She was there. But so was Ebrimuth. It doesn't fit. He wouldn't let her do that."

"So he did it for her. For love."

"No, that's pushing the edge of believability. I've known him all my life. You know him. He wouldn't."

Nikolaos was back to his plants, fiddling on the far wall of the *peristylum*. "Who else?"

"There is an unpleasant person in all this. Proba's mother, Fabia. She seethes resentment and feels the world is against her. She'd come to the breaking point, always feeling sorry for herself. She thought killing her husband would free her from worry?"

"And?"

"She hired someone or got one of the household slaves. Maybe it was the man who was with Quintinus. The one who still hasn't recovered. She bribed him and then made sure he didn't recover. It was a stroke of luck. No, that doesn't make sense. He wouldn't wound himself."

"Maybe there was a fight with Quintinus."

"Maybe... But this is all conjecture. None of this is solid. There's no evidence."

"That's the idea. A speculative look at everyone involved with Quintinus. And turn it around. What if Donicus was the prime victim, and expediency was the reason Quintinus died first?" Nikolaos finished with the plants and sat beside Argolicus.

Argolicus broke off one more piece of bread and smeared it with the herbed cheese. "Donicus was the real victim? I hadn't thought of that. And somehow Quintinus knew the killer's resentment. So, before he could say anything, he was killed first?"

"That's how this speculative thinking works. Put everyone in a new light."

"Proba and Ebrimuth?"

"Everyone."

"I understand what you are suggesting. In theory, it works. New thoughts about people. Turn everything around. But that's what Sura did with his accusations. He took facts and turned them into malicious intent."

"We're back to anger and resentment?"

"No. What I'm saying is, I have a hard time thinking of friends as murderers or benign people like Macro carrying a grudge strong enough to kill. He was my father's friend. It just can't be."

"But, that's the thing, it could be. You know how you found the right words to quiet the ruffians when they threatened the estate?"

"Yes, but I hadn't prepared a speech. It all just came out."

"You'll put the pieces together when one more piece of evidence shows. Or you'll fit two pieces together to point you in the right direction."

"So, what was this then?"

"An exercise in stretching your mind."

"This is the most challenging investigation. Nothing in Rome was this difficult. I feel like I'm disappointing Proba. But what's worse, I'm disappointed in myself." Right now, he wished for a fountain. Nikolaos had a good idea. He would get a fountain. Somehow the flowing water helped him concentrate.

"You're thinking about a fountain," Nikolaos said.

"How did you know?"

"Because you looked for one, and it wasn't there."

Boden stood in the entryway. "Master, you have a visitor."

Argolicus looked up at the sun disappearing behind the roof of the *peristylum*. "So late? Who is it?"

"Caius Larcius Sura."

# TESSERA - EMERALD

Didia crouched over her work in the workroom. The first medallion lay on a small table in front of her, so she could match the design. Alongside the medallion stood small bowls of different colored beads and skeins of thread. Light slanted in from a window. She moved her chair so her work would be illuminated. Otherwise, her eyes grew tired.

She tried to picture her mother, but the face floated out of her memory as a blur. Long dark hair, brown eyes that twinkled. She remembered the laugh, light like a rose petal. She knew roses because there were two in the garden. She could see them if she looked out the window. She'd never been in the garden. To her, it was like a dream world, filled with flowers and green leaves. Green, like the thread on the needle.

She remembered her mother laughing under green palm trees and the scent of dry air. Nothing like the humid air that seemed to press in on hot days like today.

She looked at the medallion, reached into the bowl of green beads, and threaded one onto her needle. Then she plunged the needle straight down through the layers of fabric on the new medallion in her hand.

She imagined the man who would wear the new tunic. He must be important to order all this embroidery. She never met the customers, either. Aelia, her mistress, was the only one who dealt with orders.

He would be tall. Important men were tall. And handsome. A broad brow, with arching eyebrows over dreamy brown eyes that hinted at authority. His shoulders...

"Didia." Aelia's voice cut in. "Are you dreaming again?"

# 34

Pomade scent filled the corridor before Argolicus reached the *atrium*. Sura was squinting at the newly painted frescoes. He looked the same, overdressed in colorful silks, but the lines beside his mouth were deeper as though he was turning old before his time.

"Sura," Argolicus said. "What can I do for you? I didn't expect to see you here."

They stood eye to eye. Sura glanced down, then looked up again. "I have an announcement that I'm sure will please you."

Now what? Hadn't Sura done enough?

"Yes."

"I don't know how to say this."

Argolicus waited.

Sura glanced down, then at the frescoes. Then he spoke as if addressing the pool. "I am withdrawing my accusation. I came to tell you first."

Argolicus drew back his head. His heart seemed to stop, and then pounded. What was Sura up to now? "To tell me privately that you are withdrawing your public accusation? Do you realize what repercussions you've caused already?"

"Repercussions?" Sura looked not one bit guilty, only surprised. Could he be that dull-witted?

"Yes, a formal inquisition with Vespasianus."

"Vespasianus?"

The man was exasperating.

"Yes, Vespasianus. He came here with two scribes. They recorded all my answers. Then they sent a copy to the governor."

"Venantius?"

"You accused me of murder and sedition. Did you think nothing would happen? And, it wasn't just me you targeted. You belittled my mother. And you cast doubt on my friend, Ebrimuth."

"But, Venantius. I didn't think it would go that far. And now..." He stopped, biting his lip.

"Yes, Venantius. I went to answer his questions about the inquiry. He had a copy in front of him. He repeated the questions."

Sura looked confused. "I didn't expect all this. I had no idea. And now..." He paused. Something was behind the retraction.

"And now?"

"The governor has summoned me."

Aha, fear. "So you thought if you retracted your accusations, they would go away. You'd tell the governor you were retracting your accusations, and he would nod his head and everything would go away."

"Yes, being called before the governor, I didn't expect that."

"You think that retracting, after the fact, after everyone on the council heard you, after rumors flew all over, would put everything back in a bottle, and everyone would forget. And since you are called to the governor that everyone would forget that it was you who started all this."

"Could we sit?" Sura gestured to the bench, his squinty eyes now wide and his face pale.

"Yes, let's sit. I want to know more."

Sura sank to a chair by the pool. Argolicus sat on the bench facing the pool.

Sura's white, manicured hands fidgeted in his lap. Another scent rose underneath the pomade, fear.

"I've never met the governor," Sura said. "I hear he is arbitrary. What happened when you were there?"

"You want to know what your accusations caused? I don't need to tell you. But I will. Yes, Venantius is arbitrary. There's no predicting how he will act. He's young. Younger than we are by almost ten years. What happened when I met with him is he forbade me to participate in the council for six months. In a way, that's not a major impact on my life because I was new to the council. But it is a huge impact on my honor."

"He can do that?" Concern grew on Sura's face. No apology, just anxiety about what could happen to him.

"He can do whatever he wants as long as it is within the law."

"I didn't know."

"What didn't you know, Sura? You made wild and strong accusations in front of the entire council."

"I didn't think."

Sura had stopped fidgeting. White knuckles glinted in his firmly grasped hands.

Argolicus waited for an answer as Sura struggled to speak.

"When he told me," Sura said, "I didn't know it would have so many consequences. I thought he just didn't want you at the council meetings."

Argolicus now knew his suspicions were right. Sura didn't have the brains to come up with this by himself.

"Consequences like you being called to see the governor."

Sura looked up. His brow furrowed and his eyes were mere squints. He nodded.

"Yes, I don't know what to do."

"Well, you're here now with me, telling me you are going to retract your accusations."

"Yes, I will. I'm going to tell him, I'm retracting everything I said."

"Him?"

"Yes, Vespasianus."

Argolicus sat back. Vespasianus! The man who was so sympathetic and careful. Vespasianus. He swallowed his rage for the moment.

"Did he say why?"

"No, no. He prompted me. I rehearsed. Then I made the speech. I felt bad because I was the one who invited you to the council when you moved to town."

"So, why did you do it?"

Sura sighed as if realizing the full impact of what he had done.

"As a favor. Vespasianus is a powerful man. And I, well, I owed him for my position as *curator civitatis*. That was before Donicus. And, well, Vespasianus helped me."

"So, because he helped you in the past, you wanted to repay him by smearing my reputation? But now you are worried because the governor has requested your presence."

Sura unclasped his hands and held them up and out toward Argolicus while he slumped deeper into the chair. A clump of his pomaded hair fell over his forehead. He looked up in despair.

"Yes, and that's why I wanted to ask a favor of you."

His effrontery was astounding. "A favor?"

"Yes, I was hoping, since I am going to retract my accusations, that you would go with me to meet with the governor. I could explain everything and..."

"Sura, no."

Argolicus stood. There was time enough to think about Vespasianus, now he wanted Sura out of his house. "I won't do that. You need to take responsibility for your actions."

Sura raised his eyebrows.

"That's what your father said long ago when I knocked over the vegetable stand."

"Well, now is the time to put it into practice. I'll be waiting for your retraction. Now it's time for you to leave."

⚜

"Vespasianus!" Argolicus said.

He was back in the *peristylum* with Nikolaos, sitting on the bench and longing for a fountain to cool his thoughts.

"I feel betrayed," Argolicus said. "What reason could he have to come up with a scheme like that? Why would he care? And, what was I thinking going back into politics? Was it a mistake to move to town?"

"Do you like the house?" Nikolaos said, sitting close to his master.

"I do. Yes. Of course, I do. I grew up here."

"For the moment, let's focus on Vespasianus."

"I feel like someone knocked me sideways. He's acted supportive, and now I discover it's all a sham. What reason could he have to want to smear my reputation? He's a magistrate. I've done nothing to upset the status quo. In fact, I helped resolve a potentially explosive situation."

"Jealousy?"

"Of what? I'm a newcomer to the council. I have no aspirations. What I did was something I could do. I couldn't have done it without Proba."

"That's it. He is the magistrate. You were a newcomer. Yet, you were the one who saved the town from riots and found the grain to feed the populace."

Argolicus mentally chewed on that for a minute.

"Maybe. But it seems so petty."

"It's politics."

"That it is. Still... There must be something more. Something I'm not seeing. Attacking a man's reputation is low. I'm convinced that's why he found the perfect person, Sura. Everyone knows

Sura. He's mean-spirited and out for himself. You saw him a few minutes ago. Did he apologize? No. He asked for a favor. The man is blind to his failings."

"What else have you done since you moved to town? Maybe it's not about the *curia*."

"Nothing. I met Proba. We both decided not to marry. Then she asked me to help find her father's killer. And, I have failed at that. I have no leads. I found Severa in the street. But why would Vespasianus care about that? I stopped the ruffians at the estate, but we've already covered that."

He sat pondering.

"I visited Macro, but that was a benign visit, mostly about old times with my father. I met Ebrimuth in the street. Could that be it? Does Vespasianus really think I'm in some conspiracy to subvert the local council? That I'm somehow allied with the king? That's preposterous!"

"Maybe not to him. He is the council leader. Maybe he resents Ebrimuth's new role. A rival for local power."

"But Ebrimuth's power is over The People. It has to be titular. Something Cassiodorus cooked up for the king, so the king would feel he had representation here in the South. Almost all The People live far north of here. Ebrimuth is an exception. You know, in all the time I've known him I've never heard him talk about how isolated he is... But, back to Vespasianus."

Argolicus paused. He glanced around at the vibrant plants in the *peristylum*. In a month more, the place would feel established. All it lacked was a fountain.

"Back to Vespasianus," Nikolaos prompted.

"It's a mystery," Argolicus said. "I'm going to confront him tomorrow."

"Do you have a plan?"

"No. Let's work on it now."

Nikolaos left and returned with vellum sheets, a pen, and a pot of ink.

"What do you want out of your confrontation?" he asked.

"To know why he concocted such an outrage."

"Hmm. Maybe you shouldn't phrase it like that."

Argolicus laughed. One talent Nikolaos had was getting him to laugh when he was distraught.

Nikolaos continued, "Before we write down anything, let's practice. I'm Vespasianus."

"I enter the house. We meet in the *atrium*. He may or may not ask me into his study. He'll ask why I'm there."

"And you will say..."

"I'll tell him about Sura's visit. Then I'll ask him to explain."

"No, what exactly will you say?"

"Yesterday I had a visit from Sura. He told me he is retracting his accusations. Then I'll wait to notice his response. If he explains right away, I'll have my answer."

"You're rushing ahead of yourself. What about Venantius?"

"Yesterday Sura visited, and he told me that he is retracting his accusations. I discovered he is doing this not because of a change of heart... No, no. He told me he has been called before the governor."

"Yes?"

"And then I wait for Vespasianus to explain."

"You may have a long wait."

Argolicus smiled. "Indeed. So, then I'll continue. He also told me that you prompted him to make the accusations. Then I'll wait for him to explain."

"And what will you do once he answers you?"

"I hadn't thought that far ahead."

"That's why we're practicing."

"I have no idea what his answer will be."

"Exactly, that is why you need to prepare what you'll say, so you lead him to a point where he must answer."

"What if he lies? How will I know if he's lying?"

"I think you are so angry, you've lost faith in your skills of perception."

"You're right. I can usually tell when someone is lying. But, think of it this way, he's been lying all along, and I didn't notice."

"There is that."

"You're not being helpful."

"I am. I'm helping you prepare to save your reputation."

Argolicus looked at his tutor. Then he smiled. "You've been helping me out of scrapes for many years. So, let's get started with this one."

He took in a breath and let it out slowly. "Vespasianus, I'm here today prompted by a visit from Sura yesterday. He told me he is retracting his accusations and that he will make a public statement to the council."

Nikolaos began to write.

## ❧ 35 ❧

"He told me he has been called before the governor," Argolicus said, looking into Vespasianus' eyes for a sign. He saw none.

They were in Vespasianus' study seated on opposite sides of the magistrate's worktable. So far, Vespasianus had shown no signs of anxiety. He sat with his back straight dressed in another richly embroidered tunic.

Vespasianus said, "I can understand that the governor would want to talk to Sura after meeting with you." His intonation betrayed nothing; merely a statement. "So, he plans to make a formal retraction to avoid a reprimand from the governor."

"Yes, that's his plan. But..." Argolicus looked directly at Vespasianus. "He also told me that you had prompted him to make the accusations."

Vespasianus blinked. Once.

"I never said anything like that."

"Why would he say you did?"

"Sura is Sura. Everyone knows he wheedles and cajoles. People don't take him seriously."

ZARA ALTAIR

"You performed a formal inquiry."

"I did. But that was to protect you. Once you answered the questions, and they were in writing, essentially that protected you."

"That's what I believed," Argolicus said. "But then I was called to the governor. And he thought it was something. Even though I gave the same answers, he reprimanded me."

"Reprimanded?"

"Yes. You had the notice in your hand when we last met."

"Oh, that was nothing. It's not that important."

"Barred from the council is not important?"

"You're seeing this the wrong way." Now there was a flash in Vespasianus' eyes. "You don't understand what it's like to be me. I'm in charge of the area's well-being. I had to do something. The inquiry was the best way to put this all to rest."

The conversation was heading in a wrong direction. Argolicus wanted to get back to Sura. Argolicus said, "Sura was quite definite that you prompted his accusations. He said you told him what to say."

"You needn't have bothered to come here. Sura came to me. He wanted to talk about assuming the position of *curator civitatis* again. Then he mentioned how he was the one who invited you to that council meeting. So in a way, he was the one who had saved the town. Then he started talking about how he knew you when you were younger, your father, and your mother. And how you had returned to town. Then he mentioned that man Ebrimuth. It was all Sura. My position is to maintain order in the community. This doesn't matter in the grand scheme of things."

Argolicus felt caught between two liars. "It matters to me. It's my reputation."

"You have to admit, the accusations were based on fact. This all came up when Sura came to see me. Think how you appear to others."

Argolicus instantly regretted bringing the focus on himself. But, now he understood what Vespasianus was doing. He didn't need to ask any more questions. By avoiding the answer, Vespasianus told him everything he needed to know.

Vespasianus continued. "Everything I've done is above reproach. I helped you by holding the inquiry. I have no control over Venantius. If he barred you from the council, that's not my doing."

Argolicus stood. "I'm not going to argue about this. I will follow the governor's instructions. As of now, I am leaving."

⚜

"In a way, it's a relief," Argolicus said. "Sura and Vespasianus both tell so many lies, the truth is hard to find. The main truth is that they lie."

Argolicus and Nikolaos sat in his study the next morning. Argolicus was ruminating on his encounters with Sura and Vespasianus.

"A relief to be caught between two liars?" Nikolaos said.

"Yes. I'm free from it all. If my reputation is tarnished, it doesn't make a difference. I'm out of politics. I don't know what possessed me to think I wanted to jump back in. Some idea of obligation to the community. But now I'm free."

Nikolaos kept silent.

"What?"

"There will be repercussions."

"Yes, but they can't hurt. In time the story will die out as other, more serious rumors start about something else. Some people may remember what I did for the town. It doesn't matter. But one thing I need to say..."

Nikolaos raised an eyebrow.

"If you hadn't prodded me to prepare my presentation to

Vespasianus, I might have gone off track and fallen into disputing him, or worse, attempting to defend my position. You were right to set the limits of what I had to say. It kept me from an ugly argument."

Boden, the doorman, appeared in the archway. "The lady Proba."

But she was right behind him, smiling. "I found what you needed. I made a list."

She held out a sheet of vellum. "Perhaps this will help. Now I can get back to closing the house."

"Would you like some refreshment? Stay for a moment while I go over the list."

He inclined his head toward Nikolaos. She handed the sheet to the tutor and it disappeared into his tunic.

In a few minutes they clustered around a small table with honeyed wine, plums, herbed cheese, and bread.

"Your cook seems to have something ready at a moment's notice," Proba said.

"Thank Nikolaos. He set up the household."

Proba smiled at Nikolaos who cast his eyes to the ground. "My master flatters."

"You know him better than anyone," Proba answered. "You honor him with your selection."

Nikolaos' eyes widened as if his secret had been exposed, but he said, "It is my duty." Then he strolled off to the corner where Alba, Proba's maid, stood. "Let me show you my garden."

"Let's look at the list," Argolicus said, diverting the flatteries. He gestured to Nikolaos, who came over, pulled the sheet out from the folds of his tunic, gave it to Argolicus and went back to Alba and the plants.

Argolicus studied the fifteen names and the amounts. "You need to follow up on these and claim the payments according to the terms. You have all the loan documents?"

"Yes," Proba said. "I've been busy. Once I'm settled, I will close them out one by one."

Argolicus looked at the numbers. "You'll have a substantial amount when all of these come due." He ran his finger down the column and stopped at the largest amount. Then he checked the corresponding name. "Vespasianus. He owes you a significant amount. Do you have documents that record repayments?"

"I have them, but I haven't looked. Is that important?"

"It is. Your father would have known who was current and who was late."

Proba blushed. Argolicus could tell she was thinking of Ebrimuth.

"My mind has been on my move," Proba said. "I've been in arrears in bringing all my father's business to a conclusion. Can I sell these loans as well as the grain business?"

"Perhaps, but you can collect on the loans yourself."

"Either way it would be money for my new life. I don't know how to go about collecting. That was my father's skill."

She put down her wine goblet and continued. "He was the negotiator. I'm not good with transactions or asking people for money. My skill is keeping track."

"You could hire someone to collect for you. What about that man Gregorius? You met him. He seems honest and forthright. He would be able to approach those who are in arrears and ask."

Proba's cheeks blushed again. "He... I don't think that's a good idea."

Ah, the handsome Gregorius. "Ebrimuth is jealous?"

"He's protective," Proba said, the blush spreading to her neck.

"Well, he must get accustomed to an independent Roman woman. He doesn't spend much time around women. You will be a new experience for him."

"There's so much for each of us to learn about the other. But we have the rest of our lives." Now her face glowed with love.

Argolicus was the last person to comment on long-lasting relationships. He just nodded.

"But, I will take your advice," Proba said.

"My advice?" Argolicus tried to remember if he had given any advice on love and relationships.

"Yes, you suggested I talk to Amalina if I had questions."

"I did," he said, remembering. "And, it's not my place to tell you how to live your life or suggest how to dispose of your father's estate. I apologize."

"No, we're friends. I listen. I want you to make suggestions." She picked up a plum, smiled at Argolicus, and bit into the juicy flesh.

Argolicus sat back, trying to think of the next thing to say.

"Without you," Proba said, "I would not have met Ebrimuth. You've changed my life."

Argolicus lifted the sheet with the loan list and ran down the names again.

"My life is focused on helping you, right now. That's my main objective. I told you I would help find your father's killer. I haven't had success. I feel as though I've failed you."

"Oh, no! You haven't failed me. Just knowing that you are searching reassures me. However long it takes, I know you will find him."

"Thank you for your faith. But, I want it resolved, and I want the resolution to be soon. This list is a new avenue. There may be people on this list who are unable to pay. I'll have to turn into a social gossip and see what I can discover."

"A gossip?" Proba asked.

"Yes, meet people in the forum, casual chat, mention a name listed here. Then, listen to what people say."

Proba laughed. "Is that what you men do in the forum? That's as bad as my mother and her friends."

"Yes, in a way. But that's how I can gather information. I don't know most of the people on the list. It's the fastest way to learn about them without being conspicuous."

Proba picked up her goblet of honeyed wine. "To gossip."

Argolicus raised his goblet, smiling. "To gossip. Now you know one of my secrets."

He put down the wine and continued, "Do you know any of these people?"

He held out the list.

Proba shook her head. "I only know them from grain transactions I've recorded. I don't know them as people. You'll learn more in the forum than you will from me."

"Anyone your father mentioned as difficult?"

Proba thought for a moment. "He didn't talk much about people. He talked about transactions. And, he didn't talk to me about the loans. Those were private transactions. He drew up those papers himself. That's why I had to find them and go through them to make the list. No, I don't remember him saying Fabian was difficult or Lucas balked at the sums. I'm not much help. That's why I asked for your help."

They sat in silence, watching Nikolaos proudly showing his transplants to Alba.

Proba broke the silence. "I am anxious to bring my father's estate to an end, whether we find the killer or not. I want to be free of obligations when I'm with Ebrimuth."

"Do you remember when we met, and you said you weren't unhappy?"

"I do. I wasn't unhappy. But I had no idea how happy I could be. It's as if I have a whole new life, a way of looking at the world. I didn't know I could be happy. It's different from being not unhappy."

She reached out and took his hand. "It's happened for me, I hope you find this happiness. I don't know how to tell you what it is like."

"I was married. But it wasn't what you describe. It was

pleasant but... without joy. You are joyous. Ebrimuth is joyous. I haven't experienced that."

"That's what I'm saying. I want you to have it, too."

All he could think to say was, "Thank you."

Proba laughed.

"What?"

"I'm trying to picture you in the forum gossiping."

## ✿ 36 ✿

rgolicus asked Eboric and Kunimund to wait in a corner
of the forum. He felt he didn't need the bodyguards.
Trying to return them would be an insult to his friend.
But, here they would make him conspicuous, and he wanted to
mingle without much notice.

The forum that morning was busy. The shops around the
square were busy. Slaves were buying provisions from ironwork to
fine linen. Clusters of men chatted and shifted in the morning
sun. Although the day was warm, there was a hint of autumn
coming. Maybe it was the light or a scent in the air.

Argolicus felt the aftermath of his visit to Venantius. The
rumor had spread. Whether it was Sura's accusations or Venantius' prohibition, he sensed people turning away or not making
eye contact. Friendly chatter was not going to be as easy as he had
imagined.

He spotted men he had seen at the council. Even Macro was
here. He must have come into town on business. He decided to
start with a friendly face and headed toward his father's friend
who was purchasing vellum sheets.

"Argolicus," Macro said. "Just like your father, spreading good-will at the forum."

"From the looks I've received, that is not what is happening today," Argolicus said.

"Ah, yes." Macro shook his head. "Sura causes trouble, there's no getting around that. And I heard the governor has prevented you from attending the council."

"Both true," Argolicus said.

The old man frowned as he nodded his head. His slave paid for the vellum and tucked the package under his arm.

Argolicus continued, "In a way, I am freer. Without responsibilities to the council, I can focus on what I need to do. I'm still looking for the person who killed Quintinus."

"In a way, you are fortunate. You are spared the vicissitudes of politics."

Argolicus could not help laughing. "Exactly my thoughts. When I first returned from Rome, that was my goal. I diverted from my path. Look what happened."

"Perhaps not a wise goal," Macro said, arching an eyebrow.

"Why?"

"I'm thinking of your father. He was in politics but above the fray. I think you could follow a similar path."

"Above the fray? How is that possible in politics?"

"Keep a low profile. The first thing you did at your very first meeting was stand up and volunteer for an almost impossible task. What amazes me is that you carried it off."

"It seemed the right thing to do. I thought I'd have a conversation with Quintinus and the whole thing would be solved in an afternoon."

"That's what I mean. You couldn't foresee the future. And your task became involved instead of simple. Don't volunteer. Observe. The town needs people like you."

"How can they need someone who doesn't do anything?"

"Offer advice, but not in public. Be an advisor. People will seek you out. Isn't that what they do now? People come to you for your wisdom. That's my advice." Macro smiled at his joke.

He scanned the crowd in the forum.

"There's Vespasianus," he said. "He is magistrate now, but fortune has dealt him a hard blow."

"What do you mean? How do you know these things?"

"I hear things. Vespasianus is... was... also a grain merchant. But he lost a shipment at sea. The ship sank. He couldn't deliver. He wasn't paid. This happened before you moved to town or came to the council. My understanding is he lost a year's worth of income."

Now Argolicus was curious. A disaster hid behind the pomp, the fancy clothes. "How bad is it?"

"Nobody knows. But he couldn't hide the fact that the ship sank."

An idea snapped in Argolicus. "Is he friends with Sura?"

"Nobody is friends with Sura." Macro gazed around the forum again. "Where is he? He's usually here spreading his bombast and overwhelming everyone with his scented pomade."

"Macro, you taint your observations with sarcasm."

Macro raised his eyebrow and smiled. "With Sura, it seems appropriate. But, now that you are free, you must come and visit. We can exchange books and talk philosophy. I came to town to buy some things," he gestured at the slave laden with packages. "It's always entertaining to see everyone posturing, but now it's time to go home."

"I would enjoy a visit," Argolicus said. "Plan on it. But before you go, can you tell me anything else about Quintinus? I'm determined to find his killer. I promised his daughter."

"I'm sure you did that with the same haste as telling the council you would find the missing grain."

"I didn't hesitate. But, that's neither here nor there. Can you think of anything else? Anything you may have overlooked when we talked before?"

Now Macro gazed into the middle distance as if the bustle and murmurings in the forum didn't exist. "There was talk..."

"Yes?"

"When Vespasianus lost his fortune at sea, I heard he went to Quintinus for help. But I told you how Quintinus was, he didn't talk about his dealings. So, there's no way to verify."

"He gave Vespasianus a loan. I can tell you that he did."

Macro raised the other eyebrow.

Argolicus smiled. "I see things." Then he regretted his statement.

"And so, here you are contributing to the gossip at the forum. I shall be quiet about this. Really, there's no reason to think about it. I rarely see anyone."

"Thank you for your discretion. I've been reviewing Quintinus' papers. It's something I saw."

"No need for explanation. I'll be on my way. I've decided to write a history of Squillace. For my own amusement, of course. Families, facts, as much as I can remember."

"You can read to me when I visit."

⚜

Macro's revelations about Vespasianus put the magistrate in a new light.

Back in his study, Argolicus considered what he knew about Vespasianus. He looked at Proba's list of loans. There was Vespasianus with the largest sum. Was Macro right? Was Vespasianus in debt over his head? And if he was, how did that explain his actions? He'd sent the inquiry to the governor and called attention to the entire shambles. It must be a personal vendetta. But why?

"Master," Nikolaos said, entering the study. "What did you learn today?"

"I don't know what I learned. Macro gave me advice about what I should do here in town."

"It was?"

"To refrain from public actions like looking for grain. Attend council sessions, keep a low profile."

"That would keep you out of trouble."

"And out of politics for the most part." Argolicus chuckled.

"Why are you laughing? Isn't that a wise plan?"

"Yes. Yes, it is a wise plan. But he said more. That people would come to me and I could advise them privately. He didn't say it, but he implied that I would sway politics behind the scenes. I laughed because, in a way that is more powerful than public show."

"Perhaps that is how he has lasted in politics, only now becoming the treasurer."

"He says he spends most of his time at his estate. Do you think it was unwise to move to town?"

"Your reasons for moving to town are still valid. How much you participate in politics is up to you."

Argolicus gazed at the loan list. "These doubts are probably anchored in my inability to help Proba. I feel as though I'm still going in circles. She came to me for help, just as Macro suggested others would do. But I'm not able to help her."

"You are right. You have many happy memories of this house. You'll go on to create your own memories here. And, you are helping Proba. You just haven't reached a conclusion yet."

"I'm being impatient. Nothing is better for leading to false conclusions. I do like the house, and you are right, the memories are comforting. And, rather than being impatient, I need to think about new information."

"What new information?"

"Macro told me a story about Vespasianus. He says Vespasianus is in debt." He lifted the list of loans off the table and waved it in the air. "And here is his name on oustanding loans from Quintinus. That all fits together. But, why would he single me out? Sura said it was his idea to make the accusations. But, all the time he acted supportive. It was one big lie."

"You said he lies and Sura lies. So, you have to go beyond the lies to evidence."

"There's no evidence... except this list of loans."

"And if he couldn't repay a loan, what would he do?"

"His world would fall apart." Argolicus considered the question.

"If he were desperate enough, he would try to wipe out the loan. And the only way to do that with a personal loan would be to get rid of the person who gave him the loan." He stopped. "Is he the one? Did Vespasianus kill Quintinus?"

Before Nikolaos could answer, Boden appeared with Ebrimuth in the doorway. Ebrimuth's face was pale and agitated. "Is Proba here?"

# TESSERA - MAGENTA

Cassiodorus threaded through the maze of passages in the palace on his way to the king's chambers. Then he stopped, turned around, and went back to his office, passing the scribes busy at their tables.

He carefully arranged his tunic and sat at his table, pristine and clear of any distractions, except his writing supplies. He read again the letter from Venantius, governor of his beloved Bruttium. Such an irritating young man. But, there it was, the passage about his friend Argolicus. Some nonsense about being an enemy of the state and subverting the Roman order.

He sighed, pursed his lips, and began writing.

*My dearest friend,*

*Having received a missive from the Governor of Bruttium and knowing your proclivities for recalcitrance in matters of politics, you should in all good faith write delineating the circumstances of the recent accusations and your position with regard to this man Sura.*

*Disturbances of any kind in the provinces, and especially in the province of Bruttium generate concern. While coming to my attention through the letter of the governor whose conclusions and resolutions are often tainted with personal bias, this matter...*

What was he doing? This was not a letter in the king's name. He was writing to a friend. He slid another sheet from the stack on his desk.

*My dearest Argolicus,*

But then, he was struck by an idea and knew how to resolve the issue. He would see the king, but in a different frame of reference.

## ❧ 37 ❧

"**P**roba is at home," Argolicus said, startled.

"She is not," Ebrimuth said. He twisted his shoulders, frowned, and threw up his hands. "I was just there. Her servant said she left. I thought she'd come here."

The massive man looked as if he was torn between anger and confusion.

Argolicus looked at Nikolaos. "Wine." Nikolaos was gone.

"Sit down, my friend. Tell me what has you so upset."

Ebrimuth stared blankly, then glanced at a chair and sank his frame down across from Argolicus, arranging his sword and long knife to be comfortable. Then he ran his hands through his mane of golden hair.

"I was going to show her the estate. We planned to go there, so she could decide where her things would go. That was this afternoon." He looked up at his friend. "But I came early, and she's not there."

Nikolaos returned with two wine goblets, handing one to Ebrimuth and setting the other in front of Argolicus on the table.

Ebrimuth took a long drink. He gazed around the study. "You and your books."

Argolicus ignored his remark. "There are many reasons she might not be there if you were coming this afternoon. She may have been settling some last arrangements for the house or out buying something special to wear. Women are complex."

"Ah, yes. You were married. Was Julia capricious?" He took another sip of wine.

"No, but she did things that made no sense to me."

"So, you don't think she went off to see Gregorius?"

Argolicus swallowed the laugh. "No, I'm certain it's something very mundane. I know she is eager to be with you. She told me so yesterday when she brought me this document." He lifted the list of Quintinus' loans.

Ebrimuth took a sip of wine and sat back in the chair. "I was worried."

"I understand. Proba is sensible. She takes care of details. She's not just closing up the house, she is closing her father's estate. I suggested she find someone to..."

He looked at Ebrimuth who was finally relaxed.

"Put down your wine. Let's go together to her house."

Ebrimuth, startled, put the almost empty goblet on the table. "What?"

"I made a mistake," Argolicus said. "If anything is wrong, it's my fault."

"What mistake?"

"I'll tell you on the way to her house."

⚜

Argolicus, Ebrimuth, Nikolaos, Eboric, and Kunimund stood at the door to Proba's house. Ebrimuth paced back and forth as they waited for the door to open.

"Let me talk," Argolicus said, fearing his friend would frighten Proba's slave.

When the door opened, a short but sturdy man peered out.

Recognizing Argolicus and Ebrimuth he smiled. "The mistress is out."

"Yes, where did she go?" Argolicus asked.

The man hesitated. "She doesn't tell me where she is going."

Ebrimuth stamped his foot.

Argolicus gave him a sideways look, then spoke to the doorman. "Is there someone here who would know? It's important."

The man looked confused, then said. "I'll ask."

"If anything has happened to her..." Ebrimuth punched the wall.

"We'll find out. One step at a time," Argolicus said, trying to keep worry out of his voice.

After what seemed like a long time, the doorman opened the door and pushed out a young girl. "Go ahead," he said. "Tell them what you told me."

"The mistress is closing the house and meeting various people, and she wanted to do one thing this morning. She took a long time getting dressed and asked me to help with her hair and then she..."

"Where was she going?" Argolicus cut in.

"To the magistrate, that's why she wanted to look especially good because she wanted to ask him a favor, and she was nervous, and she wanted the blue tunic and I couldn't find it..."

"Which magistrate?" Argolicus asked.

"The one with the long name, the magistrate. She was so nervous and..."

"Vespasianus?" Argolicus asked.

"Yes, yes, that's his name, how did you know? I finally found the blue tunic..."

"Thank you," Argolicus said, turning on his heels.

Argolicus led them to Vespasianus' house. Ebrimuth banged on the door. Nothing happened.

Ebrimuth glowered and banged on the door again.

At last the door opened and the large, lumbering doorman

looked at them all, taking in Ebrimuth and the bodyguards and their swords and knives. "The master is engaged," he said. "Come back another time."

Before Ebrimuth could speak, Argolicus said, "The mistress Proba? Quintina Proba?"

The man's eyes widened then closed to slits. "What about her?"

That was all Argolicus needed to hear. He knew she was inside.

"We will enter," he said, walking past the doorman, through the vestibule and into the *atrium*. The four men followed as the doorman blustered, "You can't."

The *atrium* was empty and silent. No slaves scurrying about. No one. Nothing. The doorman lumbered behind them.

Argolicus turned. "Go back to the door. I'll find your master."

The man was solid, and dumb. He followed the command.

Argolicus listened. At first, he heard nothing, then he heard Proba's voice from the back of the house.

"No."

Ebrimuth must have heard her too because he was striding toward the *peristylum*. Argolicus caught up with him, and they entered side by side.

Vespasianus stood in the center, the morning sun shining down on his dark hair and embroidery. He was gripping Proba's arm. "You owe it to your father," he said.

Proba tried to pull back, but his grip was firm. Then she saw Argolicus and Ebrimuth. Her dark eyes turned from anger to relief.

Argolicus put out his arm to keep Ebrimuth from Vespasianus. Ebrimuth stared at his friend. Argolicus shook his head. "Roman way," he said.

Vespasianus turned still holding Proba's arm. "Argolicus, this is not a good time. I was asking Quintinus Cocceia Proba to marry me. This is a private moment."

"What was her answer?" Argolicus asked.

"She hadn't given a final answer. We were just..."

"No," Proba said. "I said no." She glared at Vespasianus, her dark eyes flashing. "Let go of me."

"You're just like your father, you won't listen to reason." Vespasianus thrust back her arm. "I told him..." He stopped.

Proba ran to Ebrimuth. He cradled her in his arms.

"I have questions," Argolicus said.

"I answered your questions. Just go away. Take your barbarian friends and leave."

"In a minute," Argolicus said. "What did you tell Quintinus?"

There was a long silence. The only sound was Proba crying.

Ebrimuth moved to take her back to the *atrium*.

"Stay, we all need to hear what Vespasianus has to say."

"All of you," Vespasianus said. "You all conspired against me. Her father," he pointed at Proba, "wouldn't listen to reason. I asked to marry his daughter and he said no."

"I didn't... He never told me," Proba said, astonished.

"That's what I mean," Vespasianus said. "It was a conspiracy to bring my downfall. Your father was unreasonable. If I married you, I thought he would cancel the loan. But he wouldn't listen. He didn't care about other people, only money."

Argolicus tried to make sense of the twisted logic.

"You wanted to marry her, so he would cancel the loan?"

"Yes, he would bring me to ruin. I'm a magistrate. I have a position to uphold. It was a simple solution. And if that's not bad enough, that fool Donicus said he would tell everyone."

"Tell everyone what?"

"How I knew about the grain in the warehouses. He told me he'd made a deal with Quintinus. And when he told me before the council meeting, I knew that the town was in trouble. Everyone was out to destroy my position in the town. Quintinus with money, Donicus with my reputation."

"You knew about the extra grain? And you let the people

suffer needlessly?" Argolicus couldn't believe the man's self-centered focus.

Proba had stopped crying. She stared at Vespasianus. "My father would never..."

"Your father was an obstinate money grabber," Vespasianus said, anger rising in his voice. "It would have been so simple to make it all go away. But, no. He had to have his way."

Argolicus looked at the man trying to bluff his way through an irrational explanation. The sunlight gleamed on the bright, gold beads threaded into the tunic's embroidery. Gold beads. He knew who killed Quintinus.

"You found a way to stop him," Argolicus said. "You killed him."

"You wouldn't understand." Vespasianus' livid face grimaced. "He was in the way. Just like that fool Donicus..."

Proba flew out of Ebrimuth's arms striking Vespasianus over and over, a powerhouse of anger repeating, "My father. My father!"

Vespasianus tried to push her away, but her tiny body eluded his blows as she struck him.

Ebrimuth rushed in to pull away Proba. In a confusion of movement, Vespasianus pulled Ebrimuth's long fighting knife from the scabbard hanging from his belt. Ebrimuth tugged at Proba. But Vespasianus wrenched her away.

He stood holding Proba pressed against him trying to position the long knife against her throat.

Ebrimuth pulled at Proba as Vespasianus fumbled the knife with one hand.

Argolicus recognized a man who did not know weapons. He heard Nikolaos' voice in his head from their many practice sessions, *A knife is a death threat*. He had seconds to act before Vespasianus could position the knife.

He rushed in, body perpendicular to Vespasianus. The full force of his body slammed against the man's shoulder. At the same time, he slid his right hand up between Vespasianus' body and his forearm with the knife. He pressed the inside of the magistrate's forearm as his left hand pushed against the outside of his wrist angling his hand down. As he pushed Vespasianus' hand to angle inward, he pushed out against his forearm at the wrist. The hand bent in a tight inward angle.

Finally, Vespasianus couldn't resist the awkward pressure bending his hand. His fingers loosened and the knife clattered to the mosaic floor as Ebrimuth pulled Proba away from Vespasianus' arm.

Eboric and Kunimund grabbed Vespasianus, holding his arms.

"How did you know?" Vespasianus hissed, vainly struggling against the bodyguards.

"Your beads. Your gold beads. One fell by Quintinus at the creek," Argolicus said.

Proba looked up from Ebrimuth's arms. "Gold beads?"

Eboric and Kunimund turned Vespasianus over to the cohorts. Ebrimuth calmed Proba by taking her home. Argolicus returned to his home in town to relax and enjoy his new life. But, first, he planned a party.

## ❧ 38 ❧

**D**ays later the late afternoon sun shone down on the *peristylum* where Argolicus was hosting his first social event in his new home. In his mind, it wasn't a public event, just family and friends.

Argolicus, his mother, and his friends were finally celebrating Ebrimuth and Proba's engagement. Tables next to the chairs and benches were filled with fresh figs, plums, herbed cheese, bread, and fish cakes. Every table held a beaker of wine.

Argolicus glanced toward the entertainment room. The frescoes glowed with new colors. The craftsman Pennus had recommended had been careful and diligent. He had started with the entertainment room where everyone would eat.

"A bead," Amalina said, smiling. "You have a talent for noticing."

"That's what I thought," Proba said as she snuggled against Ebrimuth's shoulder. "There we were with that awful man trying to bully me, and Argolicus noticed a bead."

Argolicus said, "It comes from Father. I've been reading his journals. Sometimes there are details that don't make much sense when you read them, but they were important enough for him to write them down."

Proba crinkled her brow. "His vanity was his downfall. His pretense of luxury in the face of ruin. I hate him." Her eyes flashed. "He tried to bully Father, and then me."

Ebrimuth looked down at her and covered her hand with his. He turned toward Argolicus. "You never know about details, but one concerns me. What will happen to Vespasianus? You found that he killed twice. Is it up to Proba to decide? What does your Roman law say?" His large hand gently squeezed Proba's tiny one.

"According to the king's edicts, murder is a public matter," Argolicus said. "Under the old Roman law it was private. Proba can sue in court. And, also under the edicts, the punishment is death."

"If it were private," Ebrimuth said, "I would gladly oblige."

"No, my friend. That's not how it works. She must sue in court. But the case of Vespasianus is more complicated than that. He also owes on the debt to Quintinus."

"So my mother could collect?" Proba asked. "She could on anything remaining that he owns."

Proba closed her eyes for a moment. "My mother would want the debt paid, but I doubt she would go to court. She would want it to all happen without her involvement."

"It is up to you, then," Argolicus said.

Proba looked up at Ebrimuth and then at Argolicus. "It's not over, then."

"No, it's not," Argolicus said. "And there's more, and that's his public acts."

"What public acts?" Proba said, her brow furrowing.

"From what I can surmise, Vespasianus knew about Donicus hoarding the grain. I think they were working together to charge an outrageous price to the council to restore equilibrium. But everything came to a head before they could act on the plan. The

ZARA ALTAIR

money would have helped Vespasianus restore his financial stability."

"He brought it on himself?" Amalina asked, tossing her long braid as she shook her head.

"Yes, when he tried to manipulate Proba, he brought everything to a head. He threatened her life."

"One time when words were not enough," Ebrimuth said, a twinkle in his eye. "We owe Nikolaos for his years of training. Otherwise, you might have been as bumbling as Vespasianus."

Everyone turned to look at Nikolaos who was tending his plants. He turned around, shrugged, and said, "A tutor must instill the martial arts as well as mathematics and Greek."

Amalina hadn't forgotten Argolicus' words. "So he owes the council for the hidden grain, and his attempt to swindle?"

"Exactly, plus as a public debtor, he cannot appeal any decision against his act. In his case, since he was acting as magistrate, he cannot hear his own case. He will need to stand before the governor, and abide by his decree."

"All of this is making my head swim," Ebrimuth said, shifting in his seat. He wrapped his arm around Proba. "Whatever she needs to do, I will stand behind her."

Crispus, the housemaster, waddled in from the kitchen. "Dinner is ready."

Argolicus stood. "Enough of this interpretation of the law. Let's celebrate Proba and Ebrimuth." He rose and placed his arm across the shoulder of his once almost bride-to-be. "Marcus Aurelius said, *The best revenge is not to be like your enemy*."

Proba looked up at Ebrimuth and then Argolicus. She reached up to put her hand on Argolicus' hand resting on her shoulder.

"Here we are."

-The End-

# GLOSSARY

- *atrium* - The formal reception room at the front of a Roman home. Members of the family received guests here. The roof had an opening in the middle so the room was exposed to weather. Most also had a pool of water in the middle which captured rain (*impluvium*).
- *comes civitatus* - An arm of the king, far away from the throne. Under Theoderic, these men enforced the laws of The People which were different from Roman laws.
- Council - The local civic legislative body, composed of all the members of the *curia*. The Council was led by elected officials, magistrates.
- *cubiculum* - A small room in a *domus* or villa. The function differed according to what was inside the room.
- *curator civitas* - Principal in charge of the markets, finance, and administration.
- *curia* - The entire body of membership of the local Principals.
- *domus* - A house in town. The homes of local Principals were large.

- *impluvium* – The pool in the center of the *atrium*.
- magistrate – Elected official of the Council. Theoretically every member of the *curia* voted, but often official votes were limited to the Principals.
- mosaic – A picture or pattern produced by arranging together small colored pieces of hard material, such as stone, tile, or glass.
- Naming – during the Late Roman period Roman naming was shifting. Male names often kept the filiation or middle name of a noted family member rather than the immediate father. Female names shortened to the cognomen, first name, (e.g. Proba) and the filial name, the father's name or, sometimes, the mother's name. Christian names of saints also became common instead of traditional Roman names.
- *peristylum* – A large room at the back of a Roman home. The opening in the roof was larger than that of the *atrium*. The area was decorated with plants and flowers, often a fountain, and was a family gathering place.
- *praefectus urbi* – Guardian of the city, enforcing laws to keep the peace.
- Principal – A kind of oligarchy inner circle or "executive committee" of the council. Elected by the *curia*.
- *siesta* – Afternoon rest.
- *tessera* – Small piece of clay, stone, or glass. Assembled together by color to form mosaic images and patterns.
- The People – The term King Theoderic and his people used to refer to themselves. Ostrogoth was a term invented hundreds of years later by scholars.
- *triclinium* – The dining room. Furnished with tables set in the shape of a U. Diners reclined on benches, often padded, to eat. A diner would lean on an elbow to reach food with the opposite hand.

## AUTHOR NOTE
### THANK YOU!

Thank you for reading *The Grain Merchant*. Readers like you help spread the word about this unique series.

If you enjoyed *The Grain Merchant*, please consider telling your friends or posting a short review. Word of mouth is an author's best friend and much appreciated. Thank you.

You wouldn't be here if you didn't like a good mystery and delving into another time.

I love to hear from readers. Send me a message at **zara@zaraaltair.com**

Want to know when the next story is out? Join the **Fans of Argolicus** http://bit.ly/ArgolicusReader. Get a free copy of the Argolicus mystery *The Roman Heir*. I'll personally let you know what's going on with new books and share some information about the world of Argolicus.

# AFTERWORD

By the beginning of the Sixth Century, the old Roman roles for municipal government had eroded. I based my town council structure on research by Leonard A. Curchin, reported in "The end of local magistrates in the Roman Empire." *Gurion*, 2014, vol. 32, p. 271-287 and our conversations.

I am grateful to the Dipartimento di Beni Culturali, Universitá di Bologna, Ravenna, for support and guidance in early research, particularly; Antonio Carile, Professore emerito, Salvatore Cosentino, Professore ordinario, and Giorgio Vespignani, Professore associato. They pointed me to libraries, online resources, and generously contributed books to my background research.

In the United States, James J. O'Donnell, then of Georgetown University encouraged research and contributed a unique perspective to the culture of the early Sixth Century in Italy.

Astute notes from advance readers were lifeblood to adjusting details. Gratitude. Any errors are strictly mine.

*The Roman Heir*

*The Used Virgin*

*The Vellum Scribe*

*The Peach Widow*

# ABOUT THE AUTHOR

Zara Altair combines mystery with a bit of adventure in the Argolicus mysteries. *The Grain Merchant* is the fifth mystery. The series of mysteries is based in southern Italy at the time of the Ostrogoth rule of Italy under Theoderic the Great. Italians (Romans) and Goths live under one king while the Roman Empire is ruled from Constantinople. At times the cultures clash, but Argolicus uses his wit, with help from his tutor Nikolaos, to provide justice in a province far from the King's court.

Zara Altair lives in Beaverton, Oregon. Her approach to writing is to present the puzzle and let Argolicus and Nikolaos find the solution. Her stories are rich in historical detail based on extensive research.

Stay in Touch
www.zaraaltair.com
zara@zaraaltair.com